2/14 8/14

(AL) **DATE DUE**

GAYLORD   #3523PI   Printed in USA

D1402207

THE
MAN
FROM
BAR-20

Center Point
Large Print

**This Large Print Book carries the
Seal of Approval of N.A.V.H.**

THE
MAN
FROM
BAR-20

A Hopalong Cassidy Novel

CLARENCE E.
MULFORD

CENTER POINT LARGE PRINT
THORNDIKE, MAINE

This Center Point Large Print edition is published
in the year 2014. Originally published in the U. S.
in 1918 by A. L. Burt Company.

The text of this Large Print edition is unabridged.
In other aspects, this book may vary
from the original edition.
Printed in the United States of America
on permanent paper.
Set in 16-point Times New Roman type.

ISBN: 978-1-61173-968-8

Library of Congress Cataloging-in-Publication Data

Mulford, Clarence Edward, 1883–1956.
 The man from bar-20 : a Hopalong Casssidy novel / Clarence E.
Mulford. — Center Point Large Print edition.
 pages ; cm.
 ISBN 978-1-61173-968-8 (library binding)
  1. Cassidy, Hopalong (Fictitious character)—Fiction.
  2. Large type books. I. Title.
PS3525.U398M36 2014
813′.52—dc23

2013033460

Affectionately Dedicated
to
E.V.A.

CONTENTS

CHAPTER I
A Stranger Comes to Hastings

A horseman rode slowly out of a draw and up a steep, lava-covered ridge, singing "The Cowboy's Lament," to the disgust of his horse, which suddenly arched its back and stopped the song in the twenty-ninth verse.

"Dearly Beloved," grinned the rider, after he had quelled the trouble, "yore protest is heeded. 'Th' Lament' ceases, instanter; an' while you crop some of that grass, I'll look around and observe th' scenery, which shore is scrambled. Now, them two buttes over there," leaning forward to look around a clump of brush, "if they ain't twins, I'll eat—"

He ducked and dismounted in one swift movement to the vengeful tune of a screaming bullet over his head, slapped the horse and jerked his rifle from its scabbard. As the horse leaped down the slope of the ridge there was no sign of any living thing to be seen on the trail. A bush rustled near the edge of a draw, a peeved voice softly cursed the cacti and Mexican locust; and a few minutes later the shadow of a black lava bowlder grew suddenly fatter on one side. The cause of this sudden shadow growth lay prone under the bulging side of the great rock, peering out intently between two large stones; and flaming curiosity consumed his soul. A stranger in a strange land, who rode innocently along a free trail and minded his own business, merited no such a welcome as this. His promptness of action and the blind luck in that bending forward at the right instant were all that saved his life; and his celerity of movement spoke well for his reflexes, for he had found himself fattening the shadow of the bowlder almost before he had fully realized the pressing need for it.

Minute after minute passed before his searching eyes detected anything concerned with the unpleasant episode, and then he sensed rather than saw a slight movement on the mottled, bowlder-strewn slope of a distant butte. A bush moved gently, and that was all.

To cross the intervening chaos of rocks and brush, pastures and draws would take him an hour if it were done as caution dictated, and by that time the chase would be useless. So he waited until the sun was two hours higher, pleasantly anticipating a stealthy reconnaissance by his unknown enemy to observe the dead. He had dropped into high grass and brush when he left the saddle and there was no way that the marked man could be certain of the results of his shot except by closer examination. But the man in ambush had no curiosity, to his target's regret; and the target, despairing of being honored by a visit, finally gave up the vigil. After a silent interval a soft whistle from a thicket, well back in a draw, caused the grazing horse to lift his head, throw its ears forward and walk sedately toward the sound.

"Dearly Beloved," said a low voice from the thicket, "come closer. That was a two-laigged skunk, an' his eyes are good. Likewise he is one plumb fine shot."

Ever since he had listened to the marriage ceremony which had subjugated his friend Hopalong for the rest of that man's natural life, the phrase "Dearly Beloved" had stuck in his memory; and in his use of it the words took the place of humorous profanity.

Mounting, he rode on again, but kept off all sky-lines, favored the rough going away from the trail, and passed to the eastward of all the obstructions he met; and his keen eyes darted from point to point unceasingly, not giving up their scrutiny of the surroundings until he saw in the distance a little town, which he knew was Hastings.

In the little cow-town of Hastings the afternoon sun drove the shadows of the few buildings farther afield and pitilessly searched out every defect in the cheap and hastily constructed frame buildings, showed the hair-line cracks in the few adobes, where an occasional frost worked insidious damage to the clay, and drew out sticky, pungent beads of rosin from the sun-bleached and checked pine boards of the two-story front of the one-story building owned and occupied by "Pop" Hayes, proprietor of one of the three saloons in the town. The two-story front of Pop's building displayed two windows painted on the warped boards too close to the upper edge, the panes a faded blue, where gummy pine knots had not stained them yellow; and they were framed by sashes of a hideous red.

Inside the building Pop dozed in his favorite position, his feet crossed on a shaky pine table and his chair tipped back against the wall. Slow hoofbeats, muffled by the sand, sounded outside, followed by the sudden, faint jingling of spurs, the sharp creak of saddle gear and the soft thud of feet on the ground. Pop's eyes opened and he blinked at the bright rectangle of sunny street framed by his doorway, where a man loomed up blackly, and slowly entered the room.

"Howd'y, Logan," grunted Pop, sighing. His feet scraped from the table and thumped solidly on the floor in time with the thud of the chair legs, and he slowly arose, yawning and sighing wearily while he waited to see which side of the room would be favored by the newcomer. Pop disliked being disturbed, for by nature he was one who craved rest, and he could only sleep all night and most of the day. Rubbing the sleep out of his eyes he yawned again and looked more closely at the stranger, a quick look of surprise flashing across his face. Blinking rapidly he looked again and muttered something to himself.

The newcomer turned his back to the bar, took two long steps and peered into the battered showcase on the other side of the room, where a miscellaneous collection of merchandise, fly-specked and dusty, lay piled up in cheerful disorder under the cracked and grimy glass. Staring up at him was a roughly scrawled warning, in faded ink on yellowed paper: "Lean on yourself." The collection showed Mexican holsters, army holsters, holsters with the Lone Star; straps, buckles, bone rings, star-headed tacks, spurs, buttons, needles, thread, knives; two heavy Colt's revolvers, piles of cartridges in boxes, a pair of mother-of-pearl butt plates showing the head of a long-horned steer; pipes, tobacco of both kinds, dice, playing cards, harmonicas, cigars so dried out that they threatened to crumble at a touch; a patented gun-sight with Wild Bill Hickok's picture on the card which held it; oil, corkscrews, loose shot and bullets; empty shells, primers, reloading tools; bar lead, bullet molds—all crowded together as they had been left after many pawings-over. Pop was wont to fretfully damn the case and demand, peevishly, to know why "it" was always the very last thing he could find. Often, upon these occasions, he threatened to "get at it" the very first chance that he had; but his threats were harmless.

The stranger tapped on the glass. "Gimme that box of .45's," he remarked, pointing. "No, no; not that one. This *new* box. I'm shore particular about little things like that."

Pop reluctantly obeyed. "Why, just th' other day I found a box of ca'tridges I had for eleven years; an' they was better'n them that they sells nowadays. That's one thing that don't spoil." He looked up with shrewdly appraising eyes. "At fust glance I thought you was Logan. You shore looks a heap like him: dead image," he said.

"Yes? Dead image?" responded the stranger, his voice betraying nothing more than a polite, idle curiosity; but his mind flashed back to the trail. "Hum. He must have a lot of friends if he looks like me," he smiled quizzically.

Pop grinned: "Well, he's got some as is; an' some as ain't," he replied knowingly. "An' lemme tell you they both runs true to form. You don't have to copper no bets on either bunch, not a-tall."

"Sheriff, or marshal?" inquired the stranger, turning to the bar. "It's plenty hot an' dusty," he averred. "You have a life-saver with me."

"Might as well, I reckon," said Pop, shuffling across the room with a sudden show of animation, "though my life ain't exactly in danger. Nope; he ain't no sheriff, or marshall. We ain't got none, 'though I ain't sayin' we couldn't keep one tolerable busy while he lived. I've thought some of gettin' th' boys together to elect me sheriff; an' cussed if I wouldn't 'a' done it, too, if it wasn't for th' ridin'."

"Ridin'?" inquired the stranger with polite interest.

"It shakes a man up so; an' I allus feels sorry for th' hoss," explained the proprietor.

The stranger's facial training at the great American game was all that saved him from committing a breach of etiquette. "Huh! Reckon it does shake a man up," he admitted. "An' I never thought about th' cayuse; no, sir; not till this minute. Any ranches in this country?"

"Shore; lots of 'em. You lookin' for work?"

"Yes; I reckon so," answered the stranger.

"Well, if you don't look out sharp you'll shore find some."

"A man's got to eat more or less regular; an' cow-punchers ain't no exception," replied the stranger, his soft drawl in keeping with his slow, graceful movements.

Pop, shrewd reader of men that he was, suspected that neither of those characteristics was a true index to the man's real nature. There was an indefinable something which belied the smile—the eyes, perhaps, steel blue, unwavering, inscrutable; or a latent incisiveness crouching just beyond reach; and there was a sureness and smoothness and minimum of effort in the movements which vaguely reminded Pop of a mountain lion he once had trailed and killed. He was in the presence of a dynamic personality which baffled and disturbed him; and the two plain, heavy Colt's resting in open-top holsters, well down on the stranger's thighs, where his swinging hands brushed the well-worn butts, were signs which even the most stupid frontiersman could hardly overlook. Significant, too, was the fact that the holsters were securely tied by rawhide thongs, at their lower ends, to the leather chaps, this to hold them down when the guns were drawn out. To the initiated the signs proclaimed a gunman, a two-gun man, which was worse; and a red flag would have had no more meaning.

"Well," drawled Pop, smiling amiably, "as to work, I reckon you can find it if you knows it when you sees it; an' don't close yore eyes. I'll deal 'em face up, an' you can take yore choice," he offered, wiping his lips on the edge of the bar towel, both the action and the towel itself being vociferously described by his saddle-sitting friends as affectations, for everybody knew that a sleeve or the back of a hand was the natural thing. "Now, there's th' Circle S; but I dunno as they needs any more men. They could get along with less if them they has would work. Smith, of th' Long T, over in th' southwest, could easy use more men; but he's so close an' allfired penurious that I dunno as he'd favor th' idear. He's a reg'lar genius for savin' money, Smith is. He once saved a dollar out of three cents, an' borrowed them of me to start with. Then there's th' CL, over east in th' Deepwater Valley. You might get something there; an' Logan's a nice man to work for, for a few days. He allus gives his men at least two hours sleep a night, averagin' it up; but somehow they're real cheerful about it, an' they all swears by him 'stead of at him. Reckon mebby it's th' wages he pays. He's got th' best outfit of th' three. But, lemme tell you, it's a right lively place, th' CL; an' you don't have to copper *that,* neither. Th' cards is all spread out in front of you—take yore choice an' foller yore nat'ral bend."

"Logan," mused the stranger. "Didn't you say something about him before?" he asked curiously.

"I did," grunted Pop. "You've got a mem'ry near as bad as ol' Hiram Jones. Hiram, he once—"

"I thought so," interposed the cow-puncher hastily. "What kind of a ranch is th' CL?"

"Well, it was th' fust to locate in these parts, an' had its pick; an', nat'rally, it picked th' valley of th' Deepwater. Funny Logan ain't found no way to make th' river work; it wouldn't have to sleep at all, 'cept once in a while in th' winter, when it freezes over for a spell. It'd be a total loss then; mebby that's why he ain't never tried.

"But takin' a second holt," he continued, frowning with deep thought; "I dunno as I'd work

17

for him, if I was you. You looks too much like him; an' you got a long life of piety an' bad whiskey ahead of you, mebby. An', come to think of it, I dunno as I'd stay very long around these parts, neither; an' for th' same reason. Now you have a drink with me. It shore is th' hottest spring I've seen in fifty year," he remarked, thereby quoting himself for about that period of time. Each succeeding spring and summer was to him hotter than any which had gone before, which had moved Billy Atwood to remark that if Pop only lived long enough he would find hell a cool place, by comparison, when he eventually arrived there.

"Sic 'em, Towser!" shrilled a falsetto voice from somewhere. "I'll eat his black heart!" Then followed whistling, clucking, and a string of expletives classical in its completeness. "Andy wants a drink! Quick!"

A green object dropped past the stranger's face, thumped solidly on the pine bar, hooked a vicious-looking beak on the edge of the counter, and swore luridly as its crafty nip missed the stranger's thumb.

The puncher swiftly bent his sinewy forefinger, touched it with his thumb, and let it snap forward. The parrot got it on an eye and staggered, squawking a protest.

Pop was surprised and disappointed, for most strangers showed some signs of being startled, and often bought the drinks to further prove that the joke was on them. This capable young man carelessly dropped his great sombrero over Andrew Jackson and went right on talking as though nothing unusual had occurred. It appeared that the bird was also surprised and disappointed. The great hat heaved and rocked, bobbed forward, backward, and sideways, and then slid jerkily along the bar, its hidden locomotive force too deeply buried in thought and darkness to utter even a single curse. Reaching the edge of the bar the big hat pushed out over it, teetered a moment and then fell to the floor, where Andrew Jackson, recovering his breath and vocabulary at the same instant, filled the room with shrill and clamorous profanity.

The conversation finished to his satisfaction, the stranger glanced down at his boot, where the ruffled bird was delivering tentative frontal and flank attacks upon the glittering, sharp-toothed spur, whose revolving rowel had the better of the argument. Andrew sensed the movement, side-stepped clumsily and cocked an evil eye upward.

"You should 'a' taught him to swear in th' deaf an' dumb alphabet," commented the puncher, grinning at the bird's gravity. "Does he drink?" he asked.

"Try him, an' see," suggested Pop, chuckling. He reached for a bottle and clucked loudly.

Andrew shook himself energetically, and then proceeded to go up the puncher's chaps by making diligent use of beak and claws. Reaching the low-hung belt, he hooked his claws into it and then looked evilly and suspiciously at the strange, suddenly extended forefinger. Deciding to forego hostilities, he swung himself upon it and was slowly lifted up to the bar.

Pop was disappointed again, for it was the bird's invariable custom to deftly remove a portion of strange forefingers so trustingly offered. He could crack nuts in his crooked beak. Andy shook himself violently, craned his neck and hastened to bend it over the rim of the glass.

The stranger watched him in frank disgust and shrugged his shoulders eloquently. "So all you could teach him was vile cuss words an' to like whiskey, huh?" he muttered. "He's got less sense than I thought he had," he growled, and, turning abruptly, went swiftly out to his horse.

Pop stared after him angrily and slapped the bird savagely. Emptying the liquor upon the floor, he shuffled quickly to the door and shook his fist at the departing horseman.

"Don't you tell Logan that *I* sent you!" he shouted belligerently.

The stranger turned in his saddle, grinning cheerfully, and favored his late host with a well-known, two-handed nose signal. Then he slapped the black horse and shot down the street without another backward glance.

Pop, arms akimbo, watched him sweep out of sight around a bend.

"Huh!" he snorted. "Wonder what yo're doin' down here? Galivantin' around th' country, insultin' honest, hard-workin' folks, an' wearin' two guns, low down an' tied! I reckon when you learns th' lay of th' country, if you stays long enough, you'll wind up by joinin' that gang up in th' Twin Buttes country. I allus like to see triggers on six-shooters, *I* do." He had not noticed the triggers, but that was no bar to his healthy imagination. Shuffling back to his seat, he watched the indignant Andy pecking at a wet spot on the floor.

"So you didn't chaw his finger, huh?" he demanded, in open and frank admiration of the bird's astuteness. "Strikes me you got a hull lot of wisdom, my boy. Some folks says a bird ain't got no brains; but lemme tell you that you've got a danged good instinct."

CHAPTER II
A Question of Identity

Meanwhile the stranger was loping steadily eastward, and he arrived at the corral of the CL ranch before sundown, nodding pleasantly to the man who emerged from it: "Howd'y," he said. "I'm lookin' for Logan."

The CL man casually let his right hand lay loosely near the butt of his Colt: "Howd'y," he nodded. "Yo're lookin' right at him."

"Do you need any more punchers?" asked the stranger.

"H'm," muttered the foreman. "Might use one. If it's you, we'll talk money on pay-day. I'll know more about you then."

A puncher, passing the corral, noticed the two guns, frowned slightly and entered the enclosure, and leaned alertly against the palisade, where a crack between two logs served him as a loophole.

The two-gun man laughed with genuine enjoyment at the foreman's way of hiring men. "That's fair," he replied; "but what's th' high an' low figgers? I like to know th' limit of any game I sets in."

Logan shrugged his shoulders. "Forty is th' lowest I'd offer a man; an' he wouldn't draw that more'n a month. Any man as ain't worth more is in our way. It's a waste of grub to feed him. Th' sky is th' high limit—but you've got to work like hell to pass th' clouds."

"I'm some balloon," laughed the stranger. "Where's the grub shack?"

"Hold on, young man! We ain't got that far, yet. Where are you from, an' what have you been doin' with yore sweet young life?"

The stranger's face grew grave and his eyes narrowed a trifle.

"Some folks allow that's a leadin' question. It ain't polite."

"I allow that, too. An' I'm aimin' to make it a leadin' question, 'though I ain't lackin' in politeness, nor tryin' to rile you. You don't have to answer. Th' wide world, full of jobs, is all around you."

The newcomer regarded him calmly for a moment, and suddenly smiled.

"Yore gall is refreshin'," he grinned. "I'm from th' Bar-20, Texas. I'm five feet ten; weigh a hundred an' sixty; blue eyes, brown hair; single an' sober, now an' always. I writes left-handed; eat an' shoot with both; wears pants, smokes tobacco, an' I'm as handy a cow-puncher as ever threw a rope. Oh, yes; modesty is one of my glarin' faults; you might say my only glarin' fault. Some people call me 'Dearly Beloved'; others, other things; but I answer to any old handle at grub pile. My name is Johnny Nelson an' I never had no other, 'cept 'Kid,' to my friends. I'm thirty years old, minus some. An'—oh, yes; I'm from th' Tin Cup, Montanny. I get things twisted at times, an' this shore looks like one of 'em."

"Of course," grunted Logan, his eyes twinkling. "That's easy. Th' two ranches, bein' so close together, would bother a man. Sorta wander off one onto th' other, an' have to stop to think which one yo're workin' for. They should mark th' boundaries plainer—or put up a fence."

Johnny flushed. "I allus say Bar-20 when I speaks off-hand an' have more on my mind than my hair. That man in th' corral divides my attention. He flusters me. You see, I was cussed near born on th' old Bar-20—worked there ever since I was a boy. That crack in th' wall is big enough for two men to use. Thank you, friend: you near scared me to death," he chuckled as the suspicious watcher emerged and started for the bunkhouse.

"You look so much like th' boss, I couldn't help watchin' you," grinned the puncher over his shoulder.

Logan grunted something, and then nodded at the stranger.

"Cut it loose." he encouraged. "I don't get a chance like this every day, my observant friend. I allus reckoned I could cover ground purty well, but I'll be hanged if I can spread myself so I can

24

work in Texas an' Montanny at th' same time. You got me beat from soda to hock. Yo're goin' to be a real valuable man, which I can see plain. Comin' down to cases, you ain't really a cow-puncher; yo're a whole cussed outfit, barin' th' chuck waggin an' th' cook. I have great hopes for you. Tell me about it."

Johnny swung a leg over the pommel and smiled down at the man who was grinning up at him.

"Of course," he replied, "it ain't none of yore business, which we both admits. We just can't do any business on any other understandin'. But I waives that: an' here goes.

"I worked with the Bar-20 till Buck went up to run th' Tin Cup. Cow-thieves kept him so busy that our new foreman went up to help him. He stayed there. Red got lonesome for Hoppy, and shore follered. Skinny was lost without th' pair of 'em, so he up an' follered Red. Lanky, missin' Skinny, got plumb restless an' takes th' trail a month later. Then a railroad crosses our ranch an' begins layin' out two towns, so Pete gets on his hind laigs, licks a section boss, an' chases after Lanky. I'm gettin' lonesomer and lonesomer all th' time, but I manages to stick on th' job by pullin' leather, because I was drawin' down a foreman's pay. That ranch had five foremen in three months; an' they was all good ones, 'cept, mebby, me. But when I saw barbed wire on th' sidin', fence posts along th' right of way, sheep on th' hills, an' plows plumb ruinin' good grass land, I hunts up that same section boss, licks him again in mem'ry of Pete, packed my war bag, an' loped north after Pete. Th' old ranch has gone plumb to hell!"

Logan, a scowl on his face, rubbed the butt of his Colt and swore softly. "It'll be that way all over th' range, some day. Go on."

"Well, up on th' Tin Cup, Buck got married. Hoppy had been before he left Texas. Tex Ewalt's gettin' th' disease now. He quit drinkin', card playin', an' most everything worth doin'. He ain't fit company for a sheep no more. Not knowing he was framin' up th' play, I loafed along an' didn't propose quick enough. That's once more he saved my life. Th' air's plumb full of matrimony on th' Tin Cup. There was two black-eyed sisters in Twin River—Lanky takes one an' Skinny th' other. They tossed for choice. Pete, who was matrimony galled, raised such a ruction at th' doin's that there just wasn't no livin' with him. His disposition was full of sand cracks, an' he'd ruther fight than eat. We pulled off a couple of hummers, me an' him.

"Every time I'd try to get some of my friends to go to town for a regular, old time, quiet evenin' I found I didn't have no friends left; an' th' wimmin all joined hands an' made me feel like a brand-blotter. I was awful popular, *I* was! Ever try to argue with a bunch of wimmin? It's like a dicky bird chirpin' in a cyclone; he can't even hear hisself!

"We had a cook once, on th' Bar-20, that would

run an' grab a gun if he saw a coyote ten miles away. That's th' way they acted about me, all but Mary, who is Mrs. Hopalong. She had th' idea she could make me all over again; an' I wouldn't a-cared if she hadn't kept tryin' all th' time. At first all my ex-friends would sneak around an' sort of apologize to me for th' way their wives acted; an' then, damned if they didn't get to sidin' in with th' wives! Whenever I wandered into sight th' wimmin would cluck to their worse halves, an' scold me like I was a chicken hawk. An' I had lots of advice, too. It was just like my shadow, only it worked nights, too. Nobody called me 'Kid' or 'Johnny' no more. Them days was past. I was *that* Johnny Nelson: know what I mean?

"Red did sneak off to town with me twice—an' drank ginger-ale, an' acted about as free an' happy as a calf with a red-hot old brandin' iron over his flank. He wouldn't play faro because he only had two dollars, an' reckoned he might need it for somethin' before pay-day come round again. That was on pay-day, too! An' that was Red, *Red Connors!* Great polecats! Why, there was a time when Red—oh, what's th' use!

"Hopalong—you call him that now when his wife's around!—he was something on some board, or something; an' he said he had to set a good example. Wouldn't even play penny ante! Think of it! There was a time when a camel, with all his stummicks, an' a Gatlin' gun on his back, couldn't a follered th' example *he* set. I was just as happy as a bobcat in a trap—an' about as peaceful. There wasn't nothin' I could do, if I stayed up there, but get married; an' that was like hangin' myself to keep from gettin' shot. Then, one day, Mrs. Hopalong caught me learnin' William, Junior, how to chew tobacco. As if a five-year-old kid hadn't ought to get some manly habits! An', say! You ought to see that kid! If he won't bust his daddy's records for hell raisin' I miss my guess; unless they plumb spoils him in th' bringin' up. Well, she caught me learnin' him; but like th' boundin' jack rabbit I'm hard to catch. An' here I am."

Logan's grin threatened his ears. "I'm glad of it," he laughed. "There's something in yore face I like—mebby it's th' tobacco. Thanks; I will; I'm all out of it right now. How did you come to pick us out to land on? Pop recommend us to you?"

"Now don't blame me for that," rejoined Johnny. "Anyhow, he took it back later. As to stoppin' in this country, th' idea suddenly whizzed my way at them twin buttes north of town. I like this range. Things sort of start themselves, an' there's music in th' air. It reminds me of th' Bar-20, in th' old days. A man won't grow lazy down here; he'll keep jumpin'. An' I found a trace of lead at that funny-lookin' ridge east of them freak buttes; but I couldn't find where it come from. If I had, I'd 'a' salted th' mine with a Sharp's Special. You see, I'm ambidextrous—ain't that a snorter of a word?—an' when I ain't punchin' cows with one hand, I'm prospectin' with th' other. Somebody down here is plumb careless with his gun—an' he's got a good gun, too. He's too cussed familiar on short acquaintance. But it's too bad I look like you, 'though that's why I'm offerin' you my valuable services."

"I reckon it's a cross I got to stagger under," replied Logan, the smile gone from his face; "but I'll try to live it down. An' somehow my trusting nature leans toward you, though it shouldn't. Yo're a two-gun man, which acts like yeast in th' suspicious mind. I've seen 'em before; an' you looks most disconcertin' capable. Then you says Bar-20, an' Hopalong, an' Red Connors, an' th' others. You talk like you knew 'em intimate. I've heard of 'em, all of 'em. Like th' moon, you shine in reflected light. I've heard of you, too; I'm surprised you ain't in jail. Now then: If you are *that* Johnny Nelson, of *that* outfit, an' you can prove it, I yearns to weep on yore bosom; if you ain't, then I'll weep on yore grave. Th' question of identity is a ticklish one. It makes me that nervous I want to look under th' bed. As a two-gun man, unknown, yo're about as welcome on this ranch, right now, as a hydrophoby skunk; but as Johnny Nelson, of that old Bar-20, yo're worth fifty a month to me, as a starter, with ten dollars extra for each six-gun. But I've just simply got to have proof about who you are, an' where you come from. Let's pause for an inspiration."

Johnny grinned. "I don't blame you; for I've had a sample of something already. An' I've got a tail holt on an inspiration. You hunt up that pen you've had since Adam was a boy; find th' ink that you put away last summer so you'd know where it was when you wanted it in a hurry; an' then, in thirty minutes' hard labor you'll have something like this:

'Mr. William Cassidy, Senior, Tin Cup, Twin Rivers, Montanny: Dear Sir: A nice lookin' young man wants to take seventy dollars a month away from me, as a starter. His undershirt is red, with th' initials "WC" worked near th' top buttonhole in pretty blue silk thread. He wants Pete to send him that eight dollars that Pete borrowed to buy William, Junior, a .22 rifle to bust windows with. Tell Red his pants wear well. Does William, Junior, chew tobacco? He has been shot at already. What is this young man's name? Did he work on th' old Bar-20 with you? Yours truly, Logan.'

"Exhibit 1: Th' red undershirt. Hoppy has even more of 'em than Buck, 'though Rose is comin' along fast. Mary branded 'em all so she could pick 'em out of th' wash. It helped me pick this one off th' clothesline, because me an' Hoppy wears th' same size. Exhibit 2: A scab on my off ear.

30

William, Junior, was shootin' at a calf an' I stopped him. He's a spunky little cuss, all right; but they'll spoil him yet. An' Pete never did have any sense, anyhow. Th' poor kid is shootin' blanks now, an' blamin' it on th' gun. An' it was a mean trick, too. That hit about th' tobacco will get under Hoppy's scalp—he'll answer right quick. You might say to tell William, Junior, that I ain't forgot my promise, an' that I'll send him a shotgun just as soon as he gets big enough to tote it around."

"I'll shore send it," laughed Logan, whose imagination was running wild. "But outside of the identity you suits me right down to the ground. If Hopalong Cassidy says yo're all right I'll back you to my last dollar. You mentioned hearin' music in th' air. It was a tunin' up. Will you stay for th' dance?"

"Sweet bells of joy!" exclaimed Johnny, leaving the saddle as though shot out by a spring. "From wimmin', barb wire, sheep an' railroad towns, to this! I can go to town with th' boys once more! I can cuss out loud an' swagger around regardless! An' some mangey gent is careless with his gun! You can lose me just as easy as a cow can lose a tick. I feel right at home."

"All right, then. Strip off yore saddle and turn that fine cayuse loose," replied Logan, chuckling. He hoped that he might be able to coax the new man to swap horses. "Th' cook's callin' his hogs, so let's go feed."

CHAPTER III
The Wisdom of the Frogs

For two weeks Johnny rode range with the outfit and got familiar with the ranch. There was one discovery which puzzled him and seemed to offer an explanation for the shot on the trail: He had found the ruins of a burned homestead on the northern end of the ranch and he guessed that it had been used by "nesters;" and the evicted squatters might have mistaken him for Logan. His thoughts constantly turned to the man who had shot at him, and to the country around Twin Buttes; and often he sat for minutes, stiffly erect in his saddle, staring at the two great buttes, eager to explore the country surrounding them and to pay his debt.

From where he rode, facing westward, he could see the Deepwater, cold at all seasons of the year. Flowing swiftly, it gurgled and swished around bowlders of lava and granite and could be forded in but one place in thirty miles, where it spread out over a rocky, submerged plateau on the trail between the CL and Hastings, and where it grew turbulent and frothy with wrath as it poured over the up-thrust ledges. Along its eastern bank lay the ranch, in the valley of the Deepwater, and beyond it a short distance stood the Barrier, following it mile after mile and curving as it curved.

The Barrier, well named, was a great ledge of limestone, up-flung like a wall, sheer, smooth and only occasionally broken by narrow crevices which ran far back and sloped gradually upward, rock-strewn, damp, cool, and wild. It stretched for miles to Johnny's right and left, a wall between the wild tumble of the buttes and the smooth, gently rolling, fertile plain, which, beginning at the river, swept far to the eastward behind him, where it eventually became lost in the desert wastes. On one side of the rampart lay the scurrying river and the valley of the Deepwater, rolling, sparsely timbered and heavily grassed, placid, peaceful, restful; on the other, seeming to leap against the horizon, lay the grandeur of chaos, wild and forbidding.

Highest above all that jagged western skyline, shouldering up above all other buttes and plateaus, Twin Buttes peremptorily challenged attention. Remarkably alike from all sides, when viewed from the CL ranch house they seemed to have been cast in the same mold; and the two towering, steep-sided masses with their different colored strata stood high above the Barrier and the chaos behind it like concrete examples of eternity.

Twin Buttes were the lords of their realm, and

what a realm it was! Around them for miles great buttes rose solidly upward, naked on their abrupt sides except for an occasional, straggling bush or dwarfed pine or fir which here and there held precarious footholds in cracks and crevices or on the more secure placement of a ledge. Deep draws choked with brush lay between the more rolling hills along the eastern edge of the watershed where the Barrier stood on guard, and rich patches of heavy grass found the needed moisture in them. On the slopes of the hills were great forests of yellow pine, a straggling growth of fir crowning their tops. Farther west, where the massive buttes reared aloft, the deep canyons were of two kinds. The first, wide, with sloping banks of detritus, were covered with pine forests and torn with draws; the second, steep-walled, were great, narrow chasms of wind- and water-swept rock, bare and awe inspiring. They sloped upward to the backbone of the watershed and had humble beginnings in shallow, basin-like arroyos, which gradually became boxes in the rock formation as the level sloped downward.

But the chaos stopped at the Barrier, which marked the breaking of stratum upon stratum of the earth's crust. Ages ago there had been a mighty struggle here between titanic forces. To the west the earth's crust, battered into buttes, canyons, draws, and great plateaus, had held out with a granite stubbornness and strength, defying the seething powers below it; but the limestone and the sandstone, weaker brothers, betrayed by the treachery of the shales, had given under the great strain and parted. The western portion had held its own; but the eastern section had dropped down into the heaving turmoil and formed the floor of the valley of the Deepwater. And as if in compensation, the winds of the ages, still battling with the stubborn buttes, had robbed them of soil and deposited it in the valley.

One evening, when Johnny rode in for supper, Logan met him at the corral and held out his hand.

"Shake, Nelson," he smiled. "Crosby went to town today and brought me a letter from th' Tin Cup. After you have fed up, come around to my room an' see me. I want to hold a right lively pow-wow with you."

"Shore enough!" laughed Johnny, an expectant grin on his face. "Bet he laid me out from soda to hock, tail to bit, th' old pirate!"

"Well, you've got a terrible reputation, young man. Go an' feed."

Johnny was the first at the table that night, and the first away from it by a wide margin. Rolling a cigarette, he lit it and hastened to Logan's quarters, where he found the foreman contentedly smoking.

"Come in an' set down," invited the foreman. "We're goin' to do a lot of talkin'; it's due to be a long session. There's th' letter."

Johnny read it:

"Mr. John C. Logan. Dear Sir: I take my pen in hand to answer your letter of recent date. Pete paid Red the 8 dollars to even up for the pants, but nobody paid me for the shirt. Ask him why he took the best one. William, Junior, hates tobacco. We was scared h'd die. He swears most suspicious like Johnny Nelson. I hid the gun in the storeroom. It cost me $12 damages the first week, besides a calf. Can you use Pete Wilson? I'll pay 1/2 his wages the first 6 months. I'd ruther have boils than him. He's worse since Johnny left. Don't let Johnny come north again, and God have mercy on your soul. He's easy worth $70, if you are in trouble. If you ain't in trouble he'll get you there. Excuse pensil. Yours truly, Wm. Cassidy, Senior. P.S. His old job is waiting for him and he can have the shirt. It must be near wore out anyhow. Tell him it only costs 2 cents to write me a letter, but I bet hell freezes before I get one. William, Junior, raised the devil when he missed Johnny. Yes, he worked on the Bar-20. If he sends the kid a shotgun, I'll come down and bust his neck. Excuse pensil."

Johnny looked steadily out of the door, ashamed to let Logan see his face, for homesickness is no respecter of age. He gulped and felt like a sick calf. Logan smiled at him through the gloom and chuckled, and at the sound the puncher stiffened and turned around with a fine attempt at indifference.

The foreman nodded at the letter. "Keep it if you wants. They must be a purty fine bunch, them fellers. I never knowed any of 'em, but I've heard a lot about 'em. 'Youbet' Somes used to drop in here once in a while, an' he knowed 'em all. I ain't seen Youbet for quite a spell now."

Johnny managed to relax his throat. "Finest outfit that ever wore pants," he blurted. "Youbet's dead. Went out fightin' seven sheep-herders in a saloon, but he got three of 'em. Hoppy met up with two of th' others th' next summer an' had words with 'em. Th' other two are still livin', I reckon." He thought for a moment and growled: "It's th' wimmin that done it. You wouldn't believe how that crowd has changed! Damn it, why can't a man keep his friends?"

The foreman puffed slowly and made no answer beyond a grunt of understanding. Johnny folded the letter carefully and put it in his pocket. "What's th' cow business comin' to, anyhow?" he demanded. "Wimmin, railroads, towns, sheep, wire—" he despaired of words and glared at the inoffensive corral.

"An' rustlers," added Logan.

"They're only an incident," retorted Johnny. "They can be licked, like a disease; but th' others—oh, what's th' use!"

"You're right," replied Logan; "but it's the rustlers that have got me worried. I ain't thinkin' about th' others very much, yet."

Johnny turned like a flash. He wanted action, action that would take his thoughts into other channels. The times were out of joint and he wanted something upon which to vent his spleen. He had been waiting for that word to come from Logan, waiting for days. And he had a score of his own to pay, as well.

"Rustlers!" he exulted. "I knowed it! I've knowed it for a week, an' I'm tired of ridin' around like a cussed fool. I know th' job *I* want! What about 'em?"

Logan closed the door by a push of his foot, refilled and lit his pipe, and for two hours the only light the room knew was the soft glow of the pipe and the firey ends of the puncher's cigarettes, while Logan unfolded his troubles to eager ears. The cook sang in the kitchen as he wrestled his dishes and pans, and then the noise died out. Laughter and words and the thumping of knuckles on a card table came from the bunkroom, and grew silent. A gray coyote slid around the corral, sniffing suspiciously, and at some faint noise faded into the twilight, and from a distant rise howled mournfully at the moon. From a little pond in the corral came the deepthroated warning of the frogs, endless, insistent, untiring: "Go 'round! Go 'round! Knee deep!

Knee deep! Go 'round! Go 'round! Go 'round!"

The soft murmur of voices in the foreman's room suddenly ceased, and a chair scraped over the sandy floor. The door creaked a protest as it swung slowly inward and a gray shape suddenly took form against the darkness of the room, paused on the threshold and then Logan stepped out into the moonlight and knocked his pipe against his boot heel. A second figure emerged and joined him, tossing away a cigarette.

The foreman yawned and shook his head. "I didn't know how to get 'em, Nelson," he said again. "I wasn't satisfied to stop th' rustlin'. I wanted to wipe 'em out an' get back my cows; but I didn't have men enough to go about it right, an' that cussed Barrier spoiled every plan."

"Yes," said the puncher. "But it's funny that none of th' boys, watchin' nights, never got a sign of them fellers. They must be slick. Well, all right, there'll have to be another plan tried, an' that'll be *my* job. I told you that I found traces of lead over near Twin Buttes? Well, I'm goin' prospectin', an' try to earn that seventy dollars a month. Any time you see a green bush lyin' at th' foot of th' Barrier, just north of Little Canyon, keep th' boys from ridin' near there that same night. I may have some business there an' I shore don't want to be shot at when I can't shoot back. It's too cussed bad Hoppy an' Red are married."

Logan laughed: "Then don't you make that

mistake some day! But what about that feller Pete Wilson that Cassidy wants to get rid of?"

"Don't you worry about me gettin' married!" snorted Johnny. "I saw too much of it. An' as for Pete, he's too happy wallerin' in his misery. Anyhow, he wouldn't leave Hoppy an' th' boys; an' they wouldn't let him go. You couldn't drag him off the Tin Cup with a rope. Then we've settled it, huh? I'm to leave you tomorrow, with hard words?"

"Hard words ain't necessary. I know every man that works for me an' they'll stick, an' keep their mouths shut. Now, I warn you again: I wouldn't give a dollar, Mex. for yore life if you go through with your scheme. An' it'll be more dangerous because you look like me, an' have worked for me. You can give it up right now an' not lose anythin' in my opinion. Think it over tonight."

Johnny laughed and shook his head.

"Well," said the foreman, "I'm lettin' you into a bad game, with th' cards stacked against you; but I'll come in after you when you say th' word; an' th' outfit'll be at my back."

"I know that," smiled Johnny. "I'll be under a handicap, keepin' under cover an' not doin' any shootin'; but if I make a gun-play they'll begin to do some figgerin'. Gosh, I'm sleepy. Reckon I'll hunt my bunk. Good night."

"No gun-play," growled Logan. "You know what I want. How many they are, where they round up my cows, an' when they will be makin' a raid, so I can get 'em red-handed. We'll do the fightin'. Good night."

They shook hands and parted, Johnny entering the house, Logan wandering out to the corral, where he sat on a stump for an hour or more and slowly smoked his pipe. When he finally arose he found that it was out, and cold, much to his surprise.

"Go 'round! Go 'round!" said the pond. "Better go 'round! Go 'round!"

Logan turned and sighed with relief at a problem solved. "Yo're a right smart frog, Big Mouth," he grinned. " 'Go 'round' is th' medicine; an' I've got th' doctor to shove it down their throats! There's a roundup due in th' Twin Buttes, an' it's started now."

CHAPTER IV
A Feint

Pop Hayes sighed, raised his head and watched the door as hoof-beats outside ceased abruptly.

"Dearly Beloved!" said an indignant voice. "If you tries any more of yore tricks I'll gentle you with th' butt of a six-gun, you barrel-bellied cow! Oh, *that's* it, huh? I savvy. You yearns for that shade. Go to it, Pepper."

" 'Dearly Beloved'!" snorted Pop in fine disgust. "You'd think it was a weddin' tower! Who th' devil ever heard a cayuse called any such a name as that?" he indignantly demanded of Andrew Jackson; but Andrew paid no attention to him. The bird's head was cocked on one side and he sidled deliberately toward the door.

A figure jumped backward past the door, followed by a pair of hoofs, which shot into sight and out again. Andy stopped short and craned his neck, his beady eyes glittering with quick suspicion.

"I can shore see where you an' me has an argument," said the voice outside. "If you make any more plays like that I'll just naturally kick yore ribs in. G'wan, now; I ain't got no sugar, you old fool!" And the smiling two-gun man stepped into the room, with a wary and affectionate backward glance. "Hello, Pop!" he grinned. "You old Piute, you owes me a drink!"

"Like hell I do!" retorted Pop with no politeness, sitting up very straight in his chair.

"You shore do!" rejoined Johnny firmly. "Didn't you tell me that th' CL was a nice ranch to work for?"

"Yo're loco! I didn't say nothin' of th' kind!" snapped Pop indignantly. "I said they'd work you nigh to death; *that's* what I said!"

"Oh; was that it?" asked Johnny dubiously. "I ain't nowise shore about it; but we'll let it go as it lays. Then I owe you a drink; so it's all th' same. Yo're a real prophet."

Pop hastily shuffled to his appointed place and performed the honors gracefully. "So you went an' got a job over there, huh?" he chuckled. "An' now yo're all through with 'em? Well, I *will* say that you stuck it out longer than some I knows of. Two weeks with Logan is a long time."

"It's so long that I've aged considerable," admitted Johnny, smiling foolishly. "But I'm cured. I'm cured of punchin' cows for anybody, for a while. Seems to me that all I've done, all my life, was to play guardian to fool cows. I've had enough for a while. Th' last two weeks plumb cured me of punchin'.'"

He looked down and saw Andy, feathers ruffled, squaring off for another go at the spur, stooped suddenly, scooped the squawking bird into his hand, tossed it into the air, caught it, and quickly shoved it headfirst into a pocket. Andy swore and backed and wriggled, threatened to eat his black heart and to do other unkind and reprehensible things. Giving a desperate heave he plopped out of the pocket and struck the floor with a thud. Shaking himself, he screamed profane defiance at the world at large and then made his clumsy and comical way up the chaps and finally roosted on the butt of one of the six-guns, where he clucked loudly and whistled.

Johnny gave a peculiar whistle in reply, and almost instantly Pop let out a roar and jumped toward the door to drive back a black horse that was coming in.

"Get out of here!" he yelled pugnaciously. Pepper bared her teeth and slowly backed out again. Turning, Pop glared at the puncher. "Did you see that? Mebby Andy ain't th' only animal that drinks," he jabbed, remembering a former conversation.

Johnny laughed and scratched the bird, which stood first on one foot and then on the other, foolish with ecstatic joy.

Pop regarded the bird with surprise. "Well, if that don't beat all!" he marveled. "There ain't another man can do that, 'cept me, an' get off with a whole hand. Andy'll miss you, I reckon."

"He won't miss me much," responded Johnny, comfortably seating himself in Pop's private chair. "I ain't leavin' th' country."

"You won't have to. There's other ranches, where they treats punchers better'n cows. There's another chair, over there."

"No more ranches for me," replied Johnny, ignoring the hint. "I'm through punchin', I tell you. I'm goin' to play a while for a change."

"Gamblin's bad business," replied Pop, turning to get the cards.

"Mebby some gamblin' is; but there's some as ain't," grinned Johnny. "I ain't meanin' cards."

"Oh," said Pop, disappointed. "What you mean—shootin' craps?"

"Nope; I'm goin' prospectin'; an' if that ain't gamblin' then I never saw anythin' that was."

Pop straightened up and stared. "Prospectin'?" he demanded, incredulously. "Regular prospectin'? Well, I'll be cussed! If yo're goin' to do it around here; lemme tell you it won't be no gamble. It'll be a dead shore loss. A flea couldn't live on what you'll earn on that game in this country."

"Well, I ain't aimin' to support no flea, unless Andy leaves me one," laughed Johnny, again scratching the restless bird. "But I'm tired of cows, an' I might as well amuse myself prospectin' as any other way. I like this country an' I'm goin' to stay a while. Besides, when I was a kid I shore wanted to be a pirate; then when I got older I saw a prospector an' hankered to be one. I can't be a pirate, but I'm goin' to be a prospector. When my money is gone I'll guard cows again."

"Lord help us!" muttered Pop. "Yo're plumb loco."

"How can I be plumb an' loco at th' same time?"

"Andy!" snapped Pop. "Come away from there! Lord knows you ain't got no sense, but there ain't no use riskin' yore instinct!"

Johnny laughed. "Leavin' jokes aside, me an' Pepper are goin' off by ourselves an' poke around pannin' th' streams an' bustin' nuggets off th' rocks till we get a fortune or our grub runs out. We can have a good time, an'—hey! You got any fishhooks?"

"Fishhooks nothin'!" snorted Pop. "Lot of call *I* got for fishhooks. Why, I ain't heard th' word for ten years. Say!" he grinned sheepishly. "Mebby you'll get lonesome. Now, if we went off together, with some fishhooks—but, shucks! I can't leave this here business."

Johnny hid his relief. "That's th' worst of havin' a business. You certainly can't go off an' let everythin' go to smash."

"Cuss th' luck!" growled Pop. "Gosh, I'm all het up over it! I ain't done no fishin' since I was a kid, an' there must be lots of trout in these streams." Then he brightened a little. "But I dunno. You look too cussed much like Logan to be real comfortable company for *me*. I reckon I'll pay attention to business."

Johnny showed a little irritation. "There you go again! You do a lot of worryin' about my looks. If they don't suit you, start right in an' change 'em!"

"There *you* go!" snapped Pop disgustedly. "On th' prod th' first thing! You'd show more common sense if *you* did some of th' worryin'. But then, I reckon it'll be all right if you does yore prospectin' an' fishin' south of here."

"No, sir! I'm goin' to do it north of here, in th' Twin Buttes country."

Pop's expression baffled description, and his Adam's apple bobbed up and down like a monkey on a stick. "Good Lord! You stick to Devil's Gap, an' south of there!"

Johnny's eyes narrowed and he sat up very straight. "This is a free country an' I goes where I please. It's a habit of mine. I said north, an' that's where I'm goin'. I wasn't so set on it before; but now I'm as set as a Missouri mule."

Pop growled. "There ain't no chance of you havin' *my* company; an' you leave th' name an' address of yore next of kin before you starts."

Johnny laughed derisively. "I ain't worryin'. An' now let's figger out what a regular prospector needs. Bein' new at th' game I reckon I better get some advice. What I'm dubious about are th' proper things to pry th' nuggets loose with, an' hoist 'em on my cayuse," he grinned. "Ought to have a pick, shovel, gold pan for placer fussin'— 'gold pan' sounds regular, don't it?—an' some sacks to tie it up in. A dozen'll do for a starter. I can allus come back for more."

"Or you can borrow a chuck waggin; that would be handy because it would make it easy to get yore body out, 'though I reckon they'll just bury you an' let it go that way."

"They? Meanin' who?"

"I ain't got a word to say."

"There's some consolation in that," jeered Johnny.

"Yo're a fool!" snorted Pop heatedly.

"An' so that's went an' follered me down here, too," sighed Johnny. "A man can't get away from some things. Well, let's get back on th' trail. All th' prospectors I ever saw wore cowhide boots, with low, flat heels. Somehow I can't see myself trampin' around with these I'm wearin'; an' they're too expensive to wear 'em out that way. What else? Need any blastin' powder?"

"Cussed if I wouldn't grub-stake you if you wasn't goin' up there," grinned Pop. "It takes a fool for luck; an' it'll be just like you to fall down a canyon an' butt th' dirt of f'n a million dollar nugget. I got a notion to do it anyhow."

"You needn't get no notions!" retorted Johnny. "I'm goin' to hog it. Prospectors never get grubstaked unless they're busted; an' I ain't got there yet. Oh, yes; I got to get them fishhooks— you see, I ain't aimin' to cripple my back workin' hard *all* th' time. I'll fill a sack in th' mornin', eat my dinner an' rest all afternoon. Next day I'll fill another sack, an' so on. Now, what am I goin' to get for my outfit? I'll need a lot of things."

"Go see Charley James, acrost th' street. He keeps th' general store; an' he's got more trash than anybody I ever saw."

"Mebby he can tell me what I need," suggested Johnny, hopefully.

As Pop started to answer, the doorway darkened and a man stepped into the room. Pop's face paled and he swiftly moved to one side, out of range. The newcomer glanced at Johnny, swore under his breath and his hand streaked to his holster. It remained there, for he discovered that he was glaring squarely down a revolver barrel.

"Let loose of it!" snapped Johnny. "Now, then: What's eatin' you?"

"Why—why, I mistook you for somebody else!" muttered the other. "Comin' in from th' sunlight, sudden like, I couldn't see very well. My mistake, Stranger. What'll you have?"

Johnny grunted skeptically. "Yo're shore you can see all right now?"

"It's all right, Nelson," hastily interposed the anxious proprietor, nodding emphatic assurance. "It's all right!"

"My mistake, Mr. Nelson," smiled the stranger.

49

"I shouldn't 'a' been so hasty—but I was fooled. Yore looks are shore misleadin'."

"They suits me. What's wrong about 'em?" demanded Johnny.

"There you go again!" snorted Pop in quick disgust. "A gent makes a mistake, says he didn't mean no harm in it, an' you goes on th' prod! Didn't I *tell* you that yore looks would get you into trouble? Didn't I?"

"Oh! Is *that* it?" He arose and slipped the gun back into its holster. "I'll take th' same, Stranger."

"Now yo're gettin' some sense," beamed Pop, smiling with relief. "Mr. Nelson, shake han's with Tom Quigley. Here's luck."

"Fill 'em again," grinned Johnny. "Not that I hankers for th' kind of liquor you sells, but because we has to do th' best we can with what's pervided."

"Pop's sellin' better liquor than he used to," smiled Quigley. "Am I to thank you for th' improvement?"

"I refuse to accept th' responsibility," laughed Johnny.

"Well, he had some waggin varnish last year, an' for a long time we was puzzled to know what he did with it. One day, somebody said his whiskey tasted like a pine knot: an' then we knew th' answer."

"You both can go to th' devil," grinned Pop.

"Aimin' to make a long stay with us, Mr. Nelson?" asked Quigley.

"That all depends on how soon I gets all th' gold out of this country."

"Ah! Prospectin'?"

"Startin' tomorrow, I am: if this varnish don't kill me."

"There ain't never been none found around here, 'though I never could understand why. There was a couple of prospectors here some years ago, an' they worked harder for nothin' than anybody I ever saw. They covered th' ground purty well, but they was broke about th' time they started south of town, an' had to clear out. They claimed there was pay dirt down there, but they couldn't get a grub-stake on th' strength of that, so they just had to quit."

"That's where it is if it's any place," said Pop hurriedly. "Th' river's workin' day an' night, pilin' it ag'in them rock ledges above th' ford; an' it's been doin' it since th' world began."

Johnny shook his head. "Mebby; but there ain't no way to get it, unless you can drain th' river. I want shallow water—little streams, where there's sand an' gravel bars an' flats. I'm aimin' to work north of here."

Quigley forced a smile and shook his head. "I'm fraid you'll waste yore time. I've been all through that section, in fact I live up there, an' some of my men have fooled around lookin' for color. There ain't a sign of it anywhere."

"Well, I'm aimin' to go back north when I get

tired of prospectin'," replied Johnny, grinning cheerfully; "an' I figgers I can prospect around an' gradually work up that way, toward Hope. I'll drop in an' see you if I run acrost yore place. I reckon prospectin' is a lonesome game."

"Didn't you ever try it before?" asked Quigley in surprise.

"This is my first whirl at it," reluctantly admitted Johnny. "I'm a cow-puncher, got tired of th' north ranges an' drifted down here. An' I might 'a' stayed a cow-puncher, only I got a job on th' CL an' worked there for th' last two weeks; an' I got a-plenty. It soured me of punchin'. Outside of bein' cussed suspicious, that man Logan is loco. I don't mind bein' suspected a little at first; but I ain't goin' to work like a fool when there ain't no call for it. I might 'a' stuck it out, at that, only for a fool notion of his. That's where I cut loose."

Quigley looked curious. "New notion?"

"Yes," laughed Johnny contemptuously. "He got th' idea that th' night air, close to th' river, ain't healthy for th' cows! Told us to drive all of 'em back from th' river every evenin' before we rode in. I said as how we ought to blanket 'em, an' build fires under 'em. I reckon mebby I was a mite sarcastic, at that. Well, anyhow; we had an argument, an' I drew my pay an' quit."

Pop let out a howl. "Good Lord!" he snorted. "Evenin' air too wet for cows! Drive 'em back every night! An' lemme tell you that outfit's just foolish enough to do it, too. He-he-he!"

Quigley laughed, and then looked at the proprietor: "Pop, we ain't forgettin'. We both has bought, an' it usually goes th' rounds before it stops."

"Oh, I'll set 'em up," growled Pop.

"You ranchin', Mr. Quigley?" asked Johnny.

"Well, I am, an' I ain't," answered Quigley. "I'm farmin' an' ranchin' both, on a small scale. I got a few head, but not enough to give me much bother. We sort of let 'em look after themselves."

"Oh," said Johnny regretfully. "I thought mebby if I got tired of prospectin', an' short of cash, that I might get a job with you."

"I ain't got cows enough to keep me busy," explained Quigley. "We let 'em wander, an' get 'em as we need 'em. Well," he said, turning as if to leave, "I'm sorry about that fool break of mine, Mr. Nelson; an' to prove it I'm goin' to give you some real good advice: Keep away from th' Twin Buttes country. So long, boys."

Johnny looked after him, and then faced Pop, shrugging his shoulders. "I don't quite get th' drift of that," he said slowly; "but he ought to know th' country he lives in. I'll try Devil's Gap first; but I got a cussed strong notion not to!"

Pop sighed with relief. "Let's go over an' see what Charley's got for yore kit," he suggested.

53

Charley James was playing solitaire on a box laid across a nail keg and he smiled a welcome as they entered.

"Charley," said Pop. "This cow-puncher's aimin' to change his spots. He's a amatchure prospector an' wants us to pick out his outfit."

"I can believe that he's an amatchure if he's goin' to try it in this part of th' country," smiled Charley. "Nobody's ever tried it down here before."

Johnny was about to mention the two prospectors referred to by Mr. Quigley, but thought better of it.

"Oh, it's been tried," said Pop casually. "But they didn't stay long. What you got in that line, Charley?"

"I ain't shore; but first you want an axe. Come on; we'll saunter aroun' an' pick things out as they hit our eye. Here's th' axe—double bitted, six-pounder."

"Too big," chuckled Pop. "There ain't none of them there redwood trees out here; they're in Californy."

"Huh!" grunted Charley. "Mebbyso; but that's a good axe."

"Pop's right; it's too heavy," decided Johnny. "An' I don't want it double bitted because I may want to drive stakes with it."

"All right," said Charley, who had hoped to at last get rid of the big axe. "Here's a three-pounder—little Gem—an' it shore is. All right; now for th' next article."

In half an hour the outfit was assembled and they were turning to leave the store when Johnny suddenly grabbed his companions. "What about some fishhooks?" he demanded anxiously.

Charley rubbed his head reflectively. "I think mebby I got some; don't remember throwin' 'em away. There was some with feathers, an' some without; plain hooks, an' flies. Brought 'em with me when I first came out here, an' never used 'em. Ought to have some line, too; an' a reel somewheres. I'll hunt 'em up an' put 'em with yore duffle. You can cut yoreself a pole. They'll be a little present from me."

"Thank you," beamed Johnny, and forthwith Pop dragged them to his place of business.

Johnny left the following morning, and one week later he returned, trudging along beside his loaded horse, and he was the owner of a generous amount of gold, the treasure of a "pocket" upon which he had blundered. He determined to keep this a secret, for if he let it be known that he had found "color," what excuse could he offer for leaving that field? It fit too well into his plans to be revealed.

Pop grinned a welcome: "Have any luck?"

"Fishin', yes," laughed Johnny. "Bet I moved ten acres of gravel. I wasted a week; now I'm goin' north."

Pop frowned. "I reckon you'll have yore own way; but put in yore time fishin' an' prospectin', an' mind yore own business."

"Shore," said Johnny. "Look here," unrolling a bundle and producing two of the gold sacks, which were heavy and bulging. Pop stared, speechless, until his new friend opened one of them and dumped four dressed trout on the bar.

"Slip 'em in a fryin' pan with some bacon," grinned Johnny.

"Get 'em in th' river?" demanded Pop incredulously.

"You know that draw runnin' east from th' Gap—th' one with them two dead pines leanin' against each other?"

"Yes; 'tain't more'n a mile from th' ford!"

"I found 'em up there, hidin' in a bush."

"Reckon you think that's funny," grunted Pop. "Why them's *brook* trout! I ain't had any since I was a boy. Th' devil with business! I'm goin' fishin' one day a week. Now where you goin'?"

"Got some for Charley," laughed Johnny from the door.

Charley looked up from his eternal solitaire: "Hello, Nelson!"

"Look what I got," exulted Johnny, extending the bag.

"God help us!" exclaimed Charley. "Did you— did you—"

"I did. Brook trout, Pop says. Prospectin' ain't nothin' compared to fishin'. Pop's goin' one day a week, an' after you eat these mebby you'll be with him."

"Pop can't put on no airs with me," chuckled Charley. "If he can afford to close up, so can I. But you shouldn't 'a' poked no bulgin' gold sack at me like that! It was a shock. Come on; let's take somethin' for it." He grabbed the fish and led the way across the street; and for the rest of the afternoon three happy men discussed prospecting and trout fishing, but the latter was by far the more important.

CHAPTER V
Preparations

The next morning Johnny said good-bye to Pop and walked by Pepper's side, watching the big pack on her back, while Pop, shaking his head, entered his place of business and forthwith began work on a crude sign which, one day a week, would hang on his locked front door.

Well to the north of Hastings, Johnny came to a brook flowing through a deep ravine, and, forsaking the trail, followed the little stream westward and evening found him encamped in a small clearing. He spent several days here, panning the stream and fishing during daylight, and scouting in his moccasins at night. He paid a visit to Little Canyon and explored the valley he was in, and at the head of the valley he found a deep-walled pasture above a short, narrow canyon. Deciding to erect a cabin at the canyon entrance as a monument to the innocence of his activities, he prospected a sand bar near by and rediscovered the gold which he had found at Devil's Gap, which served as an excellent excuse for locating there permanently; and after a week of hard work, the cabin became a reality.

His every movement had been made upon the supposition that he was being watched; and the supposition became a fact when he discovered boot-prints along the opposite bank of the creek. These promised him a trail by which he could easily locate the rustlers' ranch, and at daylight the next morning he was following them and finally reached a great ridge, which he ascended with caution.

Below him was a deep valley, through which a stream moved sluggishly, and at the upper end was a narrow canyon, not more than ten paces wide, through which the stream escaped from another valley above. Twin Buttes were several miles to the east of him, lying a mile or more north of the valley. He looked through the deep canyon and at the corner of a stone house at its other end, and as he watched he saw several men come into view. One of them motioned toward the south and paused to speak to his companions, whereupon Johnny wriggled down the slope and set out for his camp.

Back again in his own valley, he built a sapling fence across the little canyon, cut a pile of firewood near by, and then rode to Hastings, where he nearly gave Charley heart failure by displaying a pleasing amount of virgin gold. He did not see Pop because on the saloon door he found a sign reading: "Back at 4 P.M."

It was a very cheerful cow-puncher who rode to

the new cabin that evening, for he was matching his wits against those of his natural enemies, he was playing a lone hand in his own way against odds, and the game was only beginning.

In perfect condition, virile, young, enduring, he had serene confidence in his ability to take care of himself. He admitted but one master in the art of gunplay, and that man had been his teacher and best friend for years. Even now Hopalong could beat him on the draw, but barely, and he could roll his two guns forward, backward and "mixed"; but he could shoot neither faster nor straighter than his pupil.

Johnny could not roll a gun because he never had tried very hard to master that most difficult of all gunplay, regarding it as an idle accomplishment, good only for exhibition purposes, and, while awe inspiring, Johnny had no yearning for it. He clove to strict utility and did not care to call attention to his wooden-handled, flare-butt Frontiers. There was no ornamentation on them, no ivory, inlay, or engraving. The only marks on their heavy, worn frames were a few dents. He had such a strong dislike for fancy guns that the sight of ivory grips made his lips curl, and such things as pearl handles filled him with grieving contempt for the owner.

He never mentioned his guns to any but his closest friends, and they were as unconscious a part of him as his arms or his legs. And it was his creed that no man but himself should touch them, his friends excepted. He wore them low because utility demanded it; and to so wear them, and to tie them down besides, was in itself a responsibility, for there were men who would not be satisfied with the quiet warning.

In other things, from routine ranch work to man-hunting, from roping and riding to rifle shooting, the old outfit of the Bar-20 had been his teachers and they had taken him in hand at an early age. His rifle he had copied from Hopalong; but Red had taught him the use of it, and to his way of thinking Red Connors was without a peer in the use of the longer weapon.

Johnny was a genius with his six-guns, one of those few men produced in a generation; and he did not belong to the class of fancy gun-workers who shine at exhibitions and fall short when lead is flying and the nerves are sorely tried. He shot from his hips by instinct, and that is the real test of utility. Had he turned his talents to ends which lay outside the law he would have become the most dangerous and the most feared man in the cow-country.

John Logan awoke with a start, sat up suddenly in his bunk and grunted a profane query as his hand closed over his Colt.

"It's Nelson," softly said a voice from outside the window. "Don't make so much noise," it continued, as its owner dropped a handful of pebbles on the ground. "I wanted you awake before I showed myself. Never like to walk into a man's room in th' dark, when he's asleep an' not expectin' visitors. 'Specially when he's worryin' about rustlers. It ain't allus healthy."

"All right," growled the foreman, "but you don't have to throw 'em; you can toss 'em, easy, from there. I've got a welt on my head as big as a chew of tobacco. I'm shore glad you couldn't find nothin' out there that was any bigger. You comin' in or am I comin' out?"

The door squeaked open and squeaked shut and then a chair squeaked.

"You got a musical room," observed Johnny, chuckling softly. "Yore bunk squeaked, too, when you sat up."

"It was a narrow squeak for you," grunted Logan, reluctantly putting down the Colt. "If I'd seen a head I'd 'a' let drive on suspicion. I was havin' a cussed bad dream an' was all het up. My cows was goin' up Little Canyon in whole herds an' I couldn't seem to stop 'em nohow."

"Keepin' my head out of trouble is my long suit," chuckled Johnny. "An' there ain't none of yore cows goin' up Little Canyon—not till I steal some of 'em. Been wonderin' where I was an' what I was doin'?"

"Not very much," answered the foreman. "Got a match? We been gettin' our mail reg'lar every week, an' th' boys allus drop in for a drink at Pop's; an they're good listeners. Say! What th' hell is this I hears about puttin' blankets on my cows an' shovin' 'em into th' river every night? Well, that can wait. You've shore made an impression on ol' Pop Hayes. Th' old Piute can't talk about nothin' but you. Every time th' boys drop in there they get fed up on you. Of course they don't show much interest in yore doin's; an' they don't have to. They says yo're a damned quitter, an' stuff like that, an' Pop gets riled up an' near scalps 'em. What you been doin' to get him so friendly? I never thought he'd be friendly, like that, to anythin' but a silver dollar."

"I don't know—just treat him decent," replied Johnny.

"Huh! I been treatin' him decent for ten years, an' he still thinks I'm some kind of an unknown animal. If he saw me dyin' in th' street he wouldn't drag me five feet, unless I was blockin' his door; but he's doin' a lot of worryin' about you, all right. What you been doin' besides courtin' Pop an' Andy Jackson, washin' gravel an' ketchin' fish?"

Johnny laughed. "I've been playin' cautious— an' right now I ain't shore that I've fooled 'em a whole lot. Here, lemme tell you th' thing—" and he explained his activities since leaving the CL.

At its conclusion Logan grunted. "You got nerve an' patience; an' mebby you got brains. If you can keep 'em from bein' shot out of yore head, you have. An' you say they ain't usin' Little Canyon? I know they ain't usin' it now; but was they?"

"Not since th' frost come out of th' ground,"

replied Johnny. "I can't tell you about what they *are* doin' because I'm just beginnin' to get close to 'em. Th' next time you see me I may know somethin'. Now you listen to me," and he gave the foreman certain instructions, which Logan repeated over after him. "Now, then: I want about sixty feet of rope strong enough to hold me, an' I want a short, straight iron."

"Come with me," ordered the foreman, slipping on his clothes; and in ten minutes they emerged from the blacksmith shop, which also was a storeroom, and Johnny carried a coil of old but strong rope and an iron bar.

"I never thought I'd be totin' a runnin' iron," he chuckled. "If my friends could only see me now! Johnny Nelson, cow-thief an' brand-blotter!"

"You needn't swell up," growled Logan. "You ain't th' only one in this country right now."

"Well," said Johnny, "go back an' finish yore dream—mebby you can find out how to make them cows come back through Little Canyon."

"Yo're goin' to do that," responded Logan; "an' *I*'m goin' to close that window in case *you* come back. I ain't forgot nothin' you said—an' if we don't see one of yore signs for a period of five days, we'll comb yore valley an' th' whole Twin Buttes country. So long!"

Johnny melted into the dark, a low whistle sounded and in a few minutes Logan heard the rhythmic drumming of hoofs, rapidly growing fainter.

CHAPTER VI
A Moonlight Reconnaissance

The evening following his visit to the CL, Johnny went to bed early but not to sleep. For several hours he lay thinking and listening, and then he arose and put on his moccasins, threw on his shoulder Logan's rope, now knotted every foot of its length, slipped out of the cabin and was swallowed up in the darkness along the base of the rocky wall. To cover the few yards between the cabin and the narrow crevice took ten minutes, and to go softly up the crevice took twice as long.

Reaching the top he listened intently, and then moved slowly and silently to a small clump of pines growing close to the rim of the steep wall enclosing the walled-in pasture, at a point where it was so sheer and smooth that he believed it would not be watched. Fastening one end of the rope to a tree, he lowered the rest of it over the wall and went down. Pausing again to listen, he made his way to a line of stones which lay across the creek, crossed with dry feet, and reached the northern wall of the pasture. This could be climbed at half a dozen places and he soon was up it and on his way north. After colliding with several bowlders and tripping twice he waited until the moon arose and then went on again at a creditable speed.

The crescent moon had risen well above the tops of Twin Buttes when a man in moccasins moved cautiously across a high plateau some miles north of Nelson's creek and finally dropped to all fours and proceeded much more slowly. From all fours to stomach was his next choice and he wriggled toward the edge of the plateau, pausing every foot or so to remove loose stones. These he put aside before going on again, for there is no telling where a rolling pebble will stop, or the noise it may make, when the edge of a mesa wall is but a few feet away. Coming to within an arm's length of the edge, he first made sure that the rim was solid rock and free from dirt and pebbles; and then, hitching forward slowly, he peered down into the deep valley.

Its immensity amazed him, for upon the occasion of his former reconnaissance he had viewed it from the outside; and as a picture of his own pasture flashed into his mind he snorted softly at the contrast, for where he had acres, this great "sink" had square miles. It was wider than his own was long, and it stretched away in the faint moonlight until its upper reaches were lost to his eyes. It was large enough to hold one great butte in its middle, and perhaps there were more; and from where he lay he judged the wall below him dropped straight down for three hundred feet.

"There ain't no line ridin' here, unless th' cows grow wings," he muttered.

To the south of him were four lighted windows near the forbidding blackness of the entrance canyon, and from their spacing he deduced two houses. And across from the windows he could make out a vague quadrangle, which experience told him was the horse corral. As if to confirm his judgment there came from it at that moment a shrill squeal and the sound of hoofs on wood, muffled by the distance. And from the corral extended a faint line which ran across the valley and became lost in the darkness near the opposite cliff. This he knew to be a fence.

"If this valley ends like it begins, three or four men can handle an awful lot of cows, 'cept at drive time," he soliloquized, and then listened intently to the sound of distant voices.

> . . . . *many happy hours away,*
> *A sittin' an' singin' by a little cottage do-o-r,*
> *Where lived my darlin' Nel-lie Gr-a-ay,*

came floating faintly from far below him.

He peered in the direction of the singing and barely made out a moving blot well out in the valley. As it came steadily nearer, the blot resolved itself into several dots, and the chorus had greater volume. It appeared that the group was harmonizing.

"You'll be doin' somethin' more than sittin' an' singin' at yore little cottage door one of these days," grunted Johnny savagely. It was his rebuff to the thought which came to him of how long it had been since he had ruined the silence in cornpany with his friends. "That first feller is purty good; but one of 'em shore warbles like a sick calf."

Several other dots arose suddenly from the earth and lumbered sleepily away as the horsemen approached them.

"There's some of Logan's cows, I reckon," grunted the watcher grimly. "Wish I could see better. I've got to do my prospectin' in daylight; an' I got to find some way to ride over here— waste too much time on foot."

More squealing came from the corral and grew in volume as other horses joined in it. From the noise it appeared to be turning into a free-for-all. A door in one of the distant houses suddenly opened and framed a rectangular patch of light, dull and yellow; and from it emerged a bright little light which swung in short, jerky arcs close to the ground and went rapidly toward the corral. Soon thereafter the squealing ceased and a moment later the little light went bobbing back again, blotted out in rhythmic dashes by the swinging legs beside it.

"Big Jerry fightin' again," laughed one of the

horsemen during a pause in the singing. Johnny barely was able to hear him.

Oh my darlin' Nellie Gra-a-y,
*   they have taken her awa-a-y;*
An' I'll never see' my darlin' any more
    —ANY MORE!

rumbled the harmonizers, bursting into a thundering perpetration on the repetition of the last two words.

"Th' farther off they get th' better they sound," growled Johnny as the harmonizers were swallowed up in the darkness near the opposite cliff. "They'd sound better at about ten miles."

Lying comfortably on his stomach, his head out over the rim of the wall, he was lost in thought when a sudden, startled snort behind him nearly caused him to go over the edge. A contortionist hardly could have changed ends quicker than he did; he simply went up in the air and when he came down again he was on hands and knees, one foot where his head had been. But he did not stop there; indeed, he did not even pause there, for he kept on moving until he was on his feet, his knees bent and his head thrust forward, and each hand, without conscious direction, held a gun. And almost instantly they chocked back into the holsters.

A gray shape was backing slowly into the

shadows of a bowlder, two green eyes boring through the gloom, and Johnny's hair became ambitious.

"I dassn't shoot, I dassn't run, an' I can't back up! All right; when in doubt try a bluff; but I shore hopes it's th' bluffin' kind!"

He emitted a throaty, ferocious snarl, dropped the tips of his fingers to the earth and started for the bowlder and the green eyes, on a series of back-humping, awkward jumps, like a weak-kneed calf cavorting playfully. Another snort, curious, incredulous, frightened, came from the bowlder and a great gray wolf backed off hastily, but with a hesitating uncertainty which was not as reassuring as might be hoped for.

Johnny let out another snarl, more terrifying than the first, humped his back energetically, waved his legs, and then with a low-toned but blood-curdling shriek, leaped at the wavering cow-killer. The gray silhouette lengthened and vanished, simply melting into the darkness as though it had urgent business elsewhere.

Johnny arose, a rock in his hand, and sighed with relief; and his ambitious hair settled back again into its accustomed place while the prickling along his spine died out.

"Holy smoke! What if it had been half-starved, or a grizzly! Blast you!" he growled, shaking a vengeful fist at the presumed locality of the wolf. "You just come snortin' around *my* valley!

I'll shoot yore insides all over th' landscape!"

Hanging onto the rock, he readjusted his belts and went nearer the entrance canyon to get a closer view of the houses and surroundings. When again he looked over the edge of the precipice he was directly over the corral and across from the houses, which the rays of the moon, slanting through a break in the opposite cliff, now faintly revealed.

There were three houses and they were low, long and narrow, and built of stone, with the customary adobe roofs; and they were built in echelon, the three end walls appearing as one from the canyon. He nodded appreciatively, for it required no great imagination to see, in his mind's eye, the loopholes which undoubtedly ornamented that end of the houses. The narrow canyon, straight as an arrow and fully half a mile long, lay at almost perfect right angles to the three walls. A handful of determined men, cool and accurate, in those houses could hold the canyon against great odds while their food, water and ammunition held out. Moving his head, he caught a sudden glint, and peered intently to discover what had caused it. He moved again until he saw it the second time, and then he knew. A small trickle of water flowed from a spring back near the great wall, and it passed under one corner of each house.

"That's purty good!" he ejaculated in

ungrudging admiration. He was something of a strategist himself and he was not slow to pay respect to the handiwork of genius when he saw it. "Built 'em like steps so as to cover th' canyon from all three houses; an' diverted that little stream so they could get water without showing themselves. No matter which side of them houses is rushed, there is allus three walls to face. Th' only weak spots are th' north an' south corners. If they ain't loopholed a good man could sneak right up to th' corner of th' end houses; but what he'd do after he got there, I don't know."

He studied the problem in silence and then nodded his head: "Huh! Them walls don't overhang, an' so they can't shoot down close to 'em. Mebby I've found th' weak spot—but I'll have to get a whole lot closer than I am now before I'm shore of it. An' that can wait."

He wriggled back from the wall and arose. "Seen all I can at night. Don't even know if these fellers *are* rustlin'. Bein' suspicious an' bein' shore ain't th' same. But th' next time I come up here I won't leave until I am shore, not if it takes all summer. Logan said to be shore to find out how many there are, their trail from his ranch an' th' place where they operates on th' CL. Says he's got to get 'em actually stealin' his cows on his ranch. Says he ain't got no friends out here and that th' other ranches acts like they was sort of on th' side of th' thieves. That's a hell of a note, that is! Buck, an' Hoppy, an' us: we never gave a whoop where we found rustlers if they had our cows; an' we never gave two whoops in hell what th' rest of th' country thought about it. Times have changed. Imagine us askin' anybody if we could shoot rustlers! Huh!"

He started back the way he had come up, and reached his own valley without incident; but when he wriggled toward the wall he was puzzled, and worried. There was the clump of pines up above him, ghostly in the faint moonlight; but he could see no rope. Thankful that he had been cautious in crossing the valley, he wriggled a little closer and then started back over his trail, recrossed the valley, climbed the other wall in the shelter offered by a crevice and slipped along the great ridge. All he cared about now was to get back into the cabin without being seen. All kinds of conjectures ran through his head concerning the absence of the rope, and while he thrashed them out he kept going ahead, careful to take full advantage of the wealth of cover at hand.

His senses were keyed to their highest pitch of efficiency and at times he concentrated on one of them at the expense of the others. While he used his eyes constantly, it was in his ears that he placed the most confidence. The man who does the moving about is at a disadvantage, which he keenly realized.

He did not mind so much being away from the cabin if he could make it appear to be innocent; and to that end he moved steadily toward the Hastings trail. His horse was not to be seen, and that worried him. It could have strayed, for he had neither picketed nor hobbled it, but he feared that it had not strayed.

Passing his old camp site he heard a noise, and flattened himself on the ground. It came again and from the edge of the clearing where he had spent his first few nights in the valley. Anyone foolish enough to make a noise, under the circumstances, was foolish enough to be stalked by any man who had good sense; and he proceeded to do the stalking.

It took him quite a while to get around back of the place where his tent had stood, but when he finally got there he was repaid for his time and trouble. It was not the direction from which he would be expected, if the rustlers' suspicions were aroused; and there was a certain twisting path through the brush which was devoid of twigs and sticks.

Foot by foot he crept forward until he could see the big bowlder in the clearing, and then he paused as the sound was heard again, and he tried to classify it. A twig snapped, and then another sound made him nod quickly. It was a horse; that was certain; but could it be Pepper? While he pondered and listened to the slow, interrupted steps, a dark shape moved out from the deep shadows of the trees, pricked its ears, stretched out its head toward him, nickered softly and slowly advanced.

He stared in amazement, for while it was Pepper, the saddle was on her back; and when he had left the cabin the saddle was inside. But, was it, though? In a moment his mind had marshaled in review before him all his acts of the previous day; all but one. Had he unsaddled the horse when he had ridden back from the upper end of his little valley? Of course he had; why should he have neglected to do such a thing as that? But, perhaps he hadn't. He swore under his breath and backed away, for the horse was coming nearer all the time. It was his saddle; he could tell that easily. And then all of his doubts cleared in a flash. When he had ridden in from the pasture he had started to remove the saddle, but when he thought of his boiling pots he had pushed the end of the cinch strap back under the little holding strap, and he had not shoved it home. Right now that cinch end should be sticking out in a loop. Craning his neck and shifting silently he managed to see it; and a chuckle escaped from him. He whistled softly, so softly that anyone a hundred feet away could not have heard it; but the horse heard it and nickered again. What fools these men were! Did her master think that she had to hear a whistle to know that he was about, when the wind was right and he was so close?

Pepper was a well-trained, intelligent animal, and Johnny knew it better than anyone else; and Pepper had a strong aversion to strangers, which he also knew; and knowing that, he was instantly assured that there were no strangers in the immediate vicinity because Pepper was thoroughly at her ease. The black head thrust forward into his face and the bared teeth snapped at him, whereupon he playfully cuffed the velvety nozzle. Pepper forthwith swung her head suddenly and knocked off her master's hat, and pretended to be in a fine rage.

"You old coyote!" chuckled Johnny, cuffing her again. "Cussed if you ain't th' most no-account old fool I ever saw. But I ought to be kicked from here to Hastings an' back again for leavin' that saddle on you all afternoon an' night. Will some sugar square it? Hey! Get out of my pocket—it's in th' shack," he laughed. And there was a note in his laughter that a horse of Pepper's intelligence might easily understand.

Mounting, he rode across the clearing, and when he reached the water course he followed it to his cabin. Pepper had given him the card he needed now for, in the saddle and careless of being seen, which was his best play, dangerous as it might be, he was riding home from an evening spent in Hastings. As to answering any questions about the dangling rope, he either would inform the curious that it was none of their business, or lie; and whether the lie would be a humorous exaggeration which could not possibly be believed, or adroit, plausible, and convincing would be a matter of mood.

Whistling softly he rode across the little plateau, stripped the saddle from Pepper, who waited until he returned with some sugar, and lit the lantern. Pepper was not the only member of that partnership whose nose was useful; and the faint odor of a vile, frontier cigar had lingered after its possessor had departed.

"Huh! We must 'a' swapped ends tonight; but I'll bet he's doin' more wonderin' than me. He thinks he's got a lead, findin' that rope. I know he didn't see me put it there, or go down it; an' I'll bet he don't know that I came back to it. He can watch an' be cussed."

CHAPTER VII
A Council of War

Clearing away the breakfast pans the following morning, Johnny did some soliloquizing.

"This is a nice little shack, but I ain't stuck on it a whole lot. Now that I've built it, I've got to use it or tip off my hand; an' as long as I use it they know where to find me. I've got to come back to it. At th' worst I can hold it against them for five days; an' then th' outfit'll be up here an' drive 'em off. But if it comes to trouble they won't let me get to it; they'll pick me off when I'm outside. They're gettin' more suspicious all th' time, too, judgin' from that missin' rope an' th' smell of that cigar. Nope; I don't like this shack a little bit. An' some night when I'm sneakin' back to it, suppose one of 'em is in it, waitin' for me? That wouldn't be nice. First chance I get I'll tote my tarpaulin an' some supplies out of here an' cache 'em some place not too far away."

Going into the little valley he was greatly surprised to see the rope hanging as he had left it, but he did not give it a second glance, and acted as though he was ignorant that it had been removed. He busied himself carrying firewood from the pile and heaping it up in the center of a cleared space, ready to be lit later on, and then removed the two saplings which made the gate to his rough fence and swung them aside so that they formed a V-shaped approach to the opening. Having performed these mysterious rites he passed the cabin, climbed up the crevice, recovered the rope, and returned. Carrying it into the house he carelessly closed the door behind him, went swiftly to the loose log in the rear wall and removed the things he had hidden behind it, rolling them up in the tarpaulin. Then he picked ravelings from an empty salt sack, tied them together and rolled them in the dirt on the floor until they matched it in color. After filling the water pails and chopping some firewood he took the gold pan and his rod and sought the creek, where he spent the rest of the day working and fishing.

Darkness found his supper dishes washed and put away, and, kneeling by the door, he stretched a string of weak ravelings across the opening, six inches above the sill. Cord not only would have been too prominent, but too strong; a foot would break the ravelings and never feel the contact. Whistling to Pepper, he took his saddle and the tarpaulin, stepped high over the door sill and in a few minutes was riding down the valley. Just before he came to the Hastings trail he threw the tarpaulin far into the brush without slowing the horse, and then, crossing the trail, plunged into the sloping draw which eventually became Little Canyon.

Pepper gingerly picked her way down the rough canyon trail without any directions from her rider, crossed the level, bowlder-strewn flat to the river, and stopped at the water's edge.

The Deepwater gurgled and swished, cold, swift, deep, and black, and Johnny shivered in anticipation of the discomforts due to be his for the next few hours. Unbuckling his belts, he slung them around his neck, and in his hat he placed the contents of his pockets. Giving Pepper a friendly and encouraging slap, he urged her into the river, a task which she did not like; but she overcame her prejudices against ice water and plunged in, swimming with powerful strokes. Emerging on the other bank they cantered briskly to the faintly beaten trail where Billy Atwood spent so many hours, and along it until a small, isolated clump of trees loomed up. There was a stump among them and on this Johnny placed a stone. Then he waited, shivering, until the moon came up.

A black blot arose hastily from the earth and became a cow. Two more near it also arose, and the three lumbered off clumsily, driven in the right direction by a horse that knew her work. It was her firm belief that cows had been put on earth to be bossed by her, and no matter how quickly they swerved she was always at the right place at the right time and kept them going as her master wished. She neither hurried them too fast nor pressed them too closely, for she knew that when a range cow is pushed too hard it is likely to go "on the prod" and change instantly from an easy-going, docile victim to a stubborn, vicious quadruped with no sense whatever and a strong yearning to use its horns.

It did not take long to get six cows to the edge of the Deepwater; but it took two hours of careful but hard riding, perseverance and profuse profanity to get them into the water. It was no one-man job, and with a horse that had less training than Pepper it might have proved to be an impossibility; but at last one cow preferred the water to being made a fool of, and when it went in the others reluctantly followed. Scrambling out on the farther bank they doubtless were congratulating themselves upon having escaped a pest, when the pest itself emerged behind them and drove them slowly but steadily toward Little Canyon. In it they went, and up it; and as they paused on the main trail to determine which way to go, the pest arrived and decided the question for them, drove them across it and into a small valley; and as day broke, six unhurried, placid cows wandered slowly into the crooked canyon and through the opening in the fence.

Having changed the brands from the original

CL to an equally sprawling GB, he returned to the cabin, unsaddled, and entered, stepping high over the sill. No one was there and nothing had been disturbed, but when he looked for the thread he found it snapped and lying on the floor.

Starting a brisk fire he hung his wet clothes before it on crude tripods made of sticks, hastily ate a substantial breakfast, fastened the shutter of the window, hung the gold pan over the closed door to serve as an alarm if anyone should enter, and in a few minutes was asleep.

Across the creek, high up the great ridge, a man lay behind a bowlder, a rifle in his hands, and he kept close watch on the cabin. Waiting a reasonable length of time, he finally arose, waved his hand and settled down again, the rifle covering the cabin door. In the pasture another man emerged from a thicket and hurried toward the canyon, swearing softly when he saw the changed brands. It took no second sight to tell him what the original brand had been. Emerging from the canyon he paused, glanced up at his friend, who made a significant sign, debated something in his mind, and then, pulling out a notebook, scrawled something in it and tore out the page. Creeping softly he reached the cabin door, stuck the page on it and then hurried away to join his friend. They climbed the ridge and hastened northward, conversing with animation.

When they reached the canyon leading to their

ranch a tall, rangy man advanced to meet them. "Well," he said, smiling: "what did you find out about the rope? An' what kept you so long?"

"We found out a-plenty," growled Ackerman angrily. "That feller ain't no prospector. I've said so all along. He don't know enough about prospectin' to earn a livin' on th' top of a pile of gold!"

His companion nodded quickly. "Jim's right; he's a rustler. Doin' it single-handed, on a small scale."

"*I* ain't nowise shore that rustlin' is his game, neither," said Ackerman. "If he is he's a new hand at it. I could rebrand them cows in just about half th' time it took him, an' do a better job. He's dangerous; an' he should 'a' been shot long before this. I can get him today," he urged.

"I don't doubt that; but I wouldn't do it," smiled Quigley. "An' I hope *yo're* shore he ain't Logan."

Jim swore. "Yes; but if he keeps on rustlin' he'll have Logan after him. An' that'll mean that we'll have to look sharp, an' mebby fight. You let me get him, Tom."

Quigley shook his head. " 'Tain't necessary. All we got to do is let him know he ain't wanted. Steal his cows, burn his cabin; an' shoot near him a couple of times, until he realizes how easy we can shoot *through* him. But I ain't shore I want him drove away."

"Huh!" questioned Ackerman.

"Huh!" repeated Fleming foolishly.

"Well," drawled Quigley, "for one thing Logan's purty shore to begin missin' cows before long. What puzzles me is that he ain't missed 'em long ago. Then he'll begin watchin' his range nights."

"But he won't watch up there," interrupted Fleming. "He don't know about that ford."

"There's only two breaks in th' Barrier," continued Quigley, ignoring the interruption, "that are near Nelson's valley; an' they're th' first places Logan'll watch. They're Big an' Little Canyons. Some fine night Nelson will get caught or followed. Bein' a stranger, an' once workin' for th' CL, Logan will think he's got th' rustlers. He'll find signs that'll make him look in Nelson's pasture—if they ain't there naturally we'll put 'em there. They'll find his cabin an' his rebranded herd. When they go back again they'll reckon that th' rustlin' is all over; an' we'll still be in th' game, lettin' up a little for a while, an' be better off than ever. Savvy my drift?"

Ackerman shook his head savagely. "With them six cows, an' Logan missin' hundreds?" he sarcastically demanded.

Quigley smiled patronizingly. "Findin' only a few won't mean nothin', except that he's driven off th' rest every time he has got a few together, an' sold 'em. Now if you was to take that notebook that's stickin' out of yore pocket, an' write in it some words an' figgers showin' that he's sold so many cows, an' what he got for 'em each time, it might help. We'll know when Logan's due, an' we can drop that book where he'll find it. You never want to kill anythin' till yo're shore it ain't goin' to be useful. There's one thing I'm set on: there ain't going to be no unnecessary killin'.''

Ackerman laughed grimly. "Well, anyhow; I've started things. I left a note on his door tellin' him what to do."

"What did you write?" demanded Quigley.

Ackerman told him defiantly. "An' what's more," he added, "I'm goin' to do some pot-shootin' before long."

"Well," replied Quigley, "I'd rather drive him out, an' then watch him for a while. I ain't shore he can't be scared. Do you think he suspects he's bein' watched?"

"I don't think so," answered Fleming.

"I know he does!" snapped Ackerman. "Why does he paw around that gravel bed an' pertend that he's found gold in it? There ain't no gold there!"

Quigley laughed. "He found gold, all right. Charley James saw it: an' he got it right there. He wanted Charley to take it in pay. I don't doubt that you know somethin' about prospectin' but 'gold is where it's found.' "

Ackerman thrust his head forward. "Gold in that gravel! Hell!"

"Charley saw it," grunted Quigley.

"Charley be damned!" snorted Ackerman. He looked closely at Quigley and suddenly demanded: "What makes you so set ag'in us shootin' him?"

Quigley regarded him evenly. "There was a lot of talk, when Porter was found dead. I told you all at th' time. Four men have got curious, come up in these hills an' never went out again. Twin Buttes has a bad name; an' th' next dead man that's blamed on us is goin' to make a lot more talk an' may stir up trouble.

"Now then: Pop knows that Nelson's up here, an' that means that everybody knows it. He saw me reach for my gun, an' heard me tell him to keep out of here. An' let me tell you Pop knows more about us than he lets on; an' he's as venomous as a snake when he gets riled. An' he ain't th' only one that knows things.

"Now we'll add it up: If we can scare Nelson away, or discourage him, he'll quit of his own accord; an' he won't talk because he knows that somebody knows he's been rustlin'." He turned on his heel. "Am I plain enough?"

"Wait a minute," called Ackerman. "That feller has got me worried. Mebby it would be reckless to let him disappear up here; but suppose I go on a spree in town when he's there? It's easy to start a fight with a gun-man, because he's got to toe th' mark. I can do th' job open an' above board, an' make it natural; an' that will keep us clear."

"Jim," smiled Quigley, "I don't want to lose you; an' if you pick a square fight with that man, th' even break that you demand in yore personal quarrels, we *will* lose you. I looked down his gun, an' I tell you that I didn't see him move. He's a *gun* man!"

Ackerman laughed. "We won't say anythin' about *that*. But if he did get th' worst of it in an even break an' a personal quarrel, would it hurt us up here? That's all I want to know."

Quigley thought deeply, and made a slow and careful reply. "If it wasn't bungled I don't see how it could. You'd have to rile him subtle, make him declare war an' be th' injured party yoreself; an' you'd want witnesses. But don't you do it, Jim; not nohow. I got a feelin' that he's th' best man with a Colt in this section. Yo're a wizard with a six-gun; but you ain't good enough for him. When he's around yo're in th' little boy's class; an' I ain't meanin' no offense to you, neither."

Ackerman, hands on hips, stared at Quigley's back as he walked away. "Th' hell you say!" he snorted wrathfully. " 'Little boy's class,' huh?" He wheeled and turned a scowling face to his friend Fleming. "Did you hear that? I calls that rubbin' it in! I got a notion to take that feller's two guns away from him an' make Tom eat 'em! Damned if I don't, too. You ride to town with me an' I'll show you somethin' you won't never forget!"

It may not be out of place here to say that the

time soon came when he did show Fleming something; and that Fleming never did forget it.

Mr. Quigley smiled grimly as he entered the house, for it was his opinion that Mr. Ackerman had no peer in his use and abuse of Mr. Colt's most famous invention. He hardly could ask Mr. Ackerman to sally forth and engage in a personal duel with a common enemy, for it would smack too much of asking a friend to do his fighting for him. He believed that leadership is best based when it rests upon the respect of those led. He had no doubt about the outcome of such a duel, for he implicitly believed that the stranger, despite his vaunting two guns, had as much chance against Mr. Ackerman's sleight-of-hand as an enraged rattler had against a cool and businesslike king snake. The appropriateness of the simile made him smile, because the rattler is heavily armed and calls attention to the fact, while the king snake is modest, unassuming, and sounds no war-cry. Two guns meant nothing to Mr. Quigley, because he knew that one was entirely sufficient in the hand of the right man.

He had carefully pointed out the way for Mr. Ackerman to proceed in such a situation, and then warned him in an irritating way not to go ahead. So now he sighed with relief at a problem solved, for his knowledge of Mr. Ackerman's character was based upon accurate observations extending over a long period of time.

CHAPTER VIII
Fleming is Shown

Johnny got up at noon, and when he saw the sign on his door its single word "Vamoose" told him that the valley and the cabin were of no further use to him; that the time for subterfuge and acting a part was past. That the rustlers were not certain of his intentions was plain, for otherwise there would have been a bullet instead of a warning; and he was mildly surprised that they had not ambushed him to be on the safe side.

It now remained for him to open the war, and warn them further; or to pretend to obey the mandate and seek new fields of observation. Pride and anger urged the former; common sense and craftiness, the latter; and since he had not accomplished his task he decided to swallow his anger and move. Had he been only what he pretended to be, Nelson's creek would have seen some stirring times. As a sop to his pride he printed a notice on a piece of Charley's wrapping paper and fastened it on the door. Its three, short words made a concise, blunt direction as to a certain journey, popularly supposed to be the more heavily traveled trail through the spirit world. Packing part of his belongings on Pepper, he found room to sit in the saddle, and started off for an afternoon in Hastings, after which he would return to the cabin to spend the night and to get the rest of his effects.

When he rode into town he laughed outright at the sign on Pop's door, and he laughed harder when he saw another on Charley's door; and leaving his things behind Pop's saloon, he pushed on to Devil's Gap. At the ford he met the two happy anglers returning and they paused in midstream to hold up their catch.

"You come back with us," grinned Pop. "We'll pool th' fish an' have a three-corner meal. Where was you goin'?"

"To find you," chuckled Johnny. "I'm surprised at th' way you both neglects business."

"Comin' from you that makes me laugh," snorted Pop.

Charley grinned. "Did you see that whoppin' big feller I got? Bet it'll go three pounds."

"Lucky if it's half that," grunted Pop. "If I'd 'a' got that one I had hold of, we'd 'a' had a three-pounder, or mebby a four-pounder."

Charley snorted. "Who ever heard of a four-pound brook trout? Been a brown, now, it might 'a' been that big."

"Why, I caught 'em up to eight pounds, back East, when I was a kid!" retorted Pop.

"Yo're a squaw's dog liar!" snapped Charley. "Eight-pound brook trout! You must 'a' snagged a turtle, or an old boot full of mud!"

"Bet you five dollars!" retorted Pop, bristling.

"How you goin' to prove it?" jeered Charley. "Call th' dead back to life to lie for you?"

"Reckon I can't prove it," regretted Pop. "But when a man hangs around with a liar he shore gets th' name, too."

"Nobody never called me a liar an' got off without a hidin'!" snapped Charley. "I may be sixty years old, but I can lick you an' yore whole fambly if you gets too smart!"

Pop drew rein, his chin whiskers bobbing up and down. "I'm older'n that myself; but I don't need no relations to help me lick you! Get off that hoss, if you dares!"

"Here! Here!" interposed Johnny. "What's th' use of you two old friends mussin' each other up? Come on! I'm in a hurry! I'm hungry!"

"I won't go a step till he says I ain't no liar!" snapped Charley.

"I won't go till he says I caught a eight-pound brook trout!"

"Mebby he did—how do *I* know what he did when he was a boy?" growled Charley, full of fight. "But I ain't no liar, an' that's that!"

"Who said you was, you old fool?" asked Pop heatedly.

"You did!"

"I didn't!"

"You did!"

"Yo're a liar!'

"Yo're another!"

"Get off that hoss!"

"You ain't off yore own yet!"

Johnny was holding his sides and Pop wheeled on him savagely. "What the hell *you* laughin' at?"

"That's what *I* want to know!" blazed Charley.

"Come on, Charley!" shouted Pop. "We'll eat them fish ourselves. It's a fine how-dy-do when age ain't respected no more. An' th' next time you goes around callin' folks liars," he said, shaking a trembling fist under Johnny's nose, "you needn't foller *us* to do it on!"

Down the trail they rode, angrily discussing Johnny, the times, and the manners of the younger generation.

When Johnny arrived at the saloon and tried the door he found it locked. He could hear footsteps inside and he stepped back, chuckling, to wait until Pop had forgiven him; but after a few minutes he gave it up and went around to try the window of a side room.

"What you think yo're doin'?" inquired a calm voice behind him.

He wheeled and saw a man regarding him with level gaze, and across the street was a second, who sat on one horse and held fast to another.

"Tryin' to get in for a treat," grinned Johnny, full

of laughter. "Had a spat with Pop an' Charley, an' cussed if they ain't locked me out!"

The stranger showed no answering smile. "That so?" he sneered. "Reckon you better come along with me, 'round front, till I hears what Hayes has to say about it. *I* don't believe he's home."

Johnny's expression changed from a careless grin to an ominous frown. "If you do any walkin' you'll do it alone."

Several people had been drawn to the scene and took in the proceedings with eager eyes and ears, but were careful to keep to one side. Jim Ackerman had a reputation which made such a location very much a part of discretion; and the two-gun man had been well discussed by Pop.

"I finds you tryin' a man's window," said Ackerman. "So I stopped to ask about it. As long as I've took this much trouble I'll go through with it. You comin' peaceful, or must I drag you around?"

"Mebby that's a job you'd like to tackle?" replied Johnny.

"I'm aimin' to be peaceful," rejoined Ackerman, his voice as smooth as oil; "but I allus aim to do what I say. You comin' with me?"

"If yo're aimin' to be peaceful, yo're plumb cross-eyed," retorted Johnny, slouching away from the wall.

Quick steps sounded within the building and a frightened, high-pitched voice could be heard.

"Couple of bobcats lookin' for holts," it said. "That feller Nelson is pickin' on somebody else."

The window raised and Pop stuck his angry face out to see what was going on; and his wrinkled countenance paled suddenly when he saw Ackerman, and the look in his eyes. He had a trout in one hand and a bloody knife in the other, and both fell to the ground.

"Jumpin' mavericks!" he whispered. "It's Ackerman! What's wrong, Jim?" he quavered.

"You saved us a walk," replied Ackerman, not taking his eyes from the flushed face of his enemy. "I caught *him* tryin' to open that window."

Charley thrust his head out as Pop replied. "We was playin' a joke on him. It's all right, Jim. Much obliged for yore unusual interest."

"Well, I'm glad of *that,*" smiled Ackerman; "but he looked *suspicious* an' I reckoned I ought to drag him around an' show you what I *found* tryin' to bust in. But if you *say* it's all right, why I reckon it *is!*"

"I reckon it ain't!" snapped Johnny, enraged at his humiliating position and at the way Ackerman accented his words. "An' if that itchin' *trigger*-finger of *yourn* wants to get *busy* it has my permission," he mimicked. "Pop," he said, sharply, "who *is* this buzzard?"

"No need to get riled over a thing like that," faltered Pop.

"Shut yore trap!" snapped Charley, battle in his

eyes. "That's Ackerman, relative of Quigley's; th' best six-gun man in th' country."

"Thanks," growled Johnny, staring through narrowed lids at Ackerman, who stood alert, his lips twitching with contempt. "When a dog pesters me I kick him; if he snaps at me I shoot him. I'm goin' to kick you to yore cayuse an' yore friend." He had been sliding forward while he spoke and now they stood face to face, an arm's length apart.

Ackerman suddenly made two lightning-like movements. His left hand leaped out to block his enemy's right in its draw, while his own right flashed down to his gun. As his fingers closed on the butt, Johnny's heavy Colt by some miracle of speed jabbed savagely into the pit of the scheming man's stomach with plenty of strength behind it, and Ackerman doubled up like a jackknife, his breath jolted out of him with a loud grunt. Johnny's right hand smacked sharply on his enemy's cheek, left vivid finger marks, which flashed white and then crimson, and continued on down; and when it stopped a plain, Frontier Colt peeked coyly from his hip at the surprised and chagrined gentleman across the street, who had been instructed to remain a noncombatant; and had no intention, whatsoever, of disobeying Ackerman's emphatic order. To reveal his status he quickly raised his hands and clasped them on the top of his hat, which is a more comfortable position than holding them stiffly aloft.

Ackerman was dazed and sick, for the solar plexus is a peculiarly sensitive spot, and his hands instinctively had forsaken offense and spasmodically leaped to the agonized nerve center.

"Turn around!" snapped Johnny viciously. *"Pronto!* There's dust on th' seat of yore pants."

Ackerman groaned and obeyed, and the hurtling impact of a boot drove him to his hands and knees.

"Get agoin'!" ordered Johnny, aflame with anger, slipping the right hand gun back into its holster and motioning with the other.

Ackerman, his eyes blazing, started on his humble journey, assisted frequently by the boot; and having crossed the street, he paused.

"Get up on that cayuse!" crisply ordered Johnny, making motions which increased the mounted man's uneasiness.

The further Ackerman had crawled the angrier he had become, and tears of rage streaked the dust on his face. At Johnny's last command and the kick which accompanied it, his good sense and all thought of safety left him. He arose with a spring, a berserker, trembling with rage, and reached for his gun with convulsive speed while looking into his enemy's weapon with unseeing eyes. There was a flash, a roar, and a cloud of smoke at Johnny's hip, and a glittering six-shooter sprang into the air, spinning rapidly. Ackerman did not feel the shock which numbed his hand, but leaped forward straight at his enemy's throat. Johnny swerved quickly and his right hand swung up in a short, vicious arc. Ackerman, too crazed to avoid it, took the blow on the point of his jaw and dropped like a stone.

Johnny stepped back and looked evilly at the man on the horse.

"Gimme yore gun, butt first. Thanks. You work for Quigley?"

The other nodded slowly.

"Friend of this hombre?"

"Yes; sort of."

"Then why didn't you cut in?"

"Why, I—I—" the other hesitated, and stopped.

"Spit it!"

"Well, I wasn't supposed to," coldly replied the horseman.

"Then it was talked over?"

"Not particular. Jim does his own fightin', hisself."

"Good thing for Jim, an' you, too," retorted Johnny. "When it's crowded I can't allus be polite. Who put that sign on my door?"

"What sign?"

"I'm askin' *you* questions!" snapped Johnny, his eyes blazing anew.

"Dunno nothin' about it," answered the other.

"I reckon yo're a practiced liar," retorted

Johnny. "But it don't make no difference. I'm leavin' th' valley, for I can't fight pot-shooters an' do any work at th' same time. Quigley don't own this country, an' you tell him that while he's boss of that little valley, *I*'m boss in this town. If him or any of his men come to town while I'm here I'll shoot 'em down like I would a snake. That means one at a time or all together; an' if he don't believe me, you tell him I'll be here all day tomorrow. There ain't no bushes in town, an' none of yore gang can fight without 'em. Now you say to him that I don't want no remarks made about what I was doin' up there—you savvy that? If I hear of any I'll slip up there some night an' blow him all over his shirt. An' damn you, I mean it!"

Ackerman stirred and sat up, looking around in a dazed way. When his eyes fell on Johnny they lost their puzzled look and blazed again with rage. He reached swiftly to his holster, found it empty, and shrugged his shoulders.

Johnny regarded him coldly. "Get on that cayuse, an' start goin'. This town ain't big enough for both of us at once."

Ackerman silently obeyed, but his face was distorted with passion. When he had clawed himself into the saddle he looked down on the grim master of the situation.

"Words are foolish," he whispered. "We'll meet again!"

Johnny nodded. "I reckon so. Everybody plays their cards accordin' to their own judgment. Just now I got a high straight flush, so you hit th' trail, *pronto!*"

He stepped aside to get out of the dust-cloud which suddenly swirled around him, and watched it roll northward until the dim figures in it were lost to sight around a bend. The slouch went out of his bearing as he straightened up and slid his gun into its holster, and walking over to Ackerman's glittering six-shooter he picked it up and sneered at it.

"I ain't surprised," he laughed, eying the ivory handle and the ornate engraving. Wheeling abruptly he glanced carelessly at the grinning audience and strode to the door of Pop's saloon.

"I'll be damned!" sputtered Pop, his eyes still bulging.

"Reckon you will," laughed Johnny, "unless you mends yore sinful ways."

"What you been doin' make Jim Ackerman pick a fight with you?" demanded Pop, recovering his faculties and his curiosity at the same instant.

"Here's his gun; an' here's his friend's," said Johnny. "Keep 'em for 'em. They plumb went off without 'em."

Pop openly admired Ackerman's weapon. "Bet that cost a heap," he remarked. "Ain't she a beauty?" He rubbed energetically at a leaden splotch on the cylinder.

"It was in good company," replied Johnny.

"You got to look out for him," Pop warned. "He's a bad Injun." Then he grinned suddenly. "But he come damned near bein' a *good* Injun!"

"Hey!" called a peeved voice from within. "If you reckon I'm goin' to clean *all* these fish myself, you better copper yore bets." Footsteps approached the door and Charley roughly elbowed Pop aside. "That means you, too, Nelson," he growled. "What you mean, hangin' back at th' ford? Figger we'd have 'em all cleaned before you arrove? Well, if you aim to eat any of 'em, you grab holt of a knife an' get busy!" He shuffled back into the room again, muttering: "Cripes! I'm fish from my head to my heels an' bloody as a massacre. An' what's more, I ain't goin' to clean another damned one, not nohow!"

CHAPTER IX

A Skirmish in the Night

Saying good night to his two friends, Johnny rode north along the trail, but he had not ridden more than half way to the mouth of his valley when he swung Pepper into an arroyo which he knew led to the south side of the butte behind his cabin. While heavily fringed with brush and trees it was open enough along the dry bed of the stream to permit him to push on at fair speed, and while there were rocks and bowlders in plenty, Pepper easily avoided them in the soft moonlight and went on with confidence. At last, reaching a fork, he chose the right-hand lead and pushed on more slowly for a few minutes, and then, picketing the horse, he slipped out of his chaps and boots and put on the pair of moccasins which had been hidden under the saddle flaps. Taking the rifle from the long scabbard, he slung it across his back and slipped noiselessly up the ravine.

Half an hour later he stopped suddenly and sniffed, and then glanced quickly around him. The smoke was very faint, but it was something to think about because it meant either men close at hand or a forest fire. Going on again, even more slowly, he began to take advantage of cover, and as he proceeded the smoke became steadily stronger. A sudden suspicion made him set his jaws, for he was going straight up wind and toward his cabin. Stopping a moment to consider, he turned sharply to his left and went on again, a Colt swinging loosely in his left hand. Anything close enough to be seen plainly would be near enough for the Colt, and in such poor light the six-shooter was more accurate in his hands than a rifle.

The only things about him which he could hear were the holsters, which rubbed very softly as he walked, but the sound would not carry for any distance. Having gone around the little valley near his cabin, he crawled along below the ragged skyline of the ridge and reached a point close to the cabin, when he suddenly dropped to his stomach and flattened himself to the earth.

Some restless, gambling soul could not do without a cigarette and he had detected its faint odor in time. Turning his head slowly, he sniffed deeply and swore under his breath, for he was going partly with the wind, which meant that the smoker must be somewhere behind him. Then a gentle breeze, creeping along the ridge in a back-draft, brought to him the strong and pungent odor of the fire; and he nodded in quick understanding.

The back-draft told him that the smoker was in front of him and cleared up one danger; but it also had blotted out the odor of the cigarette, and as he started forward again he put his faith in his eyes and ears. Slowly he moved along, a few feet at a time, and then he caught the brief and fragrant odor again. Worming around a great, up-thrust slab of lava he stopped suddenly and held his breath. A speck of fire, faint through the clinging ashes, moved in a swift, short arc, became brighter and moved back again, a gleaming dot of red. He could see the hand and part of the arm of the man who had just knocked the ashes from a cigarette in a characteristic and thoughtless gesture. He was sitting just around the corner of a huge bowlder not far away, his back to it, and a dull gleam of reflected moonlight revealed the end of his rifle.

From where he now lay Johnny could see the smoldering ruins of his cabin, where the flames were low and the flying sparks but few. A little current of air fanned the ashes for a few minutes and sent the sparks swirling and dancing, and the flickering, ghostly flames licking upward with renewed life. The increased light, fitful as it had been, brought a smile to his face; for he had caught sight of a pair of spurred boots projecting beyond a rock not far from the glowing embers.

"Ah, th' devil!" muttered the man near him. "I'm goin' home. He's scared out."

The speaker arose and stretched, and grumblingly leaned over to pick up his sombrero, the moon lighting his hair; and he suddenly crumpled forward and sprawled out without a groan as Johnny's Colt struck his head.

The owner of the spurred boots, down behind the rock near the cabin, wriggled backward and looked up to see what had made the noise, caught sight of a dim, ghostly figure moving past a bowlder and called up to it.

"Come on, Ben; let's get goin'. Where's Fleming?"

"Thanks to my fool idea of strategy," said a peeved voice high above the cabin, "which I borrowed from our doughty friend, Mr. Ackerman, I'm up here, smoked up like a ham. I ain't stuck on this. Shootin' a good man from ambush never did set well on my stummick. Reckon Ben's asleep, like a reg'lar sentry; he didn't have th' cussed smoke to make things interestin' for him. Hey, Ben!" he called, wearily.

"No use yellin'," warned Spurred Boots earnestly. "He ain't asleep. I just saw him move. Up to some of his fool jokes, I reckon; an' it's a damned poor time to play 'em. I'm a little nervous, an' might shoot without askin' any questions. Comin' down?"

"Yo're just whistlin' I am," growled Fleming. "It's all fool nonsense, us three watchin' an' waitin' to shoot that feller. When he finds his shack burned an' his rustlin' business busted up, he'll move out without us pluggin' him. Damn it! Didn't he say he was done? But you just listen to th' mockin' bird: If there's any shootin' to be done, he'll do his little, two-handed share. I've been eddicated today; done had a superstition knocked sprawlin'. An' so did Jim get eddicated. He made his play for that feller's right hand, when damned if he ain't left-handed. It made Jim near sick; for a minute I was scared he'd lose his dinner. An' I allus believed left-handed men came in third by two lengths; but lawsy me! What? I'm insulted! I said lawsy."

"You shore can talk!" admired Spurred Boots. "Sometimes a cussed lot too much. What in blazes is Ben doin'?" he asked petulantly, stiffly arising and working his arms and legs.

"Fixin' to jump out on us from behind a rock, an' yell 'Boo!'" grunted Fleming. "Ben, he's an original feller; allus was, even as a kid. Damn these thorns." A thin stream of profanity came from the crevice and Fleming slid down the rest of the way and rolled out into the circle of illumination. "Just like water down a chute, or a merry-hearted bowlder down a hill. Roll, Jordan, roll. Was you askin' about Benjamin, th' catcher of lightning? Benjamin Franklin Gates, his name is; an' he's done gone home. He's a sensible feller, B.F.G. is; but only in spots, little spots, widely spaced."

"You talk as much as Jim Howard's wife," grumbled Spurred Boots. "Jim he said—"

"Of course he did! wasn't it awful?" interposed Fleming. "It was just like a man. But I think it was me that told you that story; so we'll let it keep its secret. As I was sayin', getting in my words edgeways like, but shore gettin' 'em in: Ben has pulled th' picket stake, an' like th' Arabs, done went."

"You mean Arapahoes."

"Did I? I allus call 'em that for short. Have mercy, Jehovah!"

"I saw him move just before I spoke," replied Spurred Boots positively. "But that was a long time ago, before th' deluge, of words," he jabbed ironically.

"Cease; spare thy whacks. An' where th' hell did you ever hear of th' deluge? Some Old Timer tell you about it?" responded Fleming. "I been seein' things, too. All kinds of things. Some had tails but no legs; some had legs but no tails; an' to make a short tale shorter, that was a ghost what you saw. A wild, woopin', woppin' ghost. Come on, Nat; let's flit."

"Then my ghost lit a cigarette a long time back," retorted Nat Harrison. "An' then it said 'flop.' Do they smoke cigarettes?" he demanded with great sarcasm.

"Some does; an' some smokes hops; an' some smokes dried loco weed," grinned Fleming. "That was a spark what you saw, an' th' musical flop was a trout fish turnin' cartwheels on th' water. One of them sparks plumb lit on th' back of my neck, an' I cussed near jumped over th' edge an' made a 'flop' of my own for myself. An' it's a blamed long walk home," he sighed.

"There's th' lightnin's play-fellow now! See him, up there?" demanded Harrison. "Must 'a' been off scoutin'. Hey, Ben! Wait for us—be right up."

Fleming glanced up as another vagrant breeze fanned the embers, and he forthwith did several things at once, and did them quite well. Sending Harrison plunging down behind a rock by one great shove, he jumped for another and fired as he moved. "Ben hell!" he shouted, firing again. "I've seen *that* hombre before today. Keep yore head down, an' get busy!"

Two alert and attentive young men gave keen scrutiny to the ridge and wondered what would happen next. Thirty minutes went by, and then Harrison rolled over and over, laughing uproariously.

"Cussed if it ain't funny!" he gurgled. " 'Some smoke cigarettes, some smokes hops, an' some smokes dried loco weed!' Ha-ha-ha! An' I reckon yo're still seein' them woopin' woops."

"You'll see somethin' worse if you moves out into sight," retorted Fleming. "That ghost that *I* just saw was a human that ain't got to th' ghost state yet. If you don't believe me, you ask Ackerman, if you've got th' nerve."

Harrison rose nonchalantly and sauntered over toward the embers. "Come on, Art; I'm cussed near asleep," he yawned.

"You acts like you was plumb asleep, an' walkin' in it," snapped Fleming angrily. "But it's a good idea," he admitted ironically. "You stay right there an' draw his fire, an' I'll pull at his flash. You make a good decoy, naturally; it comes easy to you. A decoy is an imitation. Stand still, now, so he can line up his sights on you. *I*'m all ready."

Harrison grinned and waved his hand airily. "There ain't no human up there," he placidly remarked. "An' I don't care if Benjamin F. *is* there: she goes as she lays. What you saw was a bear or a lobo or a cougar come up to see th' fire, an' hear you orate from th' mountain top. They'll go long ways to see curious things. In th' book, on page eighteen, it says that they has great streaks of humor, an' a fittin' sense of th' ridiculous. Animals are awful curious about little things. An' on page thirty-one it says they has a powerful sense of smell; an' you know you was up purty high. An' I ain't lookin' forward with joy unconfined to gropin' along no moonlit trail with th' boss of th' wolf tribe, or other big varmits sneakin' around. I might step on a tail an' loosen things up considerable. They're hell on wheels when you steps on their tails, poor things."

"La! La!" said Fleming sympathetically. "Just because you have got yore head out of th' window it don't say you ain't goin' to get no cinder in yore eye. A lead cinder. Lemme tell you that animal wore pants an' a big sombrero. I tell you I *saw* him!"

"It was one of them sparks," grunted the other, enjoying himself. "One of 'em that plumb lit on th' back of yore neck. A spark is a little piece of burnin' wood which soars like th' eagle, an' when it comes down makes sores like th' devil. Te-de-dum-dum! Howsomeever, if yo're goin' with me, yo're goin' to start right now—I've done it already," and he walked slowly toward the creek.

Fleming arose and hesitated, scanning the ridge with searching eyes. Then he stepped out and followed his friend, who already was across the creek and climbing the steep bank.

After reaching the top of the steep part of the ridge he glanced about over the great slope and then paused for breath and reflection, peering curiously toward the tree-shaded hollow where he had seen the much-debated movement. Obeying a sudden impulse he drew his gun and went cautiously forward, bent low and taking full advantage of the cover. A deep groan at his side made him jump and step back. Cautiously peering over a large rock he started in sudden surprise, swearing under his breath. Benjamin Franklin

Gates, neatly trussed and gagged, lay against the rock on its far side, and his baleful eyes spoke volumes. There came a soft step behind Fleming and he wheeled like a flash, his upraised gun cutting down swiftly, and came within an ace of pulling the trigger at Harrison, who writhed sideways and snarled at him. Then Harrison also saw the bound figure on the ground and swore with depth, feeling, and vigor.

"Smokes dried loco weed!" he jeered sarcastically, his voice barely audible. "I feels uncomfortable, entirely too present," he whispered, sinking quietly to the ground.

"Which is unanimous," remarked Fleming, with simple emphasis. "Ben, he ain't sayin' nothin'," he added cheerfully.

An angry gurgle came from the bound figure and it rolled over to face them. Harrison grinned at it. "Under other circumstances I could enjoy this unusual situation," he remarked softly.

"Face to face with Ben, an' him not sayin' a word," marveled Fleming, his eyes busy with the rock-strewn slope. "But I can almost hear him think. Twinkle, twinkle, little star—wonder where Mr. Two-gun Nelson is located at this short, brief, an' interestin' second?"

Another gurgle slobbered from the bound man and his heels thumped the ground.

"Hark!" said Harrison, tensely. "I hears me a noise!"

"I hears me it, too," said Fleming. "But not a word; not a soft, harsh, lovin', long, short, or profane word. Not even a syllable. Not even th' front end of a syllable. All is silent; all but that mysterious drummin' noise. An' if it was farther away I'd be quite restless."

A coughing gurgle and a choked snort came from the base of the rock, and then a louder, more persistent drumming.

"An' you said Benjamin had done snuck home," accused Harrison. "I'm surprised at you. He's been here all th' time. How could he snuck when he's hog-tied, which is appropriate? Gurgle, gurgle, little man—I'll untie you if I can." He bent over, cut loose the gag, slashed the belt from the trussed feet and severed the neckerchief from the crossed wrists. "There! There! Not so loud!" he gently chided.

"Blankety dashed blank blank!" said Ben Gates. "Dashed blankety dashed blank blank! What th' hell you want to cut that belt for, you dashed dashed blankety blank of a dash! Three dollars done gone to th' devil! Just because you got a blankety-blank knife do you have to slash every dashed-dashed thing you see!"

"Sh!" whispered Fleming. "We know yo're grateful; but what happened?" he breathed, too busy to look around.

"Shut yore face!" ordered Harrison, trying in vain to stare through a great, black lava bowlder which lay on the other side of a small clearing.

"Dashed blank!" said Benjamin. "It's been shut enough, you damned pie-faced doodle-bug!"

"Yes; yes; we know," soothed Fleming; "but what happened?"

"Leaned over to get my blankety-blank hat and a dashed tree fell on my blank head!" He felt of the afore-mentioned head with a light and tender touch; and the generous bump made him swear again.

"It's that prospectin' rustler," enlightened Fleming, gratis, as he peered into the shadows behind him.

"No!" said Gates. "I reckoned it was General Grant an' th' Army of th' Potomac! Dead shore it wasn't Columbus?" he sneered.

"It was not Columbus, Benjamin," said Fleming. "Columbus discovered America in 1492 or 1942—some time around there. Ain't you heard about it yet? An' somehow I feels like a calf bein' drug to th' brandin' fire. I feels that I'm goin' to get somethin' soon; an' I ain't shore just what it's goin' to be."

"You'll get it, all right," cheered Harrison, anger in his voice withal. "It'll be a snub-nosed .45, if you don't shut up yore trap. You ain't openin' no Fourth of July celebration, or runnin' for Congress."

Ben felt for his gun and cursed peevishly. "My guns are gone: lend me one of yourn!" he said.

"Th' gentleman has quite a collection," chuckled Harrison. "Three Colts an' a Winchester. Good pickin', says he. Good enough, says I. True, says he; but, he says, I have hopes of more. Ta-ta! jeers I."

"Shut *yore* face!" growled Fleming, writhing.

"I want a gun, an' I wants it now!" blazed Gates, pugnaciously.

"Fair sir, how many guns do you think we pack?" demanded Harrison.

"You got a rifle an' a Colt!" snapped Gates. "I wants one of 'em!"

"He only wants one of 'em," said Fleming.

"I was scared you'd be a hog," said Harrison. "Here; take this Winchester, an' *keep* it. Bein' generous is all right; but it has its limits."

Gates gripped the weapon affectionately and sat up. "No use of stayin' here like we done took root," he said, rising to his feet. "We wants to spread out. Mebby he's still hangin' around."

"Yes; an' shoot each other," growled Harrison. "I'm goin' to spread out, all right; an' when I quits spreadin' I'll be in my little bunk. He's a mile away by now; but if he ain't, don't you let him have that gun; he's got enough now."

He stopped suddenly, and their hair arose on their heads as a long-drawn, piercing scream rang out. It sounded like a woman in mortal agony and it came from the ridge above them. From the upper end of the rock-walled pasture below came

113

a howl, deep, long-drawn, evil, threatening. They turned searching eyes toward the nearer sound and saw a crescent bulk silhouetted against the moon. It lay in the top of blasted pine, and as they looked, it raised its chunky head and neck and screamed an answering challenge to the lobo wolf in the canyon.

Ben moved swiftly, and a spurt of flame split the night, crashing echoes returning in waves. The crescent silhouette in the tree-top leaped convulsively and crashed to the ground, breaking off the dead limbs in its fall, and then there ensued a spitting, snarling, thrashing turmoil as the great panther scored the earth in its agony.

Ben's friends forsook him as though he were a leper and melted into the shadows, cursing him from A to Z. They wanted no ringing notice of their presence broadcasted, and the flash and roar of the heavy rifle had done just that.

As they faded into the darker shadows farther back a crashing sounded in the brush and they peered forth to see the great panther plunging and writhing through the bushes, smashing its way through the oak brush in desperate plunges. Reaching the edge of a small clearing it gave one convulsive leap, another harrowing scream and thudded against a bowlder, where it suddenly relaxed and lay quiet.

"There's near a quart of corn juice up in my bunk, an' I'm goin' for it," said Harrison, moving swiftly up the rough trail. "I need it, an' I need it bad!"

"That cat's mate ain't fur away," remarked Fleming thoughtfully. "It's due hereabouts right soon. I'm stickin' closer than a brother, Nat. Lead me to th' fluid which consoleth, arouseth anger and dulleth pain; blaster of homes, causer of headaches, damn it! Ben, he's a great hunter, a wild, untamed, ferocious slayer of varmints; he can stay here an' argue with th' inquirin' mate, if he wants, while we wafts yonder an' hence. It won't be draped up in no tree, neither; somehow I can just see it sniffin' at th' beloved dead an' then soft-footin' through th' brush, over th' ridges an' around th' bowlders, its whiskers bristlin', its wicked little ears pointed back, an' its long, generous tail goin' jerk-jerk, tremble-tremble. Lovely picture. Fascinatin' picture. It is lookin' real hard for th' misguided son-of-a-gun that killed its tuneful mate. Nice kitty; pretty kitty; lovely kitty! I votes, twice, for that whiskey. I votes three times for that whiskey. Lead th' way, Nat; an' for my sake keep yore eyes peeled."

Quick, heavy steps behind them made them jump for cover, turning as they jumped, and to peer anxiously back along the trail.

Ben walked into sight, the rifle held loosely in front of him as he peered into the shadows. "You acts like you has springs in yore laigs," he derisively remarked.

115

"An' you acts like you had sour dough for brains," courteously retorted Harrison. "An' it's so sour it's moldy. Go away from here!"

"Yo're a great little, two-laigged success," sneered Fleming. "Reg'lar Dan'l Boone. I hopes if any gent ever trails me for my scalp it will be you. You wants to buy yoreself a big tin whistle an' a bass drum when you go out ambushin'!"

"I claims that was a good shot," complacently replied Ben. "What with it bein' near dark, an' a strange gun, an' my head most splittin', I holds it was. Must 'a' been to make you long-winded ijuts so damned jealous."

"Trouble is, yore head didn't split enough," grumbled Harrison pleasantly. "It should 'a' been split from topknot to chin. Next time *I* goes manhuntin', *you* stays home with yore pretty picture books."

"Suits me," grunted Ben placidly. "Yore company hurts my ears, offends my nose, an' shocks my eyes. An' as for th' excitement, why I done got enough of that to—look *out!*" he yelled, firing without raising the gun to his shoulder.

An answering flash split the darkness between two bowlders further up the slope and Ben pitched sideways. His companions fired as if by magic; the instant return fire sent Harrison reeling backward. He tripped on a root and fell sprawling, the gun flying from his hand. Fleming leaped toward a huge rock, firing as he jumped, and slid

116

behind the cover, where he sighed, and groped for his gun with trembling hands. Groans and muttered curses came from the trail, and Fleming, raising himself to a sitting position, his back against a rock, saw Harrison dragging himself toward his gun and a clump of brush.

"You stay where you are," said an ominous voice, "an' put up yore hands!"

Lying in a patch of moonlight, Harrison could do nothing but obey; but Fleming nerved himself and picked up his gun, still able to fight and only waiting for his enemy to show himself. Several minutes passed and then a hand darted over the rock and wrenched Fleming's gun out of the weak hand that held it.

"You ain't goin' to get hurt no more if you acts sensible," said the new owner of the gun. "Where you hit?"

"Thigh an' shoulder," muttered Fleming weakly.

The stranger fell to work swiftly and deftly and in a short time he arose and moved toward the two men in the clearing. "You'll be all right after yore friends get you home," he said over his shoulder. Reaching the two figures on the trail he first took their guns and then looked them over.

"This feller with th' lump on his head is my old friend, th' smoker," said Johnny. "He's got a crease in his scalp. Barrin' a little blood an' a big headache, he'll be all right after a while. Where'd I get you?" he demanded of Harrison.

"Arm," grunted Harrison. "Through th' flesh. I done tripped an' fell—must 'a' near busted a rock with my fool head when I lit," he said, as if to explain his subsequent inaction. "We reckoned you'd left th' country till we found th' package you tied up an' left."

"I come back for th' rest of my stuff," replied Johnny. "I was scared to come up th' valley."

"You acts like you'd scare easy," admitted Harrison. "I'm sorry you ain't got more nerve," he grinned despite the pain in his arm.

"Here," said Johnny, squatting beside him, "lemme tie up that arm. I wasn't aimin' to shoot nobody till I was cornered," he grinned. "I heard what you fellers said, back in th' valley, an' that's why. I was plumb peaceful, tryin' to slip away, when that gent up an' let drive at me. Bein' in a pocket made by them fool bowlders I couldn't get out, so I had to cut down on you with both hands. Th' dark shadows helped me a lot; you couldn't see what you was shootin' at. An' anyhow, I *owe* him somethin'. I was under that tree when he up an' dumped that pleasant cougar down on top of me, right in my arms. Never was more surprised in all my life. An' to make matters worse, this is my best pair of pants."

"Show 'em to me!" begged Harrison.

Johnny stepped back for inspection and waved his hands at the trousers; and Harrison had to laugh at what he saw. What was left of them formed a very short kilt, and the underwear was torn into bloody strips.

Harrison wept.

"I'm pullin' my stakes," continued Johnny pleasantly. "This layout is too excitin' for a man of my bashful an' retirin' disposition. You can tell Quigley he don't have to set no more ambushes in that valley, an' also that th' first time I meet him I'm goin' to smoke him up with both hands. I'm honin' for to get a look at him, just a quick glance. Give my regards to yore friend Ackerman; his gun, an' that other feller's, is with Pop Hayes; but mebby they ought to wait till I leave th' country before they go in for 'em."

He turned on his heel and walked slowly away, with a pronounced limp, a present from the cougar. When he reached the edge of the clearing he paused and faced about.

"You two fellers will be all right in a little while, an' if you can't get yore friend home, you can send them that can. I'll take yore six-guns along with me so there won't be no accidents; but I'll leave this rifle over here on this rock, empty. Th' cartridges are on th' ground on th' other side of th' rock. That cougar's mate is some het up about now, I reckons, an' you may need it. Better not come for it for a couple of minutes. There's been enough shootin' already. *Adios*," and he was gone as silently as a shadow.

Harrison sat cross-legged and waited

considerable more than two minutes and then walked slowly toward the rifle. As he picked it up there came a haunting scream and a rolling fusillade of shots from the south. Then a distant voice called faintly.

"I got th' mate, an' lost th' rest of my pants. *Adios!*"

"I'll be damned!" grunted Harrison, going toward his friend at the rock. "That feller is one cheerful hombre. If I was Quigley, I'll bet four bits I wouldn't show my face in Hastings till he was a long way off. No, ma'am; not a-tall. Here, Art; you take th' gun till I go back an' see how Dan'l Boone is comin' along. He's a rip-snortin', high-class success, *he is!* I'll bet you he'll *brag* about droppin' that cougar, you just wait an' see. *Hello,* you wild jackass! How you feel!"

"You can go to hell" snorted the man with the creased scalp, sitting up. "An' I don't care a cuss when you starts, or how you goes. I'm fond of excitement, thrive on it an' get fat; but I serves notice, here an' now, that I'm quittin'. Any man that takes th' trail with you two fools is a bigger fool. Great guns! I won't have no head left after a while!"

"You never did have one that amounted to anythin'," said Harrison cheerfully. "I admit that it's a handy place to hang a hat, but when that is said, th' story is ended. Amen. You set right where you are till you are able to walk, an' then we'll get Art home."

"Takin' Art home is what we should 'a' done long ago; we're doin' this thing backwards, th' damn fool!" moaned Ben. "We'd 'a' been home long ago if it wasn't for him."

"Huh?" muttered Harrison. "Well, I'll be damned! Say! If it wasn't for you pluggin' that cat we'd 'a' been home, whole an' happy, sleepin' th' sleep of th' innercent. When you got that bright idea, you shore touched off a-plenty. He was pullin' his stakes, aimin' to get out peaceful, when you dumped that panther right down plumb around his neck! Man! Man! But I wish I'd 'a' seen that! Benjamin, if you only knowed what I'm thinkin' about you! Words ain't capable of revealin' my thoughts; they fall far short; an' if I used enough words I'd strain my vo—vocabulary, till it never would be any good any more. An' I can only swear in English, Spanish, Navajo, an' Ute. An education must be a grand thing."

"Th' breaks was ag'in us," explained Benjamin.

"Lord, please hold me back!" prayed Harrison.

Well to the south of them a limping cow-puncher, with no trousers at all now, and blood-soaked strips of underwear pasted to his torn and bleeding legs, pushed doggedly toward his horse, swearing at almost every painful step and avoiding all kinds of brush as he painstakingly held to the middle of the dried bed of the creek.

His shirt tail, cut into ragged strips, flapped in the cold breeze where not held down by the weight of the sagging belts and holsters; and in his hands he carried the captured Colts.

Reaching his horse he fastened the extra weapons to his saddle, carefully drew on his chaps, coiled up the picket rope and climbed gingerly astride.

"Come on, Pepper!" he growled. "Pull out of this. I got a pair of pants wrapped up in that tarpaulin at th' mouth of th' valley; an' I wants 'em bad. You shore missed somethin' this evenin', you lucky old cow!"

When day broke it revealed a shivering, grumbling cow-puncher washing his cuts and gashes in the cold, pure water of Nelson's creek. Retiring to the pebbly bank, he tore up a clean shirt and used it all for bandages, after which he carefully drew on a pair of clean underdrawers and covered them with a pair of well-worn trousers. The chaps came next as a protection against whipping branches and clinging brush. Rolling up the tarpaulin he fastened it behind his saddle and, mounting stiffly, started for Hastings.

Some hours later he lolled at ease and related to the grinning proprietor the strange and exciting occurrences of the night. Pop was swung from one extreme to the other as the tale unfolded, while Andrew Jackson chuckled, whistled, and laughed until the narrator's scratching fingers lulled him into a deep and soul-stirring ecstasy.

"You shore started some fireworks," chuckled Pop when the tale was finished. "An' yo're cussed lucky, too. When Ackerman showed his hand yesterday I knowed trouble was fixin' to ride you to a frazzled finish. Now what damned fool thing are you goin' to do?" he demanded anxiously.

"I'm goin' to keep out of that valley," reluctantly answered Johnny. "It ain't got no charms for me no more. They've burned my cabin, an' I reckon I got all th' gold there was, anyhow. When my legs get well I'm goin' to try it again somewhere else. Twin Buttes are too unlucky for me."

"Now yo're shoutin'," beamed Pop. "You just set around here an' take things easy for a few days, while me an' Charley fixes that tarp so it'll be a pack cover an' a tent that *is* one. No prospector wants to build a shack unless winter ketches him in th' hills or he finds a rich strike. Me an' you an' Charley will go fishin' a few days from now an' have a reg'lar rest. I'm all tired out, too. Business is shore confinin'." He looked Johnny over and chuckled. "Cussed if I wouldn't 'a' give six pesos, U.S., to 'a' seen that cougar a-fannin' you! He-he-he!"

CHAPTER X

A Change of Base

Johnny, upon leaving Hastings, struck south from it and spent the night west of the Circle S after a journey of twenty miles on foot. Pepper was again a pack horse, and the diamond hitch which held the bulging tarpaulin in place would have dispelled any doubt as to Johnny's abilities to cut loose from civilization and thrive in the lonely places. And he had cut loose when he placed a note under a rock behind a certain tree near the ford; for when "Hen" Crosby, riding for the mail, saw the agreed-upon sign on the tree, it would not be long before Logan had the note.

Following the line of least resistance, the second day found him bearing westerly, and the next three days found him crowding the pack on Pepper's back and riding due north through a country broken, wild, and without a trail. The way was not as difficult as it might have been because the valleys joined one another, and through them all flowed creeks, which made a trail that left no tracks. To an experienced man who had plenty of time the difficulties were more often avoided than conquered.

At noon of the fifth day he drove Pepper slantingly up the wall of a crumbling butte, and reaching the top, looked around for his bearings. They were easily found, for Twin Buttes looked too much alike, even from the rear, to be easily mistaken; and they loomed too high to be overlooked. Almost on a direct line with the Twins lay Quigley's cabins, a matter of fifteen miles from him; which he decided was too far. That distance covered twice daily would take up too much time. Returning to the valley he built a fire, had dinner, and, hanging the edible supplies on tree limbs for safety, whistled Pepper to him and departed toward the Twins.

Two hours later he left the horse in a deep draw and crawled up the eastern bank. Crossing a bowlder-strewn plateau he not long afterward wriggled to the edge of Quigley's valley and looked down into it.

The size of the enclosed range amazed him, for it was fully thirteen miles long, eight miles across at its widest, the northern end, and three miles wide at the middle, where massive cliffs jutted far out from each side.

The more he saw of it the better he liked it. The grass was better and thicker than even that in the prized and fought-for valley of the old Bar-20. He judged it to contain about eighty square miles and believed that it could feed two hundred cows to the mile. The main stream, which he named Rustler Creek, flowed through a deep ravine and was fed, in the valley alone, by six smaller creeks. There was a sizable swamp and six lakes, one of them nearly a mile long. It was singularly free from bowlders and rocks except at a place near the upper wall, where a great collection of them extended out from a broken cliff.

Except at three places the canyons which cut into the cliffs were blind alleys and he could see that two of them had narrow waterfalls at their upper ends. The three open canyons were the only places where cattle could leave the great "sink," as Johnny called it; and they were strongly fenced. The first was the entrance canyon, near the houses; the second was a deep, steep walled defile at the northwest corner of the range, and it led into another, but smaller valley, also heavily grassed. Through it ran a small stream which joined Rustler Creek at the swamp. The third canyon, at the northeast corner of the valley, was wide enough to let Rustler Creek flow through it and leave room for the passing of cattle; and judging by the gates in the heavy fence which crossed it, Johnny knew this to be the exit through which the drive herds went. Where that drive trail led to he did not know, but he believed it to pass well to the west of Hope.

Taking it all in all, it was the most perfect range he ever had seen. Rich in grass so heavy and thick as to make him wonder at it, naturally irrigated, blessed with natural reservoirs, surrounded by a perpendicular wall of rock which at some places attained a height of three hundred feet, the water courses lined with timber, its arroyos and draws heavily wooded, and with but three places, easily closed and guarded, where cattle could get out, it made the Tin Cup and the Bar-20, large as they were, look like jokes. Its outfit could laugh at rustlers, droughts, and blizzards, grow fat and lazy and have neither boundary disputes nor range wars to bother them. There were no brands of neighboring ranches to complicate the roundups and not a cow would be lost through straying or theft.

Having located the valley, he slipped away, mounted his horse and rode back the way he had come, looking for a good place to pitch his camp. Five miles from the valley he found it—a cave-like recess under the towering wall of a butte, half way up the wooded slope which lay at the foot of the wall. From it he could command all approaches for several hundred yards, while his tarpaulin would be screened by bowlders and trees. It was high enough for purposes of observation, but not so high that the smoke from his fire would have density enough when it reached the top of the butte to be seen for any distance. A spring close by formed pools in the hollows of the rocks below him. The great buttes lying to the east of the fire would screen its light from any wandering member of Quigley's outfit.

"This is it," he grunted. "We'll locate here tomorrow."

The following day, having put his new camp to rights, he rode up the western slope of the great plateau which hemmed in Quigley's ranch, picketed his horse in a clearing, and after a cautious reconnaissance on foot he reached the edge of the cliffs, and the valley lay before him. Cattle grazed near a little lake, but at that distance he could not read the brands. He first had to find out if any of the outfit ever rode along the top of the cliffs, and he struck straight back to cross any such trails. By evening he had covered the western side of the ranch without finding a hoof-print, or a way up the sheer walls where a horseman could reach the top. There were several places where a cool-headed man could climb up, and at one of these Johnny found several burned matches.

The next day was spent on the plateau north of the ranch, and the third and fourth days found him examining the eastern side; and it was here that he found signs of riders. There were three blind canyons on this side, and the middle one had a good trail running up its northern wall, and it appeared to be used frequently. At the top it divided, one branch running north and the other south. It was the only place on that side of the valley where a horseman could get out.

Now that he had become familiar with his surroundings he began his real work. If Quigley had rustled, the operations could be divided into two classes: past operations, now finished; or present operations which were to continue. It was possible that enough cattle had been stolen in the past so that the natural increase would satisfy a man of modest ambitions. In this case his danger would decrease as time passed and eventually he would have a well-stocked range and be above suspicion. If he were avaricious the rustling would continue, if only spasmodically, until he had made all the money he wanted or until his operations became known.

Johnny early had discovered that Quigley's brand was QE and this increased his suspicions, for the E could not be explained. Logan's brand was childishly simple to change: The C could become an O, Q, G, or wagon-wheel; the L would make an E, Triangle, Square, or a 4.

Satisfied that the foundation of Quigley's brand had been the CL, Johnny had to discover if Logan's cattle still were being taken to swell the Quigley herds. Logan's inaction and his easy-going way of running his ranch jarred Johnny, for the foreman had confessed that for the last few years the natural increase, figured in the fall roundups, had not tallied with the number of calves branded each preceding spring. But Logan was not altogether to blame, because the Barrier had given him a false security and there was nothing to fear from other directions. It was the last spring roundup and its tally sheets which had stirred him; and a close study of his drive-herd records and the use of a factor of natural increase suddenly brought to his mind a startling suspicion. Even then he wavered, fearing that he was allowing an old and bitter grudge to sway him unduly; and before he had time to make any real investigations, Johnny had appeared and demanded a job.

Among Quigley's cattle the proportion of calves to cows was so small that Johnny could not fail to notice it. He was satisfied that the QE, so prominently displayed, originally had been CL, but when he caught sight of a crusty old steer near the mouth of the second canyon all doubts were removed. While the mark was an old one, the rebranding had been done carelessly. The segment which closed the original C had not been properly joined to the old brand, and there was a space between the ends of the two marks where they overlapped. A look at the ears made him smile grimly, for Logan's shallow V notch had become a rounded scallop; and there was no honest reason why Quigley should notch the ears of his cows when there was no chance of them getting mixed up with the cattle of any other ranch. The scallop had been made simply to cut out the telltale V notch.

CHAPTER XI
Nocturnal Activities

Light gleamed from Quigley's ranch houses and an occasional squeal came from the corral, suggesting that "Big Jake" was getting up steam for more deviltry. Occasionally a shadow passed across the lighted patches of ground below the windows and the low song of Rustler Creek could be heard as it swirled into the long, black canyon. Save for the glow of the windows and the rectangles of light below them everything was wrapped in darkness, and the canyon, the range, and the rims of the cliffs were hidden.

"A miner, 'forty-niner, and his daughter, Clementine," came from the middle house as Art Fleming dolefully made known the sorrowful details of Clementine's passing out. He put his heart into it because he had troubles of his own, for which he frankly and profanely gave Ben Gates due discredit.

Ben, tiring of the dirge, heaved a boot with a snap-shooter's judgment and instantly forsook the heavy inhospitality of the house for the peace and freedom of the great outdoors. He plumped down on a bench and immediately arose there-from.

"Look where yo're settin', you blunderin' jack-ass!" snarled a hostile voice from the same bench. "Yo're a big a nuisance as a frisky bummer in a night herd!"

"A bull's eye for Mr. Harrison," chanted the man inside.

"You two buzzards are about as cheerful an' pleasant as a rattler in August," snapped Gates belligerently. "Like two old wimmin, you are, *both* of you! Settin' around in everybody's way, tellin' yore troubles over an' over again till everybody wishes Nelson had done a better job. How'd *I* know you was sprawled out, takin' up all th' room? You reminds me of a fool dog that sets around stickin' its tail in everybody's way, an' then howls blue murder when it's stepped on. Think yo're th' only people on this ranch that has any troubles?"

"A miss for Mr. Gates," said the irritated voice within the house. "An' if he will stick his infected head in that door, just for one, two, three, he'll have more troubles," prophesied Mr. Fleming, facing the opening with a boot nicely balanced in his upraised hand. "If it wasn't for him, we—"

"Shut up! *Shut up!*" yelled Gates, enraged in an instant. "If you says that much more I'll bust yore fool neck! For God's sake, is that all you know, Andrew Jackson?"

132

"If it wasn't for you," said the man on the bench very deliberately as his hand closed over a piece of firewood, "I said, if—it—wasn't—for—you, we'd be ridin' with the boys tonight, instead of stayin' around these houses like three sick babies."

"Another bull's eye for Mr. Harrison," said the man inside.

Gates wheeled with an oath. "An' if it wasn't for *you* sound asleep in th' valley; an' Fleming sound asleep up on that butte, I wouldn't 'a' been lammed on th' head an' tied up like a sack! It's purty cussed tough when a man with nothin' worse than a scalp wound has to lay up this way!"

"Bull's eye for Mr. Gates," announced the man in the cabin, with great relish.

"If you'd been wide awake yoreself," retorted Harrison, "you wouldn't 'a' been tied up! You didn't even squawk when he hit you, so we'd know he was around. Was you tryin' to keep it a secret?" he demanded with withering sarcasm. "An' as for them bandages, how did *I* know th' dog had been sleepin' on 'em? Cookie gave 'em to me!"

"Bull's eye for Mr. Harrison," said Fleming. "But he was awake," he continued with vast conviction. "He was wide awake. He ain't got no more sense awake than he has asleep. When he's got his boots on, his brains are cramped an' suffocated."

"You got him figgered wrong," said Harrison. "His brains are only suffocated when he sets down."

While the little comedy was being enacted at the bunk-houses, the main body of rustlers followed Quigley down the steeply sloping bottom of a concealed crevice miles north of the ranch house of the CL. The five men emerged quietly and paused on the edge of the curving Deepwater, and then slowly followed their leader into the icy stream. The current, weakened by a widening of the river at this point, still flowed with sufficient strength to make itself felt and the slowly moving horses leaned against it as they filed across the secret ford. Reaching the farther bank the second and third men rode quietly to right and left, rapidly becoming vague and then lost to sight. The three remaining riders sat quietly in their saddles for what, to them, seemed to be a long time. Suddenly a low whistle sounded on the left, followed instantly by another on the right; and like released springs the rustlers leaped into action.

Vague, ghostly figures moved over the open plain, finding cows with uncanny directness and certainty. Two riders held the nucleus of the little herd, which grew steadily as lumbering cows, followed inexorably by skilled riders, pushed out of the darkness. There was no conversation, no whistling now, nor singing, but a silence which, coupled to the ghost-like action and the dexterous swiftness, made the drama seem unreal.

There came an abrupt change. The two men riding herd saw no more looming cattle or riders, which seemed to be a matter of significance to them, for they faced southward, guns in hand, and pushed slowly back along the flanks of the little herd. Peering into the shrouding gray darkness, tense and alert, eyes and ears straining to read the riddle, they waited like sooty statues for whatever might occur, rigid and unmoving.

A sudden thickening in the night. A figure seemed to flow from indefinable density to the outlines of a mounted man. A low voice, profanely irritant, spoke reassuringly and grew silent as the rider oozed back into the effacing night.

"Shore," muttered a herder, relaxing and slipping his gun into its holster. He moved forward swiftly and turned back a venturesome cow. His companion, growling but relieved, shrugged his shoulders and settled back to wait.

Minutes passed and then another lumbering blot emerged out of the dark, became a cow, and found reassurance in numbers as it willingly joined the herd. The escorting rider kept on, pushed back his sombrero and growled: "They're scattered to hell an' gone tonight; but," he grudgingly admitted, "they acts plumb docile. S'long."

Another wait, long and fruitless, edged anew the

nerves of the herders. Then Quigley, Ackerman, and Purdy moved out of the obscurity of the night and took up positions around the herd, urging it forward. When they had it started on its way, Ackerman dropped back and became lost to sight, engaged in his characteristic patrolling, suspicious and malevolent.

The little herd, skilfully guided over clean patches of rock which led deviously to the water's edge and left no signs on its hard surface, at last reached the river, where a shiver of hesitancy rippled through it and where the rear cows pushed solidly against the front rank, which appeared to be calling upon its inherent obstinacy. The craft and diplomacy of Quigley's long experience won out and the uncertain front rank slowly and grudgingly entered the stream, the others following without noticeable hesitation. As the last cow crossed and scrambled up the western bank, Ackerman rode down to the water's edge, pushed in and crossed silently, only the lengthening ripple on the black surface telling of his progress. As he climbed out he squirmed in his wet clothes and swore from sudden anger, which called forth a low ripple of laughter from the base of the Barrier, where the others took their discomforts lightly.

"Scared you'll shrink, Jim?" softly said an ironic voice.

"Or dissolve, like sugar?" inquired another scoffingly.

"Sugar?" jeered a third. "Huh! He's about as sweet as a hunk of alum!"

Ackerman's retort caused grins to bloom unseen, and the miseries of wet clothes and chilled bodies were somewhat relieved by the thought that Ackerman felt them the most.

Up the crevice in orderly array, docile as sheep, climbed the cattle, and when they reached the top of the plateau they moved along stolidly under guidance and finally gained the outer valley leading to the QE by a trail west of and parallel to the one which showed the way to Hastings.

Back on the QE, Fleming and his friends, having awakened the cook at an unseemly hour by their noise, finally turned in and found some trouble in getting to sleep, thanks to the energetic efforts of the boss of the kitchen, who most firmly believed in the Mosaic Law, and had the courage of his convictions. But things finally quieted down and peace descended upon the ranch.

Outside the bunk-house and behind it, a blot on the ground stirred restlessly and slowly resolved itself into a man arising. He moved cautiously along the wall toward the lighted cook shack and then sank down again, hand on gun, as the door opened.

Cookie threw out a pan of water, scowled up at the starry sky and then peered intently at a chicken-coop, visible in the straggling light from the door, from which a sleepy cackle suddenly broke the silence. Muttering suspiciously he reached behind him and then slipped swiftly toward the shack, a shotgun in his hands. Going around the coop he stood up and shook his fist in the darkness.

"You can dig up my traps, an' smell out my strychnine, but you can't dodge these buckshot if ever I lays th' sights on you. Dawg-gone you, I owes *you* a-plenty!" he growled. Striking a match he looked in the coop and around it. "Had two dozen as nice pullets as anybody ever saw, only three weeks ago; an' now I only got sixteen left. *There,* blast you!" he swore, as the second match revealed the telltale tracks. "There they are! O, Lord! Just let me get my gun on that thievin' ki-yote! Just once!"

He stared around belligerently and went slowly back to the house, swearing and grumbling under his breath. It is the cook's fate to be the sworn enemy of all coyotes, and let it be said without shame to him that he seldom is a victor in that game of watchfulness and wits. And also let it be said that often with tears of rage and mortifi-cation, and words beyond repetition, he pays unintentional tribute to the uncanny cunning of the four-legged thieves. With guns, dogs, traps, and poison is he armed, but it availeth him naught. And as bad as the defeat are the knowing grins of the rest of the outfit who, while openly cheering on the doughty cook, are ready to wager a month's wages on the coyote.

The man on the ground moved again, this time toward the canyon, and soon was feeling his way along the great eastern wall. Reaching the other end, he stopped a moment to listen, and then went on again, groping along by the edge of the stream until he stumbled over a dead branch, which he picked up. Then feeling for and finding a certain rock, he stepped on it and with his foot felt for and found another, which was partly submerged in the creek; and by means of this and others he crossed dry-shod to the opposite bank, using the branch as a staff.

Daylight was near when Johnny wriggled to the edge of the cliff opposite the houses and hid behind a fringe of grass on the rim. An hour passed and then his keen ears caught distant sounds. Below him the cook was rearranging his traps and swearing at the cleverness of his four-footed enemy. Suddenly he arose and hastened to the kitchen to serve a hot breakfast to the men who soon drove a bunch of cattle out of the canyon and into the small corral.

While the others hastened in for their breakfast, Quigley and Ackerman loitered at the corral.

"Purty good for five men, with one of 'em playin' sentry," said Quigley. "We'd do better if we didn't have to scout around first."

"Scoutin's necessary," replied Ackerman. "It's

too wide open. This bunch ain't worth gettin' wet for. That river's cussed cold!"

Quigley chuckled. "Huh! I've swum it when th' ice was comin' down."

"You did," retorted Ackerman. "That was th' night Logan burned our houses. You had to swim an' freeze, or stay out an' get shot. You went in *pronto*, that night!"

"You beat me in by forty yards, an' out by sixty!" snapped Quigley.

Ackerman ignored the remark. "Not satisfied with nestin' on a man's range, you had to start a little herd. We didn't bring no cows with us, nor buy any afterward—but what's th' use? Let's eat," and he led the way toward the cook shack.

Johnny waited a few minutes and then, returning to his horse, started for his camp. He was puzzled, for no place near Big or Little Canyons was devoid of shelter, and he knew of no other places where cattle could pass the Barrier. He had noticed that the backs of the cows were dry, which meant that they had forded the river, and he was certain that the crossing had not been made at the ford near Devil's Gap. He had to learn the location of the place they visited and that unknown ford; and he wanted to learn the date of their next raid.

"We'll have to trail 'em, Pepper," he growled. "An' then bust all runnin' records to get Logan and th' boys. Get agoin'; I'm sleepy."

CHAPTER XII
Yeasty Suspicion

Ackerman walked to the small corral, where two straight irons were in a fire and where three men were cinching up in preparation. Fleming, Harrison, and Gates, lolling on the ground, kept up a running fire of comment, and Ackerman stopped and looked down at them.

"Three cheerful fools," he grinned.

"Here's Little Jimmy," remarked Fleming; "an' by all th' Roman gods, he's actually grinnin'! Look, fellers! Behold an' ponder! Mr. Ackerman wears a smile!"

"Sick?" solicitously inquired Harrison.

"Drunk?" suspiciously questioned Gates.

"Three children," grunted Ackerman. "An' scabby. Two sentries an' a hunter."

Holbrook poked the fire. "Kit Carson, Dan'l Boone, an' Californy Joe. Three scouts. Th' ambushin' trio."

"Faith, Hope, an' Charity," chuckled Purdy.

"You called it," grinned Holbrook.

"If Custer had only had 'em," said Ackerman, "there'd been no massacre."

"Huh!" grunted Gates. "What could I do, with them two fools herdin' with me?"

"Not so much herdin' with you, as tryin' to herd you," said Harrison blithely.

Gates sought escape by creating a diversion, and shouted: "Hey, look at him!" and pointing at the cook, who staggered past under a great load of saplings and poles.

"Hey, Cookie!" he shouted stentoriously. "Why don't you put them birds in th' house nights, an' sleep in th' coop, yoreself?"

"Or give him some of that there strych-nine that we got for you?" yelled Sanford. "There's a lot of it left," he chuckled, remembering the cook's futile rage when he had found the poisoned carcass half covered over with dirt.

The cook, his glistening face crimson, carefully lowered the forward end of the poles to the ground, eased them upright with his shoulder and wiped the perspiration from his face with a grimy sleeve. Turning a red countenance toward his grinning friends he started to speak, muttered something, spat forcibly, shouldered carefully under his load again and staggered away with as much dignity as he could command.

"That's right, Cookie," commended Gates. "Don't you waste no words on 'em a-tall. They're a lazy, worthless, shiftless lot. If they wasn't they'd help you tote them trees. But I wish you'd tell me what yo're aimin' to do, because if yo're goin' to rig up a scaffold for that ki-yote, I want to be around when he's hung." He turned and surveyed the group. "You ought to be ashamed of yoreselves, lettin' him tote that load hisself. He works harder than any man on this ranch, an' I can prove it. I can prove it by him. What with buildin' stockades an' scaffolds, diggin' holes for his traps, poisonin' baits, an' settin' up nights with his shotgun, he's a hard workin' member of this outfit. He ain't got no time to set around an' loaf all day like some I could name if I had a mind to."

"Hard workin'!" snorted Purdy. "That ain't work; that's fun! He's as happy doin' that as others is playin' cards or somethin'. He'd get mopey if that ki-yote died. A man allus works harder at his fun than he does at his work. Allus!"

"Shore!" grunted Holbrook. "I've seen men so lazy that they growled because th' sun kept 'em movin' to stay in th' shade; but show 'em a month's good huntin' an' they'd come to life quick! They'll climb an' hoof it all day to get a shot at somethin'; but if their wife asked 'em to rustle a bucket of water you could hear 'em holler, clear over in th' next county."

"Would you look at him settin' them poles!" chuckled Gates. "He's shore goin' down to bedrock!"

Holbrook pulled an iron out of the fire, glanced at it, shoved it back again and arose. "Let her go," he said.

143

At the word two men vaulted into their saddles and rode into the corral. A cow blundered out and was deftly turned toward the fire, and at the right instant a rope shot through the air, straightened and grew taut; and the cow, thrown heavily, was hog-tied, branded, its ears cut to conform to the QE notch, and released in a remarkably short time. Arising it waved its lowered head from side to side and stared to charge Holbrook. Gates stepped quickly forward, kicked a spur of dirt in its face and a clever cow-pony sent it lumbering out through the gate in the fence and onto the range.

"Maverick," grunted Holbrook, waiting for the next. "Logan shore is careless in his calf round-ups. That's four of 'em we got in th' last two raids. Reckon he thinks brandin' is more or less unnecessary, th' way he's located. An' damned if here don't come another! Nope; it's a sleeper. Somebody took th' trouble to cut th' notch."

Ackerman did his share of the work, silent and preoccupied, and when the last cow had been turned onto the range he wheeled abruptly, looked around, and walked over to Quigley, who was approaching.

"I reckon I better go off on a little scout," he said. "I ain't satisfied about Nelson; an' th' more I mills it over, th' less satisfied I am. You can grin; but *I*'m tellin' you it ain't no grinnin' matter!" he snapped, eyeing the group. "I'm tellin' you what *I*'m goin' to do, an' that's all."

"That's for you to say," smiled Quigley. "Nobody's goin' to try to stop you; but we reckon yo're only makin' trouble for yoreself. He's quit th' Twin Buttes country. I understand he's prospectin' south of town."

"He ain't prospectin' none," retorted Ackerman. "An' he wasn't prospectin' up here, neither; he was runnin' a bluff, an' makin' it stick. *I* looked into that gravel bed!"

Fleming laughed. "He was coverin' his rustlin' operations. His real prospectin' was to be done with a rope an' a runnin' iron."

"Yes," grunted Stanford; "an' now he's doin' th' same thing down south, I'll bet. Th' Circle S has got a lot of sleepers an' mavericks runnin' on their outlyin' range. Holmes has been threatenin' for two years to round 'em all up; but when he's ready, th' Long T ain't; an' t'other way around."

"Our friend is goin' to set right down on a rattler if he starts rustlin' down there," grinned Purdy. "Them two ranches are wide awake. I know, because I've looked 'em over."

"He'll tackle th' job," said Harrison; "because he's somethin' of a pinwheel hisself."

"That's how I figger it," said Holbrook quickly. "A burned child loves th' fire, if it's stubborn. Let him alone; don't stir him up. We don't want him up here, an' that's our limit. What he does down there ain't no game for us to horn into. Let 'em fiddle an' dance an' be damned."

Ackerman regarded them pityingly and shrugged his shoulders. "I pass! Ain't there no way to get it through yore heads that I don't believe he's interested in anythin' but *us?* It's like drillin' in granite. I hammer an' hammer, twist th' drill an' hammer some more; an' after hard work all I got is a little hole, with a cussed sight more granite below it! I feel like rammin' in a charge of powder an' blowin' it to hell an' gone. *Look* at me! *Listen!* Put away yore marbles, an' *think!*"

"Why don't you fellers listen?" grinned Fleming.

"Just because he went south don't say he *stayed* there," hammered Ackerman. "He wasn't scared away; not by a damned sight. *I* know that. Fleming, Gates, an' Harrison know it. We *all* know it. He went south. But he can turn, can't he? If he can't, he's in a hell of a fix! No tellin' where he'll end up—Patagonia, mebby. All right, he can turn. It's only a question of *where!* He's goin' to turn; an' when he does, I'm goin' to be there an' see him do it. I'm goin' to make it my business to find him, watch him, an' trail him. If he turns north I'm goin' to *get* him. An' if you'll take any advice from me, you'll *all* begin to take long rides, north, east, south, an' west; mostly southwest an' west. You'll ride in pairs, an' you'll keep yore fool eyes open. Th' time has passed for loafin' around here, shootin' craps an' swappin' lies. Yo're smokin' on an open powder keg; an' *damn you,* you ain't got sense enough to know it!" He raised his clenched fists. "I *mean* it! Damn you—you—ain't—got—sense— enough—to—know—it!"

Quigley laughed, although uneasily; for Ackerman's earnestness carried unrest with it. "Jim, Jim," he said kindly, "we've been up here a long time; an' we've given these hills a name that guards 'em for us. Them that bothered us disappeared; an' th' lesson was learned."

"Was it?" shouted Ackerman. "*He* didn't learn it! *He* come up here, plump in th' face of yore warnin', in spite of what he had heard in Hastings! *Why?* Because it's his *business* to come! Because he's *paid* to come! *He* ain't one of them Hasting's loafers! *He* ain't no sleepy puncher, satisfied to draw down his pay, an' th' hell with th' ranch! I tell you you never *saw* a man like him before. Can't you see it? Logan found out that he was a *real* man, a *gun* man, an' not scared of hell an' high water. Then he quits Logan, an' comes up here. Can't you *see* it? *Can't* you? *Think,* damn it; THINK!"

"I did; have been, an' am," snapped Quigley angrily. "Thinkin' is one thing; goin' loco, another. *I* think yo're a damned fool!"

Ackerman threw up his hands in a helpless gesture. "All right; have it yore own way. I give it up. I pass before th' draw. But I ain't swallerin' no pap an' gazin' at th' moon. I'm goin' to keep my eyes on Nelson."

"You want to; he's a bad hombre," said Fleming uneasily.

Ackerman wheeled and smiled at the speaker. "He is; an' he's a damned *good* man. I takes off my hat to him; an' I wish to heaven we had a few Nelsons up here; this ranch would *hum*. An' you'd 'a' done better if you'd follered yore own advice. I won't make th' same mistake twice. Th' minute he makes a false move I'll plug him. I underrated him before; now I'm goin' to overrate him, to be on th' safe side. But *you* ain't got a thing to say: three to one, an' you let him make fools out of you!"

"I admits it," said Fleming. "An' that's why I'm tellin' you to look out for him. He's as quiet as a flea; an' as harmless as blastin' powder. I wish you luck."

"I ain't so harmless myself, retorted Ackerman. "An' now I know what I'm buckin'. You'll see me when you see me; I'm preparin' to be gone a month or more."

They watched him enter the bunk-house, and when he came out again he had his saddle and a blanket roll; and when he rode into the canyon without a backward glance or a parting word he had his slicker, a generous supply of food, and plenty of ammunition.

Quigley watched him until he rode out of sight

beyond the canyon, and turned toward his outfit, shaking his head. "He's so all-fired set on it that I'm gettin' a little restless myself. Jim ain't no fool; an' he don't often shy at a shadow. It won't do us no harm, anyhow; an' we can take turns at it. I'll start it off by takin' one side tomorrow, an' Holbrook can take th' other. Later on we'll figger it out an' arrange th' shifts. Mebby he's right."

CHAPTER XIII
An Observant Observer

Jim Ackerman strode into Pop Hayes' saloon, where he found the proprietor and Charley James squabbling acrimoniously over the value of a cribbage hand.

"Not satisfied with gettin' a twenty-four hand," snorted Charley, "he tries to make it twenty-seven, shovin' 'em around like he was playin' three-card monte! You old fool! You've counted them runs once more'n you oughter; but I don't care how much you mills 'em; it's twenty-four!"

"I ain't done no more countin' than they'll stand!"

"I dunno what *they'll* stand; but I knows what *I'll* stand. It's twenty-four!"

"Soon as you gets two bits up," sneered Pop, "you lose yore nerve. You can play all day for fun, an' never loose a yelp; but when you've got money up you acts like you was stabbed!"

"That so? You forget how to count when there's money up!"

"When yo're winnin' everything is lovely; but when yo're losin' you go on th' prod!"

"You don't have to go; yo're allus rarin' around on yore hind laigs, a-pawin' th' air an' snortin'. Leave it to Ackerman. I dare you!"

"I'll leave it to anybody but you. You hadn't ought to even play for th' drinks. Jim, look at that twenty-seven hand an' tell that fool what it counts, will you?"

Ackerman moved it around and grinned. "Fifteen eight; two pairs is twelve, an' four runs of three makes that twenty-seven hand count just twenty-four. An' it's a cussed good hand, too; you shore knows how to discard."

Charley nodded emphatically. "There! I told you so!"

Pop raised his hands helplessly to heaven. "How much longer have I got to keep th' peace? Two more like you an' Charley an' this country would go plumb to th' dogs! Yo're two fools."

"Now who's stabbed?" jeered Charley. "You can get more out of one crib hand than most folks can find in two. 'Four, five, six,'" he mimicked. "Why don't you shift 'em around an' work six, five, four; an' five, six, four; an' four, six, five? A genius like you ought to get thirty-six out of a twenty-four hand an' never turn a hair. I'm such a stranger to a hand like that that I'd be satisfied with twenty-four. I ain't no genius at figgers."

"If I told you what you are, you'd get insulted!"

"Anybody that could insult you could make cows live on malpais an' get fat," sneered

Charley. "I've done called you a liar, an' a cheat, an' a thief—"

"Hey! Stop that!" interposed Ackerman. "Quit it; an' have a drink with me. You'd let a man die of thirst, *I* believes."

Pop shuffled around behind the bar and sullenly produced the bottle and the glasses. "I know, Jim," he apologized; "but you don't know how my patience gets tried!"

Charley snorted. "If they ever tries yore patience they'll lynch it. Here's how, *Jim*."

"Good luck," said Jim, tossing off the drink.

Charley, walking back toward the card table, caught sight of the well-loaded horse outside; and Pop, taking advantage of the situation, reached swiftly under the bar and slid two Colts toward Ackerman, who frowned and pushed them back. "Some other time," he growled. "Ain't goin' back right away." He pushed his hat back on his head. "Any news?"

"There ain't never any news in this place," answered the proprietor. "But I hear as how th' Circle S has fired Long Pete Carson for stayin' drunk. Long Pete was all het up over it an' lets drive at Holmes. Bein' unsteady he missed Dick an' nicked Harry Kane. Then Dick took th' gun away from him an' give him a beatin'. Dick's hands are shore eddicated. Th' Long T near lost three hosses in that quicksand near Big Bend; an' Smith come near goin' with 'em. An' that Nelson is prospectin' somewhere near th' Circle S, if he ain't left th' country."

"What makes you think that he's mebby left th' country?" inquired Ackerman casually.

"He had his spirit busted when his cabin burned. Said this country was too full of dogs to live in. But I reckon he'll work around th' Circle S or th' Long T a while before he quits for good."

Charley turned and grunted derisively. "That's all you know about it. He crossed the river near th' Circle S, over Rocky Ford, an' went to Bitter Creek hills."

"How'd you know he did?" demanded Pop. "I was told by th' man that saw him do it."

"Who was that?" asked Pop, indignant because he had not been told about it before.

"Yo're a reg'lar old woman," jeered Charley. "You can guess it."

"Funny he didn't tell me," sighed Pop.

"Mebby he reckoned it was his own business," retorted Charley. "Mebby he knowed you'd blurt it out to everybody you saw."

"I keep things under my belt!"

"Yes; food an' likker," chuckled Charley, enjoying himself. "If nobody come around for you to tell yore gossip to, cussed if you wouldn't tell it to th' sky, night an' mornin', like a ki-yote."

"So, he's still prospectin'," laughed Ackerman. "He'll starve to death."

"I ain't so shore about that," said Charley. "He

weighed his gold on my scales an' it was one pound an' eleven ounces. It was all gold, too; I saw it."

"He-he-he!" chuckled Pop. "If yore scales said one eleven he only had about half a pound. Them scales are worse than a cold deck."

"That's a lie; an' you know it! Them scales are honest!"

"Then they ain't 'pervious to their 'sociations," grinned Pop. He reached behind him, picked up a package and turned to Ackerman. "Did you say you was goin' near th' Circle S?" he inquired.

"He did not," said Charley gleefully. "Didn't I say you was an old woman?"

Ackerman laughed, winked at Charley and went out; and the two cronies listened to the rapidly dying hoof-beats.

Pop wheeled and glared at his friend. "Now you've done it! Ain't you got no sense, tellin' *him* where Nelson is?"

"If I had much I wouldn't hang out with you," grinned Charley. "But I got a little; an' if he crosses th' river he won't find Nelson. A Circle S puncher saw him hoofin' it into th' southwest. *Quién sabe?*"

"Sometimes you do have a spark of common sense," said Pop. "Sort of a glimmer. It's real noticeable in you when it shows at all, just like a match looks prominent in th' dark. Pick up them cards an' don't do no more fancy countin'."

"Countin' wouldn't do me no good while yo're multiplyin'. Get agoin'; I got to get my four bits back before I go home."

Well to the south of the two friends in Hastings, Jim Ackerman loped steadily ahead, debating several things; and as he neared the Circle S range a man suddenly arose from behind a rock. There was nothing threatening about this gentleman except, perhaps, his sudden and unexpected appearance; but Ackerman's gun had him covered as soon as his head showed.

"Turn it off me," said the man behind the rock, a note of pained injury in his voice. "My intentions are honorable; an' plumb peaceful. Yo're most scandalous suspicious."

Ackerman smiled grimly. "Mebby I am; but habit is strong. An' one of my worst habits is suspicion. What's th' idea of this jack-in-th'-box proceedin' of yourn? You've shore got funny ways; an' plumb dangerous ones."

"Reckon mebby it does look that way," said the man behind the rock. "I neglects caution. I should 'a' covered you first an' then popped up. That shows how plumb innercent an' peaceful I am. Yore name's Jim Ackerman, ain't it?"

"You can't allus tell," replied Ackerman.

"That's where yo're figgerin' wrong. I can allus tell. Havin' told me yore name, I'll tell you mine. I'm Pete Carson, known hereabouts an' elsewhere as Long Pete. Some calls me Long-winded Pete; but it's all th' same to me. Pint that a little mite more to th' sky; thank you, sir. I was punchin' for th' Circle S, but th' Circle S punched me; then it fired me. I've got to eat, so I got to work. Th' Long T ain't hirin'; an I'd starve before I'd work for Logan. I ain't no slave, not me.

"I'm settin' there in th' sun whittlin' a stick an' arguin' with myself. I was gettin' th' worst of it when I hears yore noble cayuse. Not bein' curious I riz up instanter an' looked plumb into yore gun—just a little mite higher; ah, much obliged."

"What's all this to me?" demanded Ackerman impatiently.

"That's what I'm aimin' to find out. I saw you comin'—up a little more; thank you. Then I think I got a new chance. I want a job an' I want it bad. Hold it in yore left hand; yore right hand is tired, an' saggin'. Any chance for a close-mouthed man up yore way? One that does as he's told, asks no questions, an' ain't particular what kind of a job it is? Better let me hold that; I can see yo're gettin' tired. Thank you, sir. I'm desperate, an' I'm hungry. What you say? Speak right out—I'm a grand listener."

Ackerman grunted. "Huh! I ain't got nothin' to say about hirin' th' men where I work. As a matter of fact we ain't got work enough for another man. An' I reckon you don't understand nothin' about farmin', even in a small way; but if yo're hungry, why, I can fix that right soon. Got a cayuse?"

Pete nodded emphatically. "I allus manage to keep a cayuse, no matter how bad things busts; a cayuse, my saddle, an' a gun. Why?"

"Climb onto it an' come along with me. I'm aimin' to make camp as soon as I run across water. That's a purty good animal you got."

"Yes; looks good," grunted Long Pete; "but it ain't. It's a deceivin' critter. I'm yore scout. There's a crick half a mile west of here. I'm that famished I'm faint. Just a little more an' I'd 'a' cooked me a square meal off of one of th' yearlin's that wander on th' edge of th' range. That was what I was thinkin' over when I heard you."

"You shouldn't do a thing like that!" exclaimed Ackerman severely. "Besides, you shouldn't talk about it. An' if you *do* it you'll get shot or lynched."

"A man does lots of things he shouldn't. An' as for talkin', I'm th' most safe talker you ever met. I allus know where I'm talkin', what I'm talkin' about, an' who I'm talkin to. Now, as I figger it, I'd rather get shot or lynched than starve in a land of beef. What do I care about killin' another man's cows? I'm plumb sick of workin' on a string that some bull-headed foreman can break; an' I'm most awful sick of workin' for wages. *I* ain't no hired man, damn it! What I wants is an equal share in what I earns. An' you can believe me, Mister Man, I ain't noways particular what th' work is. I never did have no respect for a man

157

that gambled for pennies. No tin-horn never amounted to nothin'. He can't lose much; but yo're cussed right he can't *win* much, neither. If th' stakes are high an' th' breaks anywhere near equal, I'll risk my last dollar or my last breath.

"As to what I am, you lissen to me: When I'm sober I stays strictly sober, for months at a time; an' when I'm drunk I likeways stays drunk for days at a time. I ain't like some I knows of, half drunk most of th' time an' never really sober. Me, I just serves notice that I'm goin' off on a bender, an' I goes. An' when I comes back I'm sober all th' way through. Here's th' crick. An' I never get drunk when there's work to be did. You can put up that Colt now an' watch me get a fire goin' that won't show a light for any distance or throw much smoke. I tell you I know my business."

Ackerman unpacked and turned the horses loose to graze, and by the time he was ready to start cooking, Long Pete had a fire going in a little hollow near the water.

"Now you just set down an' watch me cavort an' prance," quoth Long Pete pleasantly. "Reckon mebby you might not move fast enough for my empty belly. Chuck me that flour bag—I'm a reg'lar cook, *I* am. You just set there an' keep right on thinkin' about me; weigh me calm an' judicial."

Ackerman smiled, leaned back against his

saddle and obeyed his verbose companion, pondering over what his deft guest had said. He knew of Long Pete by hearsay, and he now marshaled the knowledge in slow and orderly review before his mind.

The cook handed him a pan, a tin cup, and a knife, fork, and spoon. Then he waved at the pan. "Take all you want of this grub, an' take it now. This bein' a one-man outfit I'll eat off th' cookin' utensils—utensils sounds misleadin', don't it?—somethin' like tonsils or a disease. Now I warn you: dig in deep an' take all you kin eat, for there won't be no second helpin' after I gets *my* holt. Want yore coffee now?"

"Later, I reckon," smiled Ackerman. "You shore can cook. Better take th' cup first if you wants yore coffee now. I'll use it later."

"Soon as we open one of them cans I'll have a cup of my own, an' we're goin' to open one tomorrow," grinned Long Pete, opening his pocketknife and attacking the frying pan. When the pan had been cleaned of the last morsel Pete emptied the cup, washed it in the creek, refilled it and handed it to his companion. Rolling a cigarette with one hand, he lit it, inhaled deeply and blew a cloud of smoke toward the sky.

"Cuss me if that don't hit me plumb center," he chuckled. "An' plumb center is th' place for it. I'd ruther eat my own cookin' in th' open, than feed in th' house after some dirty cook got through messin' with th' grub. At first I thought you was another prospector; but when I looked close I saw that you didn't have th' rest of th' outfit. Now don't you say nothin'. I ain't lookin' for no information; I'm givin' it. You see, I shoots off my mouth regardless, for I'm a great talker when I'm sober; an' tight as a fresh-water clam when I'm drunk. A whiskered old ram of a sky-pilot once told me that I was th' most garrulous man he'd ever met up with. After I let him up he explained what garrulous means; an' th' word sort of stuck in my memory. I know it stuck in his; he'll never forget it."

Ackerman coughed up some coffee. "He won't," he gasped. "But what—made you think—I might be prospectin'?"

"Just a little superstition of mine," explained Long Pete. "There's some coffee runnin' down yore neck. You never ought to laugh when yo're drinkin'. Good thing it wasn't whiskey. Things allus comes in bunches. That purty near allus holds good, as mebby you've noticed. I have. I saw one prospector, a cow-puncher gone loco, hoofin' it in th' dirt alongside his loaded cayuse. Of th' two I thinks most of th' cayuse. It was a black, of thoroughbred strain, steppin' high an' disdainful, with more intelligence blazin' out of its big eyes than its master ever had. So when I sees you ridin' along with a big pack I reckoned mebby that you must 'a' eat some of th' same weed an' had got th' same kind of hallucerna-tions. They's different kinds, you know. But this is once th' rule fails. There won't be no bunch of prospectors, an' I know why; but that's a secret. There won't be no third."

Ackerman looked keenly at him through narrowed lids, speculating, wondering, puzzled. Then he leaned back and yawned. "*Is* there a prospector down here?" he asked incredulously. "You don't mean it."

Long Pete coolly looked him over from boots to sombrero. "I'm duly grateful for this sumptious feed, an' I know what is th' custom when you breaks bread with a man; but I *do* mean it; an' I don't lie even when my words are ramblin' free. I reckon, mebby, you ought to remember that. We'll sort of get along better, day after day."

"No offense! I was just surprised. Which way was th' fool headin'?"

"Mebby I am a little too touchy. We all have our faults. He was headin' th' same as us because we're on his trail, right now. I sort of follered it here to keep my hand in. You never can tell when yo're goin' to need th' practice. Our fire is built on th' ashes of hisn. His fire an' smoke was well hid, too. What a two-gun cow-puncher, with a Tin Cup cayuse like that, wants to go hoofin' off on a fool's errand for, is more than I can figger out. But two heads are better than one; an' a man hears an awful lot of talkin' up in

Old Pop Hayes' place. Strange old polecat, Pop is."

Ackerman stared thoughtfully into the fire for a few moments. Then he looked squarely and long into Pete's placid, unwavering eyes, and what he saw there must have pleased and piqued him.

"Pete, yore habit of usin' words reminds me of a gravel bed I once panned. It was a big bed an' I panned a terrible lot of gravel; but you'd 'a' been surprised if you knew how much gold there was in it. I was a rich man until I hit town." He waved his hands expressively. "You've said a whole lot, but it pans out strong. Anybody that won't listen to you is a fool. Let's have a pow-wow, without hurtin' any feelin's. Speak plain; keep cool. What you say?"

Pete waited until he rolled another cigarette and drew in another lungful of smoke. Then he recrossed his long legs, hitched comfortably against his saddle, and nodded.

"Meanin' to swap ideas an' personal opinions, ask questions regardless, an' if things don't come out like we'd mebby like 'em, keep our mouths shut afterwards an' not hold no hard feelin's?"

"Just that," Ackerman acquiesced. "Just what was you aimin' at in yore talk?"

Pete scrutinized the fire. "Well, I hit what I was aimin' at—you allus do with a scatter gun. An' for th' ease of my conscience, an' th' rest of my calloused soul, let me confess that I had a gun on you while I was talkin' to you. One arm was folded across behind my back an' a little old Colt was squeezin' against my side an' th' other arm, lookin' right at you. Carelessness ain't no sin of mine; I got enough without it. But, shakin' some of th' gravel out, let's see what I got.

"I wants a job. It's funny how many times I've wanted a job, an' then threw it sprawlin' after I got it. Bein' desperate, I was aimin' to stick you up an' take your outfit. Then when you got near an' I saw who it was, I knowed I'd have to shoot to kill; an' first, too. That's why I didn't tackle that other feller, too. An' just then my perverted mind says two an' two is four. An' it most generally is. Then I knowed you needed me. So I let th' gun slip an' got real friendly. But, as I was sayin', I want a job. Now you pay attention.

"We knows what's rumored around about Twin Buttes; an' we knows who lives up there; an' we knows there ain't never been no farm products come out of that section. That's th' biggest mistake you fellers ever made; you should 'a' run a garden. Likewise, we knows that tin-horns don't gamble with things that belong to other people, if th' other people packs guns. An' specially they don't gamble with no cows an' hosses. 'Tain't popular, an' folks don't like it. A tin-horn ain't man enough to risk a bullet or a rope. Now then, you just let me draw you th' picture of a dream I've often had.

"I can see a bunch of husky cow-punchers, among which I see myself, an' we're punchin' cows that we never bought. We're poolin' our winnin's an' sharin' th' risks. I can even see me rustlin' cows, an' there's men with me that I could name if my memory wasn't so bad. There's a big rock wall, an' a deep, swift river that's so damned cold it fair hurts. An' somewhere back in th' buttes, which is in a section plumb fatal to strangers, all but one, is a little ranch, with a drive trail leadin' north or west. That's th' dream. Ain't it hell what fool ideas go trompin' an' rampagin' through a man's mind when he's asleep, 'specially if he ain't satisfied to work for wages? Did you ever have any?"

Ackerman grinned to hide his surprise. "Yo're a grand dreamer, Pete. I've had dreams somethin' like that, myself; an' so far's I'm concerned yourn can come true; but I only got one vote. An' as I ain't goin' back for some time, I don't know just what to say."

"Not knowin' what to say never bothered me," chuckled Long Pete. "I can talk th' spots off a poker deck; I'll show you how, some day. But as long as you mentioned dreams, it reminds me of another I've had. Not long ago, neither. I saw a two-gun prospector leavin' an unpleasant location. He was a *reg'lar* two-gun man; a wise feller could just see it a-stickin' out all over him. I kept right on bein' hungry. Then, quite a little later I saw another man, a cow-puncher, ridin' along his trail; an' he had so much grub it fair dazzled me. An' bein' friendly, in my dream, I up an' tells th' second man where th' other feller was headin'. An' if th' dream hadn't 'a' stopped there I could 'a' told him which way th' two-gun prospector an' his black, Tin Cup cayuse went on th' mornin' follerin' th' day I saw him. Funny how things like that will stick in a man's memory. An' I've heard tell that lots of people believes in dreams, too. Seems like you only got to know how to figger 'em to learn a lot of useful an' plumb interestin' things. A fortune-teller told me that. Why, once I dreamed that I had shot a feller that had been pesterin' me; an' when I got sober, damned if I hadn't, too!"

Ackerman slammed his sombrero on the ground and leaned quickly forward over the fire. "Pete, I ain't got much money with me—didn't expect to have no call to use it. I ain't got enough for wages for any length of time; but I've got grub, plenty of it. An' if you wants to make that first dream of yourn come true, you stick to me an' with me, come what may, an' I'll see you a member of a little ranch back in some buttes, or we'll damned well know th' reason why. We need brains up there. Are you in?"

"Every damned chip; from my hat to my worn-out boots; from soda to hock," grinned Long Pete. "You got your cayuse, yore shootin' irons, an' th' grub; I got my cayuse, mean as it is, my guns, an' a steady-workin' appetite. Pass them pans over; allus like to wash things up as soon as they've been used. It'll be yore job next meal. I believe in equal work. Better hang up that pack —there's ants runnin' around here."

"Yo're a better cook than me," said Ackerman cheerfully, as he obeyed. "You do th' cookin' an' leave th' cleanin' up to me. I'd rather wrastle dirty pans than eat my own cookin' any day. That fair?"

"As a new, unmarked deck," replied Long Pete contentedly. "An' while we're talkin' about washin' pans, I want to say that that two-gun hombre went due north, ridin' plumb up th' middle of this here crick. An' since yo're trailin' him, I reckon he kept goin' right on north. I allus like to guess when I don't know."

"Yo're a damned good guesser," grinned Ackerman. "Let's roll up in th' blankets early tonight an' get an early start in th' mornin'."

"Keno. That suits me, for if there is one thing that I can do well, it's rollin' up in a blanket. I should 'a' been a cocoon."

CHAPTER XIV
The End of a Trail

Johnny ducked down behind a bowlder, for a horseman, sharply silhouetted against the crimson glow of the sunset, rode parallel to the edge of the cliff; and, judging from the way he was scrutinizing the ground, he was looking for tracks. While he searched, another horseman rode from the north and joined him. They made a splendid picture, rugged, lean, hard; their sharply-cut profiles, the jaunty set of the big sombreros, their alert and wiry cow-ponies, silhouetted against the crimson and gold sky; but to the hidden watcher there was no poetry, no art, in the picture, for to him it was a thing of danger, a menace. Their voices, carelessly raised, floated to him distinctly.

"Find anythin'?" asked Ben Gates ironically.

"Just what I reckoned I'd find, which was nothin'," answered Harrison. "Ackerman's loco. But I reckon it's better than loafin' around down below. I was gettin' plumb fed up on that."

"It's all cussed nonsense. Nelson's cleared out for good. He ain't no fool; an' there's too many of us."

"Seen th' others?"

"Only when they left. They ought to be ridin' back purty soon I reckon. This finishes this side, don't it?"

"Yes; they'll comb th' west side tomorrow; an' then take th' north end. Ridin' in daylight ain't so bad; but I got a fine chance seein' anythin' at night. An' I hope he *has* cleared out; a man on a bronc looks as big as a house."

"Don't ride at all; lay up somewhere near th' canyon trail an' let *him* do th' movin'. But hell! He's gone out of this country."

"That's just what I was aimin' to do. I could ride within ten feet of a man in th' dark, with all th' cover there is up here, an' not see him. Don't you worry about yore Uncle Nat; he's shore growed up. But it's all fool nonsense, just th' same."

"Oh, well; it'll make things pleasanter down below," grinned Gates. "It'll stop th' arguin'. Quigley's gettin' near as nervous as Ackerman. He's gettin' scared of shadows since Jim laced it into him. Well, I'm goin' on; if I meets Holbrook I'll tell him to take th' south end. So long."

They separated and went their respective ways, and while Johnny watched them he suddenly heard a murmur of voices below him, and he squirmed between two big bowlders as the sounds came nearer.

"Well, we've shore combed this side," said one

of the newcomers. "An' that ends part of a fool's errand."

"We shore have," grunted another. "An' it did us good, too. We all have been gettin' too cussed lazy for any account. I reckon a certain amount of work is th' best friend a man has got."

"Mebby; anyhow, I know that my appetite is standin' on its hind laigs yellin' for help," laughed the third. "An' we have th' satisfaction of knowin' everythin' is all right out here. Cussed if I couldn't eat a raw skunk!"

"But that ain't what I'm drivin' at," said the first speaker, his voice growing fainter as they rode on. "I claims if he is workin' for th' CL he only has to get one look in our valley to tell him all he wants to know. If he's up here, or has been up here, that would be enough. He wouldn't stay here day after day like a dead dog in a well."

As the words died out in the distance Johnny started to slip out from between the bowlders, when a sharp *spang!* rang out at a rock near his waist, and a whining scream soared skyward. An opening made by a split in the bowlder had partly revealed his moving body to a pair of very keen eyes on the lookout for just such a sign. A second later the flat report of the shot cracked against his ears, but he was on the other side of the bowlders and leaping down the steep hillside when he heard it. As he cleared a big rock he landed almost upon a slinking coyote, which instantly destroyed distance at an unbelievable speed. It shot up the hill, over the crest, and sped like an arrow of haze across the open table-land. Another shot rang out and a laughing voice shouted greeting.

"Hi-yi! Who-o-p-e-e-e! Scoot, you streak of lightnin'! Cookie's layin' for you with nine buckshot in each barrel. But I'm a drunk Injun if you didn't fool me."

A peeved voice raised loudly in the twilight. "Hey! Damn you! Look out where yo're shootin'! That slug ricochetted plumb between our heads! Ain't you got no sense a-tall?"

"That's right! Start kickin'!" retorted Gates at the top of his voice. "Didn't you ever hear a slug before? Don't you know that th' slug you can hear is past you?"

"That so? How'd *you* like to listen to one *now?*" angrily shouted the objector. "How do *I* know that th' *next* one is goin' past?"

"Ah, go to hell!" jeered Gates. "Little things make big bumps on *you,* you sage hen!"

"*Little* things!" roared a second voice. "*Little* things! Would you *listen* to him? It sounded like a train of cars to me, damned if it didn't!"

"Thinks he's treed another cougar," laughed a third voice.

The three appeared upon the plateau and rode toward the disgruntled marksman, their hands up over their heads in mock anxiety and surrender.

170

Down from the north rolled a swift, rhythmic drumming, and Harrison, eagerly alert, his rifle balanced in his hands, slid to a dusty stop.

"What is it?" he demanded.

"Reckon it was Cookie's pet ki-yote," grinned Gates. "There ain't nothin' with wings, even, can beat 'em. He just melted."

"Yo're a damned fool!" swore Harrison angrily.

"Huh! I could 'a' told you that long ago," observed Purdy. "You just catchin' on?"

"I saw somethin' move," retorted Gates. "It slid past that crack an' th' sun caught it purty fair, so I let drive. How th' devil do you suppose *I* knowed it was a ki-yote? Think I'm one of them mejums an' has second sight?"

"Never!" chuckled Fleming. "People make mistakes, but th' man don't live, free an' unrestrained, that would think you had second sight. He might even be doubtful about th' first sight. You want to practice second *look*. Look twice, pray, an' then count ten, Dan'l, old trapper."

"He oughta be penned up nights," growled Sanford. "He's a cussed sight more dangerous than a plague."

Another rider joined them from the south. "Dan'l Boone at it again?" he asked, grinning.

"He is!" snapped Purdy.

Harrison quieted his horse. "You fellers take him home with you, an' keep him there. He shoots at anythin' that moves! I'm goin' to make root right here till he gets down below. Mebby he might take me for somethin' suspicious."

"If I'd 'a' got that chicken-thief," placidly remarked Gates, "I'd 'a' slipped it into Cookie's coop tonight, cussed if I wouldn't!"

"You keep away from his coop," warned Fleming, with a solemn shake of his head. "He's another that shoots at anythin' that moves."

Holbrook looked at Harrison. "You takin' th' north end tonight?"

"Yes; but I'm stayin' right here till Davy Crockett gets down on th' range. Don't you move, Frank; he'll likely blow you apart if you do."

"Glad he ain't ridin' in yore place. Good night, fellers."

The group split up and four of the riders rode toward the canyon trail.

"Take th' lead, Art," said Purdy. "You know that ledge better'n we do."

Holbrook and Harrison watched them disappear, consulted a few moments and then separated.

At the bottom of the steep eastern bank of the plateau, Johnny, a vague blur in the fading light, hastened stealthily into the brush. When assured that he was safe from observation he swung north and made the best time possible in the darkness over such ground, eager to reach his horse, which was picketed more than a mile away.

"Huh!" he grunted. "So they're combin' th' country an' patrolin'. Hereafter an' henceforth

I've got to play Injun for all I'm worth. An' if they comb th' west side tomorrow I've got to move my camp at daylight."

To the southwest of the rustlers' ranch Ackerman and his new friend had sworn day after day, for they found no tracks to follow. After riding up several creeks to their head-waters they gave up such careful searching and went blindly ahead in the direction Ackerman thought their enemy would take; and the ashes of dead campfires from time to time told them that they had decided right.

At last they came to a point due west of the little valley of the burned cabin, and Ackerman did not choose to pass the stream which flowed from that direction. As the day was about done they camped on the bank of the little tributary and planned the next day's work. Arising early the following morning Ackerman divided the supplies and gave part of them to Long Pete.

"Well," he said, smiling grimly; "here's where we separate. We're north of Twin Buttes, an' that means we are about even with th' south end of our ranch. He could 'a' turned off any place from here on because when he got this far he had just about arrived.

"Now I reckon I better keep on follerin' th' big creek, for I got a feelin' that I know purty well just about where he's located. But we can't overlook no bets. You foller this crick to th' end, or till you see where he left it. An' you meet me tonight, if you can, at th' south end of that big butte up there, th' one with th' humpback.

"I've told you he's dangerous, chain-lightnin' with his guns; an' I'm tellin' you now to make shore you won't forget it. If you run across him, shoot first, as soon as you see him. You can't beat him on th' draw; an' while I don't like to shoot a man that way, I'm swallerin' my pride in this case because he's a spy, or else he'd never ride up th' cricks for forty miles. I never heard of anybody bein' so cautious an' patient *all* th' time. We got to get him; if we don't there'll be hell to pay."

"Don't you get no gray hair about me," growled Long Pete. "I know what it means, damn him!" A smile flitted across his face. "But I shore has to laugh at th' son-of-a-gun! An' me thinkin' he was a prospector, an' loco! I'd feel ashamed of myself if I really *did* think he was a prospector. You see, I've seen prospectors before. You mustn't mind me makin' a break like that once in a while; I've had to fool so many folks I can't sort of get my bearin's now. I'd be prouder of gettin' a man like him than anythin' I ever done. Did you gimme plenty of grub? All right; I'm movin' on now. So long."

"So long; an' good luck," replied Ackerman, going north along the creek.

Long Pete rode carefully up his own watery

way, thoroughly alert and closely scrutinizing both banks.

"Settin' on a cayuse, out here, don't set well on my stummick," he muttered uneasily. "I'd mebby be more prominent cavortin' around on a mountain top, or ridin' upside down on th' under side of a cloud, but I ain't hankerin' after no prominence. Nope; I'm a shrinkin' violet. An' *splash! splash!* says th' bronc. *Splash! splash!* reg'lar as a watch, for th' whole wide world to hear, observe, an' think about. Long Pete, yo're a fool. Long Pete, yo're several, all kinds of fools. What you should oughta do is picket th' bronc an' perceed with more caution, on yore belly like a silent worm, or at least on yore kneecaps an' han's, like a—like a—a—who th' hell cares what? Day after day we been temptin' Providence. 'Hurry up!' says he. 'Hurry be damned!' thought I. But we hurried. Yes sir. But it must be did. Damn th' *must.* All my sinful life there was a *must* or a *mustn't.* It's a *must-y* world. He-he! That ain't a bad one, or I'm a liar!

"All serene. Both banks lovely. Lush grass an' mosquitoes an' *flies. Splash! Splash! Ker-*splash! *Ker-*plash! Slop inter it, bronc. Don't mind my stummick. Keep lungin' on, pluggin' right ahead, stubborn as th' workin's of hell. *Long Pete! Long Pete! Ker-splash! Here's Long Pete!* Tell him, bronc; grease th' chute for yore boss. Even th' frogs got more sense; they shut up when they hears us. It's a gamble, bronc; a toss-up. Our friend, Mr. James Ackerman, says: 'Here, Long Pete. We done reached th' partin' of th' ways. He could 'a' left th' crick any place, now. Over east yonder is where he was burned out. You take that way, an' I'll go on north where I reckon I know mebby where he oughta be.' That's what he *said,* bronc. But what he kept a damp, dark, deep secret was: 'But I know he ain't. He's east, where he knows th' lay of th' land. Where he feels at home. An' anyhow, Long Pete, you know too damned much about our affairs.' He's a friend of ours, bronc; we know that—but he's a better friend of hisself.

"We must watch both banks, bronc; watch 'em close. All right; but this time we'll just bust hell out of Mr. Must. We'll square up, right now, for th' way Mr. Must has horned inter our affairs all our fool life. Come on; get out of this! That's right. Now you stand there an' drip. I'm going to travel humble an' quiet. I don't want no fife an' drum to lead *me* to war; no ma'am; not a-tall."

Long Pete's low, muttered chatter ceased as he wriggled through the cover. Minutes passed as he went ahead, glancing continually at the banks of the small creek for the telltale signs. He wormed around some scattered bowlders and came to the edge of a small, rock-floored clearing, where he paused.

A movement half way up on a mesa close by caught his eye, and he backed over his trail, wriggled around the little clearing and began to stalk that particular mesa ledge. Yard after yard was put behind him, nearer and nearer he approached the ledge and a nest of bowlders three hundred yards from it. The bowlders were his objective, for, once among them, he would have the view he wished. Leading to them was a brush-covered ridge and toward this he cautiously advanced, rifle at the ready and every sense alert. But he never reached it.

Behind him and two hundred yards to his right a man slowly arose from behind a rock and, resting a rifle on the bulwark, took slow and careful aim at the gray shirt crawling close to the ridge. There was a flash, a puff of smoke, a sharp report. Pete, a look of great surprise on his face, tried to rise and turn to pay his debt, crumpled suddenly and lay inert, sprawled grotesquely on the ground.

The man behind the rock mechanically re-loaded and walked slowly toward his victim, waving his sombrero in a short arc. On his face was an expression of triumphant joy. Up on the ledge of the mesa wall another man arose, acknowledged the signal and began to climb down the wall as hurriedly as safety would permit. When he reached the prostrate figure he found the successful marksman standing like a man in a trance, a look of blank wonderment on his face, his lower jaw sagging loosely.

"Good for you!" said the man from above; and then he paused. "What's th' matter?" A ghastly suspicion flashed into his mind and he leaped forward to see who the victim was. He arose relieved, but as surprised as his companion. "Lord! I was scared you'd got one of th' boys, from th' way you looked! Who th' devil is *this* feller? An' what's he doin' up *here?* I've seen him before; who th' devil *is* he?"

The other drew a long breath. "It's Long Pete, of th' Circle S; but what he's doin' up here is past me. Look at his shirt, his hat, an' say he don't look like Nelson from th' back! He only wears one gun, but I couldn't see that; th' grass an' brush hid it. But, just th' same, he was stalkin' you! If you'd 'a' shoved up yore head, he'd 'a' drilled it, *shore!*"

"But why should he stalk *me?*" demanded Harrison. "He didn't have no business up here; he didn't have no reason to sneak along, an' he didn't have no call to stalk me! Say! Mebby he's throwed in with Nelson! If he has, mebby his outfit has throwed in, too! Mebby they're up here strong, an' closin' in from all directions, for a show-down! We better warn th' boys, an' get back to Quigley; an' damned quick!"

"Go ahead," said Gates. "I'll get his cayuse an' foller close. Where's Art an' Frank?"

"They went on north—I'm off after 'em," snapped Harrison. "Let his cayuse be. You hotfoot it to Quigley!"

"Come on!" growled Gates, wheeling. "They may be on both sides of th' ranch!"

Jim Ackerman, riding slowly along the bank of the main creek, saw everything that could be seen by a man with keen eyes; and he felt nervous. There was cover all about him, good cover; and any of it might be sheltering the man he was hunting. There was no sense for him to ride along the bank, an inviting target that a boy hardly could miss; there was no sense in riding at all; so he picketed his horse and went ahead on foot.

Gaining Humpback Butte, the meeting place he had mentioned to Long Pete, he worked along its eastern base, noiselessly, cautiously, alertly; and he stopped suddenly as he caught sight of the ashes of a dead fire; stopped and looked and listened and sniffed. It did not smell like a fire that had been dead very long, he thought; and then a playful little whirlwind, simulating ferocity, spun across the partly covered ashes and caught up a bit of charcoal which glowed suddenly as if winking about what it knew and could tell.

Ackerman flitted back into the brush and when he again reached the side of the butte he was north of the camp, and had viewed it from all angles. Pausing for a moment he started back again, on a longer radius, and soon found Pepper's newly made tracks in a moist patch of sand, and hurried along the trail until he saw where it entered the creek. No need for him to wonder which way the submerged and obliterated trail led; for it must lead north. Otherwise he would have met his enemy. Swearing in sudden exultation he whirled and ran at top speed to gain his horse.

Ackerman knew Humpback Butte and its surrounding valley and canyons as he knew the QE ranch, for he had spent days hunting all over that country; and he knew that the great slopes of the valley grew steadily steeper as they reached northward until they became sheer cliffs without a single way up their walls that a horse could master. A mile above Humpback Butte the walls curved inward until only a scant six hundred yards lay between them; and on the southern side of the eastern cliff, which jutted out into the valley, hidden behind an out-thrust point, was a narrow canyon leading into the valley which formed the northwestern outlet of the QE ranch. For nearly five miles north of Humpback Butte extended the valley, now a great, wide canyon; and not one of the several blind canyons in its great walls gave a way out. Anyone passing the hidden canyon would hunt in vain for an exit and have to return again.

Reaching his horse, Ackerman mounted and rode north at top speed, guiding the animal over grass as he threaded his way in and out among the obstructions. Speed was the pressing need now, for if he could gain the hidden canyon before his enemy found it on his return, he had him trapped. There was an up-thrust mass of rock, covered with brush and scrub timber, which lay before the entrance of the canyon; once up on that he could command both the canyon and the valley, the greatest range not over five hundred yards.

Dismounting in a thicket close to the entrance, he slipped to the canyon and looked for tracks. Finding none he clambered up on the mass of rock and searched the valley for sight of Nelson. For a quarter of a mile he could follow the winding creek and he watched for a few minutes, studying the whole width of the valley.

"I've beat him; an' he ain't come back yet," he chuckled grimly. "I got five minutes to look in th' canyon an' be dead shore!"

For a hundred yards the little creek flowed along the north wall of the canyon and he wasted no time on it; any man who would ride for forty miles in creeks would not forsake the water for a mere hundred yards. Running at top-speed he dashed around a bend, eager for what he would find. There was a six-foot drop in the bottom of the canyon, and a small waterfall, where a rider would be forced to forsake the creek to climb the ridge. A quick glance at a wide belt of sand running out from the ledge at a place where it had crumbled into a steep slope told him that no one had passed that way, and he wheeled and ran back to gain the great pile of rock outside.

"Got you!" he panted triumphantly. "Yo're a clever man, Mr. Nelson; but you can't beat a stacked deck. Here's where I pay for a certain day in Hastings!"

As he reached the mouth of the canyon he heard a crashing in the brush near where he had left his horse and he dove into cover like a frightened rabbit. The crashing continued and then he heard the animal tearing off leaves, and the swish of the released branches. As he slipped forward, cursing under his breath, the horse emerged and walked slowly up on a ridge, where it paused to look calmly around.

"Damn you!" raged Ackerman, leaping forward. "I'll learn you to stay where I put you! Hell of a cow-pony *you* are!"

Grabbing the reins he kicked the horse on the ribs and dragged it back into the thicket, where he tied it short to a tree. As soon as the knots were drawn tight he scurried along the ridge, slipped through a clump of scattered brush and climbed frantically up the side of the mass of rock. A swift glance about reassured him, and, settling behind a rock, he patted his rifle and softly laughed.

An hour passed, and then suddenly he heard a plunging in the thicket below him. Pivoting like a flash, he faced about and threw himself flat on the ground, his rifle cuddled against his cheek. To his utter amazement his own horse walked into view again, the broken reins dangling and dragging along the ground. A gust of rage swept over him and he came within a hair of shooting the animal; only the need for silence kept his tightening trigger-finger from pressing that last hundredth of an inch. White with rage, choking with curses, he writhed behind his breastwork, for the horse was on the ridge again, a bold, skyline target for any eye within a mile.

"Th' journey home will be yore last!" he gritted furiously, slipping down the steep incline as rapidly as he dared. "We'll see if you can bust my rope, doubled twice! If you strain at th' rig *I*'m goin' to fix, you'll choke yoreself to death, damn you!"

Driving it back into the thicket he fastened it to a sapling with the lariat, doubled twice; and the noose around the animal's neck was a cleverly tied slip-knot.

"Now, damn you!" he blazed, kicking the horse savagely. "Take *that,* an' *that, an' that!*"

Reaching up to readjust the rope he suddenly froze in his tracks as a crisp voice hailed him.

"Keep 'em up!" said Johnny, stepping into view. "Turn around—*keep 'em up!*"

Cool as ice and perfectly composed, Ackerman slowly obeyed and scowled into the muzzle of a leveled Colt, waiting for his chance.

"A man that treats a cayuse like that ain't hardly worth a bullet," said Johnny. "If you'd 'a' looked at them reins you'd 'a' seen th' knife-pricks."

Ackerman smiled grimly with understanding, but made no answer.

"Sorry that human ramrod ain't with you," continued Johnny. "If I'd knowed he was a friend of yourn I'd 'a' stopped him cold down south of Hastings."

Ackerman scowled. "Talk's cheap. Th' man with th' drop can find a lot to say, if he's a tin-horn."

Johnny slipped the Colt into its holster and slowly raised his hands even with his shoulders. "I want you to have an even break," he muttered. "But I ain't goin' to stay here till that Circle S puncher blunders onto us. I'll wait one minute. It's yore play."

"I've been waitin' for a chance like this," said Ackerman. "Remember how you kicked me? I allus pay my debts. Th' next time—" He sprang aside with pantherish speed and the heavy Colt glinted as it leaped from his holster and flashed in an eye-baffling arc. A spurt of flame flashed from his hip and a rolling cloud of smoke half hid him as he pitched forward on his face.

Johnny staggered and stepped back out of the smoke-cloud which swirled around him and fogged his vision. A trickle of blood oozed down his cheek and gathered in his three-days beard.

Peering at the huddled figure, he pushed his gun back into its holster and wiped the blood from his face.

"There ain't many as good as you with a gun, Ackerman," he muttered. "Well, I got to get out of here. Them shots will shore call some of th' others; an' I'd rather let 'em guess than know."

He sprinted to Ackerman's horse, released it and stripped it of saddle and bridle, turning it loose to freedom and good grass; and then, slinging the pack of supplies on his back, hastened to his own horse and rode away.

All day long Pepper moved ahead as fast as the country would permit, first north, then east, and finally south; and when she was stopped in mid-afternoon she was under the frowning wall of the southern Twin, three miles east of Quigley's stone houses and less than half a mile from the trail used by the rustlers when they rode abroad.

The very audacity of his choice of a camp site tended to make it secure; and it was in the section combed by the rustlers only the day before; it was under the most prominent landmark for miles around and practically under the nose of the QE outfit. His camp-fire and its almost invisible streamer of smoke from carefully selected dry wood was screened on the south and east by the great side of the southern Twin, and on the north and west by the bulk of the northern Twin; and by the time the filmy vapor reached the tops of those towering walls it would have become as invisible as the air of which it was a part. And because of the tumbled chaos of rock, ridge, arroyos, bowlders, shrubs, and trees, the little tent easily could be overlooked by anyone passing within twenty feet.

It had been his intention the day before to watch that out-bound trail in hope of following the next raiding party and learning what Logan wanted to know; but now he was forced to change his plans.

"All right," he muttered as he finished putting the new camp to rights. "As long as you know I'm here, an' are huntin' me down, it's time I showed my teeth. I'm goin' gunnin': it's a game two can play."

Having had his supper and lashed a small pack of food and ammunition on his back, he led Pepper farther down the chasm between the two buttes and let her graze where she pleased, knowing that she would not stray far. Then he plunged into the tangled cover and headed toward the entrance canyon of the QE ranch.

CHAPTER XV
Blindman's Buff

It was nearly dark when he came to the long slope leading to the plateau behind the QE ranchhouses and he went on with infinite caution, at last looking down upon the buildings, which showed no lights.

Had they gone on another raid and had he missed the opportunity of trailing them? He shook his head. There would be no more raids until they were sure that no one was watching them. Suddenly he grinned. The Circle S puncher, when last seen, was gong straight toward the ranchhouses. It was simple now. Having been told all that the Circle S man knew, they knew that only one man was watching them and would plan accordingly.

"Layin' low an' settin' traps for me," he grunted. "Bet th' three canyons are guarded—an' that trail down th' blind canyon farther along this wall. That's th' easiest for me, so I'll slip up there an' look around; but first I'll take a look down in th' main canyon."

A short time later he peered over the rim of the

chasm and chuckled, for a small fire, cunningly placed so as not to shine in the eyes of anyone in the houses, burned at the base of the great wall and made sufficient light to show a watching marksman every rock and hollow across that part of the canyon.

"They can set in th' house at a loophole an' keep a good watch," he muttered. "There ain't a man livin' could cross that patch of light. An' if they're guardin' one end they're guardin' th' others—an' I'll exchange compliments with one bunch."

Squirming back from the edge he started north, and he stopped only when the plashing of water told him that he was near his objective.

"If *I* was watchin' that trail I'd stay down below," he thought. "It would be near th' narrowest part of the ledge an' where nobody could shoot down on me. I know th' place, too; glad I learned th' lay of th' land around this sink."

He crept forward confidently, his rifle strapped across his back, for he decided to depend on his Colts. Reaching the head of the trail he dropped to all fours and crept onto it; instantly a flash split the darkness ten feet below him, the bullet ripping through his sombrero. He did not reply, but wriggled against the base of the wall, where an out-cropping stratum of rock gave him shelter. As he settled down he heard a sound above him and a pebble clicked at his side and bounced out into the chasm.

Here was a pleasant situation, he thought. They were guarding the top of the trail when they should have been guarding the bottom. There was an outlaw below him and another above him, and at the first streak of dawn he would find himself in a bad fix. Glancing up at the sky he saw that the ledge protected him from the man above; but it would take the man above only half an hour to run back along the canyon, round its upper end and appear, ready for business, on the farther side, in which case a certain member of the CL outfit would be neatly picked off at the first blush of daylight.

"I was hell-bent to get down here," he soliloquized in great disgust; "an' now I'm hell-bent to get back again. What business have they got to watch *this* end?"

He looked back up the trail and could see nothing. Then he held out his hand and could not see that. "That fool didn't see me; he *heard* me! I'm glad I didn't shoot back. He'll wait a while, doubt his ears an' think mebby that he's loco."

But Ben Gates, firing on a guess, thought he saw what he fired at when the flash of his gun lit up the trail in front of him. True, the smoke interfered; but Gates was backing both his eyes and his ears.

Johnny waited half an hour, and then grew anxious. His enemies were not doing anything, but appeared to be copying the patience of the noble red men, and waiting for dawn.

"Cuss th' dawn!" mused Johnny fretfully. "If th' feller below still thinks he heard me, th' feller up above may get dubious an' reckon his friend pulled at nothin'; an' he's th' man I got to gamble with an' th' sooner th' better."

He wriggled backward an inch at a time until he had gained a few yards and then he softly turned around. Another pebble fell on the ledge close to the place he had just evacuated. The instant he heard it he moved a little more rapidly because he was now east of the man above. A soft shuffle came to his ears and he swore under his breath when the sounds stopped at the head of the trail. The man above was now east of him, and painfully alert.

Slowly arising, Johnny hugged the wall and felt it over carefully. There were knobs and slight footholds and small cracks in it, and he took the only way open to him, desperate as it was. He judged the rim to be thirty feet above him, and setting his jaws he started to climb it. The shuffling again was heard and it now passed to the west of him.

"Cuss him!" gritted Johnny. "He acts like he don't know what to do with hisself. Why th' devil can't he stay where he belongs?"

Stepping back on the trail again Johnny stooped over and ran silently toward its upper end, thankful that he was wearing moccasins; and he had come within ten feet of it when the shuffling sound again passed him, eastward bound.

"There!" grumbled Johnny. "I *knowed* it. He acts like a bobcat in a cage. All right, damn you! I'll give you some music to shuffle to!"

Finding several pebbles, he threw them, one at a time, over the rim and about over the place where he had found shelter. A muttered expletive came from above and the shuffling went rapidly toward the sounds. Below him on the trail he heard a slight stir, but ignored it as he sprinted up the trail, silent as a ghost, and gained the shelter of a bowlder. Here he waited, grim and relentless, for the sentry's return.

Shuffle Foot was peeved, and cared not a whit who knew it. Just because he was hitched to a fool was no reason why he should endure asinine practical joking; so he peered over the canyon's rim and spoke softly:

"What th' hell do you think yo're doin'?"

The silence below was unbroken; but the astonished Mr. Gates longed passionately for the power of thought transmission. It was all right for Nat Harrison to go wandering around and braying like a jackass; he wasn't lying almost nose to nose with the most capable two-gun man that had ever cursed the Twin Buttes country.

"'Sleep?" queried Harrison. "What did you shoot at; 'nother ki-yote?" Receiving no answer he became exasperated. "If it was anybody but you I'd pay some attention to it. First you shoots a cougar out of a tree when we're all holdin' our breath to keep quiet. Then you let drive at a measly ki-yote, which you opined was a he-man. Next you plugs Long Pete, thinkin' he was Nelson. An' *now* what do you think you see? If I poke my head out far enough, even though I'm *talkin'* to you, I'll bet you'd let loose at it, thinkin' th' Lord only knows what. Why don't you *say* something? Do you think we're playin' some kid's game, where th' feller that keeps still longest gets th' apple? Did you make that noise?"

Gates writhed in impotent rage; but he suffered in silence, which only increased the pressure of his anger.

"Mebby you done shot yoreself," suggested Harrison hopefully. "Didn't see somethin' down by yore feet, an' shoot off yore toes, did you? What's th' matter with yore mouth? You can use it enough, th' Lord knows when nobody wants to hear it. *Say* somethin', you locoed polecat."

The pause was fruitless, and he continued, cheerfully:

"Mebby he's clubbed you again," he said. "Clubbed yore stone head with th' butt of his gun an' gagged you with yore own handkerchief; yore very much-soiled handkerchief. But I hardly reckon he did, because any blow heavy enough to send a shock through that head of yourn would 'a' been heard at th' houses, an' I didn't hear nothin' like that. Goin' to say somethin'?"

Harrison chuckled, and tried again: "Well, if you ain't talkin' I'll bet yo're thinkin'. Bet yo're wishin' I'd find a million dollars, get elected president of th' country an' not have nothin' to worry about all th' rest of my life. Ain't you, Dan'l Boone?

"You must be scared 'most to death," he continued after a pause. "Any time you can't find a chance to talk you shore are in a bad fix. I'm beginnin' to lose my temper. You make me plumb disgusted, you do. What th' devil do you think *I* was doin' out here all night? Think anybody got past me to go down there for *you* to shoot at? If there's anybody down there he come up from below an' crawled over you before you woke up."

Suddenly he cocked his head on one side and listened as a low gurgle sounded in the canyon.

"Cuss my fool hide!" he whispered. "Mebby he *did* see something! Mebby somebody come *up* th' trail, tryin' to get out of th' valley before daylight! Mebby it wasn't Ben at all that did th' shootin'! Hey, Ben; *Ben!* For heaven's sake, *say* something, *any*thing!"

Gates, stung into a blinding rage which swept aside every thought of caution, did say something. Nature seemed to shrink from the stream of throbbing profanity which came shouting up out of the black canyon, whose granite walls flung it back and forth until the chasm reverberated with it.

Harrison listened, entranced, his open mouth, refusing to shut, testifying to the great awe which held him spellbound. Never in all his sinful life had he heard such a masterpiece of invective, epithet, and profane invocation. The words seemed to be alive and writhing with venom; he almost could hear them crackle in the air. He heard himself called everything uncomplimentary which a frontier vocabulary saved for just such situations. He heard his ancestors described back to the time of Adam; sweeping up to the present, himself, his relatives, his ambitions, habits, and personal belongings were dissected by the man below. And then his future and the prophesied future abode of his spirit were probed and riddled and described by a furious, vitriolic tongue. His hair, eyes, ears, nose, gait, and manners were gathered up and torn apart for microscopic examination and the descriptions were shouted at the top of his companion's voice, which bellowed and boomed, rasped and coughed, screeched and shrilled down in the blackness forty feet below him. Then there fell a sudden calm, a silence which seemed doubly silent, unreal, because of the contrast. A convulsive, retching, strangling fit of coughing broke it, and then a hoarse, rasping voice asked mildly, anxiously, a mild question:

"Is there anything I forgot?"

Johnny, standing up behind the smaller bowlder that he might not lose a word or an inflection of the masterpiece, lost in admiration, forgetful of purpose and the situation, danced gleefully and gave a joyous shout: "Not a cussed thing!"

Harrison fired at the sound, and a sharp, lurid flashed replied to his own. He staggered back as he fired again, and an answering flash doubled him up. Gamely he pulled the trigger again and two spurts of flame, so close to each other that they seemed almost to merge, sent him staggering and reeling toward the edge of the canyon. Tripping over an inequality in the earth he threw out his arms, fought to regain his balance and with a sob plunged over the wall into the darkness below.

Down on the trail Gates muttered in sudden horror as he felt the wind of the hurtling body, and he leaned against the wall, white, sick, shaken. A muffled, sickening sound came up from the pit, and Gates dropped to his hands and knees, not daring to stand erect.

"Nat!" he cried. *"Nat!* Was that you? *Nat! Nat!"*

At the top of the trail a rapier-like flash of fire split the darkness, and then a series of lurid spurts of flame stabbed in short jets, rapidly, regular as the ticking of a clock, marking the place where two heavy guns crashed and jumped as they poured forth a stream of lead down the narrow rock shelf that formed the precarious trail.

The canyon roared in one prolonged reverberation and the bullets whined and spatted and screamed in high falsetto as they cleared the wall or struck it to glance out into the valley below.

Gates, on his hands and knees, shaken, sick with horror, crept slowly downward, oblivious to the crashing, rolling thunder and the flying lead.

"I didn't mean it, Nat!" he muttered over and over again. "I didn't mean it; not a word of it!"

A sharp *spang!* sounded on a rock close to his head and a hot splinter of lead cut through his cheek. He stopped and spat it out, his nerve returning as a cold rage swept over and steadied him. Jerking his gun loose he emptied it up the trail, and, methodically reloading, emptied it again, slowly, deliberately, moving it a little at each shot so as to cover a short arc. Another spurt stabbed the darkness above, and his gun, again refilled, replied to it. Again the canyon sent roaring echoes crashing from wall to wall as flash answered flash. Then suddenly the gun below grew silent, and the guns above spat twice spitefully without a reply, and they, too, ceased.

Gates stirred and slowly raised himself on an elbow, groping blindly for his gun. His trembling hand struck it blunderingly and knocked it over the edge of the trail as his numbed fingers sought to close over it. Dazed, racked with pain, he sobbed senseless curses as he slowly dragged himself down the trail, desperately anxious to reach his picketed horse before his reeling senses left him.

After an unmeasured interval, as vague and unreal as an elusive dream, he stumbled over the picket rope and sprawled full length. Arousing himself he felt along it and managed to loosen it from around the rock which served as a picket pin; and then, slowly, by a great effort he crawled along the rope and staggered to his feet to grasp the pommel of his saddle, where he clung and rested for a moment.

The restless horse, scenting blood, tossed its head and moved forward; but Gates, by a great, supreme effort, crawled heavily into the saddle and bound himself there with his lariat. Then, spurring clumsily, he started the animal toward the ranch-houses, fighting desperately to keep his wandering senses.

An hour later two men stole to the door of the end house and listened, questioning each other. Actuated by a common impulse they slipped out toward the corral, gun in hand, and found Gates, unconscious and weak, but alive, huddled forward on the horse's neck.

CHAPTER XVI
The Science of Sombreros

Johnny rubbed his eyes and sat up, wondering. It was still dark, but a grayness in the east told of approaching daylight. He was puzzled, for it had been mid-forenoon when he had gone to sleep. Unrolling stiffly from the blanket, he sat up to listen and to peer about him. From his thicket he could see the tent, with the soles of his boots and part of his blanket showing. Arising he stretched and flexed his muscles to ease the ache of them, and then approached the ashes of the fire, and found them and the ground underneath to be stone cold. Rubbing his eyes, he laughed suddenly: he had slept for nearly twenty hours!

"Shore made up for th' sleep I been missin'!" he grunted. "An' ain't I hungry!"

Having eaten a hearty breakfast he scouted along his back trail, acting upon the assumption that the Circle S puncher might have gone back again, picked it up and followed it. Reassured as to that he started back to camp, and on the way topped a little rise and caught sight of Pepper grazing in the narrow canyon.

"That won't do, at all," he muttered, thoughtfully. "She's a dead give-away—an' now I can't take no chances."

Returning to his camp he packed up food and spare ammunition, and then, hurrying down the canyon, whistled to the horse, who followed him closely, as he searched in vain for a safe place to put her. He was growing impatient, when he chanced to look closely at the face of the southern Twin, and then nodded quickly. If there was water on its top, that was the place for the horse. Half an hour later, after some careful climbing, he reached the high plateau, dropped the reins down before Pepper's eyes and made a swift examination of the top of the butte. His hopes were rewarded, as he had expected them to be, for in a deep bowl-like depression lying at the foot of a high steep ridge he found a large pool, the level of which was considerably below the high-water mark on the wall. This meant concentration due to evaporation, and he tasted the water to be sure that it was fit to drink. Whistling Pepper to him, he picketed her so that she could reach the edge of the pool and range over enough grass to satisfy her needs, cached the pack and departed.

When he reached the canyon he went around the butte and started for his camp along its southern side, critically examining the sheer wall as he fought the brush and the loose shale under his feet. There was one place where he thought it possible for a cool headed, experienced man to climb to the top, if he put his mind to the task and took plenty of time. Giving it no further thought he plunged on, glad that the horse was out of the sight of any scouting rustler and picketed so she could not get near the edge, where she would have shown up sharply against the sky, visible for miles.

Swinging past his camp and turning to the south he cautiously crossed the rustlers' main trail and climbed the wall behind it, and as he went forward he tried to figure out what his enemies thought of the situation. If they believed that several enemies opposed them they would be likely to stay in the houses, or not stray far from them; but if they thought only one man fought them they would most certainly take the field after him. Such was his summing up; and, bearing in mind that Long Pete, when last seen by him, was headed toward the houses, he took full advantage of the cover afforded.

Approaching the cliff by a roundabout way, he at last wriggled to the edge and peered over. A gun-barrel projected from the crack of the door in the last house; a man lay behind a bowlder on the cliff across the valley, facing eastward; and almost directly below him a sombrero moved haltingly as its wearer slowly climbed up the cliff at one of the few places where it could be scaled.

"They've figgered right," thought Johnny; "an'

they're goin' to make things whiz for me. Red Shirt, over there, must be a thousand yards away; but this sink is deceivin'."

He looked down at the climber, who was about half way up the bluff. "Huh! I don't want to shoot him without givin' him a chance; but he just can't come up. Le's see: one, two, three; an' one in th' house, wounded, is four. There's a couple more somewhere, layin' low I reckon, waitin' for me to move across their sights."

He looked across at Red Shirt and grinned. "He's layin' on th' wrong side of that rock an' don't know it. I'll tell him, an' get rid of that climber at th' same time. Hope he busts his neck gettin' down."

Wriggling back from the edge so that the man in the house could not locate him by the smoke, he took deliberate aim at Red Shirt and gently squeezed the trigger. Red Shirt soared into the air and dove over the bowlder headfirst and with undignified speed.

"Knowed it was deceivin'," growled Johnny. "Shot plumb over him. Can't be more'n eight hundred yards. An' that's a fool color of a shirt to wear on a job like this."

Johnny's shirt had been blue, a long time back; but now its color hardly could be described by a single adjective. Sun, wind, and strong lye soap had taken their toll; and it had not been washed since he had left his little valley.

Wriggling back to the patch of grass, a quick glance below showed the climber frantically descending; and the man in the house was making lots of smoke on a gamble. Across the valley a gray-white cloud puffed out above the big rock and a little spurt of sand forty feet to Johnny's left told him that Red Shirt, too, was guessing.

"Must 'a' been asleep not to see my smoke," muttered Johnny.

More smoke rolled up from the bowlder and soon some pebbles not ten feet away from him scattered suddenly, while a high-pitched whine soared skyward.

"He's pluggin' at every bit of cover he can see," mused Johnny, wriggling back behind a rock. "An' he'll prospect that bunch of grass—*knowed it!* He can shoot," he exclaimed in ungrudging praise; "an' he's got th' range figgered to a foot. An' he's workin' steady from th' north to th' south; an' when he tries for that clump of brush over there he's got to show his head an' shoulder."

A puff of dust and sand fifty feet to his right told him to get ready; and then a bowlder south of the sandpuff said *spat!*

Johnny lowered his rear sight and cuddled the stock of the heavy Sharp's to his cheek. Slowly a red dot moved up in front of his sights and he again squeezed the trigger, and again missed. But he had no way of knowing that Art Fleming was spitting sand and that his eyes had not escaped the little shower.

"I got to guess too much," swore Johnny. "That front sight hides him. I wonder how many times I was goin' to file it sharp?"

As he reloaded, his sombrero suddenly tugged at his scalp and a flat report sounded behind him. He quickly rolled into a shallow depression and another bullet sprayed him with sand.

"Repeater," he growled. "I got as much sense as a sheep-herder!"

There now was plenty of cover between him and Repeater, but there was still too little distance between him and Fleming; and the latter was a disconcertingly good shot. Two quick reports sounded from the house and Johnny smiled; the man at the door was seeing things, and backing his imagination with lead.

Johnny was watching a ridge behind him. "Me an' Repeater are goin' to argue," he remarked, and almost fired when a sombrero slowly arose on the skyline.

"Cussed near bit," he chuckled; "but you got to have yore head in that bonnet before I lets drive."

A matted tuft of grass on the top of the ridge moved so gently that only a very observant eye would have detected it. Johnny's Sharp's roared, and instantly was answered from a point a yard away from the stirring clump of grass, the bullet fanning his face.

"Yo're too cussed tricky," grunted Johnny; "but I got a few of my own."

Leaving his rifle lying so that its barrel barely projected into sight, he slipped into a gulley and crept toward the west, a Colt in his hand.

Repeater again stirred the grass tuft, and then he found a rock about the size of a man's head and pushed it up to the skyline of the ridge. Nothing happened. "If my hair wasn't so red," he murured, "I'd take a peek. It's an awful cross for a man to bear."

He was a cheerful cattle-thief and did not get easily discouraged. Also, he was something of a genius, as he proved by putting his sombrero on the rock and raising the decoy high enough in the grass for the hat brim to show.

"Shoot, cuss you!" Repeater grunted, leveling his rifle; and then as the uneventful seconds passed he grew fault-finding and used bad language. Suddenly a suspicion flashed across his mind.

"That would fool a man with second sight," he muttered. "Somethin's plumb wrong; an' I think I better move. That bowlder over there looks good." And as he crawled behind it a pair of keen eyes barely caught sight of his disappearing heel.

"That man's got th' right to wear expensive hats," grinned Johnny, squatting behind a great mass of lava; and his grin widened as he glimpsed the sombrero-topped rock. "Yes, sir: he's got a head worth 'em; an' if I don't watch him close I'll grab holt of th' wrong end of somethin'."

Across the valley Fleming, having cleared his eyes of sand, was rapidly recovering his normal vision and was preparing with cheerful optimism to bombard everything which looked capable of sheltering his enemy, when a movement north of and far behind the suspected area acted upon him galvanically. He threw the rifle to his shoulder without elevating the sight, raised it instinctively to the angle of maximum range and squeezed the trigger. He did not expect a hit, and he did not get one; but he caused his friendship to be strongly doubted.

Repeater ducked, and when his face bobbed up again it wore an expression of outraged trust, and he raised a belligerent fist and muttered profanely in hot censure of the distant experimenter. Fleming, chuckling at his friend Sanford's anxiety, raised his sombrero and waved it, seeming to regard this as ample reparation.

"He's gettin' as bad as Gates," growled Sanford, eying a leaden splotch on a bowlder a foot above his head; "but he can shoot like th' hinges of hell with that blasted Sharp's."

He suddenly leaped closer to the bowlder and behind its sheltering bulge, for Fleming, having apologized, fired again. The marksman was frantically waving his sombrero, seemingly indicating a southerly direction.

Sanford scowled at him. "Does he want me to go south, or does he mean that that feller is south of me?"

Fleming, with no regard for the cost of Sharp's Specials, fired again and Sanford heard the slobbering, wheezing hum of a nearly spent bullet turning end over end in the air and trying to ricochet after it struck.

"He's shootin' south of me," said Sanford; "an' I stays here. Somethin' tells me that th' feller that does th' movin' is goin' to die. No red-head ever made a handsome corpse, an' bein' th' red-head which I mentions, I'm goin' to stick to this hunk of granite like a tick to a cow."

Johnny, hands on hips, was glaring defiance at the cheerful spendthrift, sorry that he had left his rifle behind. He regarded Fleming as a meddlesome busybody who took delight in revealing his every movement. Also, the optimist was a good shot; but he derived no satisfaction from the fact that the closest bullet had been ricochet, for a key-holing slug makes an awful mess if it lands.

"I'll bust yore neck!" quoth Johnny, shaking a fist at the persistent nuisance; and then he jumped aside as a sudden sharp *spat!* came from the bowlder. "You can shoot near as good as Red Connors, but if he was here he'd show you what that little difference means." He raised his voice: "Hey, Repeater! Who is that fool?"

Sanford laughed softly and made no answer; but he carelessly showed a shirt sleeve, and when he jerked it back under cover it needed a patch.

"What th' hell you doin'?" demanded Sanford heatedly.

"Who's Red Shirt?"

"Ackerman."

"Then he's better with a Sharp's than a Colt."

"That's a Spencer carbine."

Johnny laughed derisively: "If it is he'll strain it."

"It's a Winchester," chuckled Sanford.

"Yo're a liar!"

"Yo're another! She's a single-shot, .40-90."

"Then he's changed guns. He had a Winchester repeater in Hastings. I saw it."

"You'll see too much some day. You'll see a slug in yore eye."

"I'm waitin'," replied Johnny, and ducked. Fleming was getting good again, and Johnny was glad that he could not see where his bullets were landing, for as it was he was shooting by guess.

"He'll get you yet," encouraged Sanford.

"Think I'm goin' to wait for it?" indignantly demanded Johnny.

"Gimme a look at you," urged Sanford genially. "Stand up an' take it," retorted Johnny.

"Reckon I'm scared to?"

There was no reply, for Johnny had slipped away and was running at top speed along a gully, where he was out of sight of the hard-working Fleming. A few minutes later he had reached his rifle and was cuddling it against his cheek; and he was causing Sanford a great amount of mental anguish and wriggling progress.

"Some people calls this strategy," muttered Johnny, "but I calls it common sense."

Raising his head cautiously he looked across the valley but saw no sign of Fleming; and he figured that it would be an hour before that interesting person could cross the valley and get close enough to be a menace. What concerned him most were the two rustlers' friends, who must certainly have heard the shooting. Out of deference to the curiosity of those individuals he crawled into a partly filled-in crevice, whose sides were steep rock and whose floor was several feet below the level of the surrounding plateau.

Peering out from between two rocks he saw Sanford's sombrero disappear from the ridge, and then it cautiously arose again; and Johnny's eyes narrowed, for he knew the numerous uses of sombreros.

"Keep stickin' it up," he muttered. "An when I get tired shootin' at it you'll stick yore head in it an' get a good look around. Most generally when a man pokes up an empty hat th' crown don't tip back as it rises; it just comes up level. An honest hat slants back more an' more as it comes up. 'Cause why? Why, 'cause. 'Cause a man uses his neck to raise his head with. Now, if he kept his neck stiff an' raised his whole body, from th' knees up, plumb straight in th' air, then th' hat would come up level. An' I asks you, Ladies an' Gents, if a man layin' down behind a little ridge can raise his whole body stiff an' straight, plumb up an' down? No, ma'am; he can't. He raises his soiled an' leathery neck, an' th' top of th' useful sombrero just naturally leans backward; just like that.

"Look, Mister; there it comes again; an' it don't tip back at all. I shall ignore it, deliberate an' cold. But when it tips back, lifelike an' natural, like a' honest hat should, then I'll pay attention to it, me an' my little Sharp's Special.

"Oh, I've done made a study of appearin' hats. I'm a reg'lar he-milliner. It was Red Connors an' Hoppy that directed my great intelligence to that important science. Tex Ewalt knowed about it, too. Tex was eddicated, he was. He said it is in th' little things that genius showed. He said somethin' about genius payin' attention to details, an' havin' infernal patience. Now, Ladies an' Gents, a hat is a detail; an' right now I've got th' infernal patience. Lookee! There she comes again! Level as a table. So, you see; I'm a genius. An' ain't he a persistent cuss? He's got infernal patience, too; but he ain't no genius. He ain't strong on details."

He looked around and grinned. Another hat, to the west of him, was in plain sight.

"Huh! Two hats in sight are two corners of a triangle; an' sometimes th' most dangerous corner is th' third, where there ain't no hat. Somewhere east of me there's a feller sneakin' up; an' he's th' feller I got to ventilate with my long-distance ventilator. An' mebby th' second hat's boss is circlin' around bareheaded; but it is still a triangle. Mebby it's a four or five or six cornered triangle. An' me, I'm all alone; so I'll crawl east an' hunt for company."

He dropped the monologue and took up the science of wriggling swiftly and silently; and when he stopped he was in the middle of a nest of rocks and bowlders at the base of a great pile of them.

The second hat still could be seen, but he gave most of his attention to the opposite direction.

"If I'm wrong, why did Number Two stick up his hat? I'll bet a peso that him, or Red Shirt, or their friends are stalkin' me from th' east. An' I'll bet two pesos that I'll cure him of such pranks. There's only two ways of explainin' that second hat. One is that th' owner is loco. Th' other is that he left his sign hangin' up to show me where he ain't. Th' other is that he left it so I'd think he wasn't there, but he is. An' th' other is that he figgered I'd think he left it to show me where he ain't an' that I'd think he was, so he moved on an' ain't there at all. Jumpin' mavericks! It makes my head ache. Havin' settled it with only four ways left to guess, I'll stay pat, right here, an' let them do th' openin'."

The shadows were growing longer and reaching out from bowlders and brush like dark fingers of destiny, and the sun hung over the western buttes and set them afire with brilliant colors. A lizard flashed around a rock, regarded the prone and motionless figure with frank suspicion until a slight movement sent it scurrying back again.

To the left a bush trembled slightly and he covered a rain-worn crease which cut through the top of a ditch bank. To the right a pebble clicked and behind him came the faint snapping of a twig.

"*Three* of 'em stalkin' me!" he muttered angrily. "I got to shoot on sight an' not waste a shot. An' they knowed where I was, judgin' from th' way they're closin' in on that crevice."

In front of him a red line showed and, rising steadily into view, became the back of a bare head. Then, very slowly, a brown neck pushed up, followed by the shoulders. Johnny picked up a small rock and arose to a squatting position.

Sanford was now on his toes, crouching, the tips of his left hand fingers on the ground, while in his other hand, held shoulder high, poised a Colt, ready for that quick, chopping motion which many men affected.

Johnny took careful aim and threw the stone. Sanford jumped when the missile struck near him, and wheeled like a flash, the Colt swinging down. He saw a squatting figure, a dull glint of metal and a spurt of flame. Johnny wriggled swiftly back among the rocks and awaited developments.

"They don't know who fired," he mused, "an' they dassn't ask."

If it had been a miss the silence would have been unbroken, as before, until a second shot shattered it; and if it had killed the rustler the silence also would remain unbroken; but if Sanford had scored a kill he instantly would have made it known. Being uncertain they were sure to investigate.

"Cuss it, there's at least two left; an' there may be four or five," grumbled Johnny. "I stay right here till dark."

Suddenly he heard a soft, rubbing sound, and he guessed that someone wearing leather chaps was crawling along the rocky ground behind the pile of bowlders which sheltered him. The sound grew softer and died out, and a panic-stricken lizard flitted around a rock, stopped instantly as it caught sight of him, wheeled and darted between two stones. Johnny smiled grimly and waited, the gun poised in his hand. Again the rubbing sounded, this time a little nearer, and he softly pushed himself further back among the bowlders. Something struck his left hand holster and he glanced quickly backward, and paled suddenly as he saw the copperhead wrestling to get its fangs loose. He drew in his breath sharply and his hand darted back and down, gripping behind the vicious, triangular, burnished head; and instantly a three-foot, golden-brown, blotched band writhed around his wrist and arm, seeming to flow beneath its skin. Jerking his hand forward again he broke the reptile's neck, tore it from his arm, shoved it back among the rocks, picked up the Colt again, and waited.

There sounded, clear and sharp, a sudden shirring rattle and the rubbing sound grew instantly louder. Again the fear-inspiring warning sounded and he heard pebbles rolling, where a creeping rustler made frantic efforts to get back where he suddenly felt that he belonged. A rattlesnake ready for war is not a pleasant thing to crawl onto.

"This is a devil of a place!" muttered Johnny, cold chills running along his spine. "It's a reg'lar den! As soon as that cow-thief gets far enough away, that rattler will slip in among these rocks—an' my laigs ain't goin' to be back there when he arrives!"

He wriggled softly out of the narrow opening and found more comfort on a wider patch of ground, where he could sit on his feet. As he settled back he saw the rattler slipping among the stones at his left.

"It all belongs to you an' yore friends," muttered

Johnny, getting off his feet. "I'll risk th' bullets, cussed if I won't!" And he forthwith crawled toward the side where he had heard the rubbing sounds.

The shadows were gone, merged into the dusk which was rapidly settling over the plateau, and he had to wait only a little longer to be covered by darkness; but he preferred to do his waiting at a point distant from a snakes' den. Creeping along the edge of the bowlder pile, alert both for snakes and rustlers, he at last reached the southern end and stopped suddenly. A leather-covered leg was disappearing around a dense thicket, and he darted to the shelter of a gully to wait until darkness would hide him on his return to camp.

CHAPTER XVII
Treed

Johnny awakened at the shot and softly rolled out of his blanket. The fire was nearly out, but an occasional burst of flame from the end of the last stick served to show him the outlines of the little tent and the glistening hobnails in the soles of the protruding boots. A bush stirred and a careless step snapped a twig with a report startlingly loud in the night. A voice some distance behind him called out to a figure which appeared like a ghost upon the edge of the little clearing.

"Get him, Purdy?"

Boots scraped on stone at his right and another voice raised out of the dark. "If he didn't, there'd be some cussed rapid shootin' about now!"

"Course I got him!" snorted Purdy.

Johnny cautiously backed out of the thicket while the men behind him crashed through the brush and swore at the density of the growth.

The man at the end of the clearing stopped and stood quietly regarding the vague boots, his rifle at the ready. Somehow he did not feel that everything was as it should be. The boots appeared to be in the same position as when he had espied them a moment before. He must have made a lucky brain or heart shot, or—. He raised his hand swiftly and backed into the oak brush again, where Mexican locust in the high grass stabbed him mercilessly. Again his rifle spoke. The boots did not move.

"You got him th' first time," laughed Fleming, walking rapidly toward the tent; but he was not confident enough in his claim to put up his Colt.

"Shore," endorsed Holbrook. "It was good judgment, an' good luck."

Fleming, Colt ready, leaned swiftly over, grasped a boot and gave a strong pull—and went down on his back, the Colt exploding and flying one way while the boot, showering pebbles and small bits of rock, soared aloft and went the other way.

"Damn him!" swore Purdy, diving back into the brush and giving no thought to the thorns. "Cover, fellers! Quick!" he cried.

His warning was hardly needed, for Holbrook had dived headfirst into a matted thicket and landed on some locust with but little more than passing knowledge of its presence. Fleming bounded to his feet, scooped up his Colt on the run and jumped into another thicket, unmindful at first of the peculiar odor which assailed his nostrils. He had no time, then, to think about skunks, or whether or not they were hydrophobic.

The silence was deep and unbroken, except for an occasional faint swish or scrape, for three men had settled down where they had landed, there to remain until daylight, not far off, came to help them.

Out of the clearing a small, striped animal moved leisurely and defiantly, tainting the air, and entered the tent. It instantly became the cynosure of three pairs of anxious eyes, for while August was a long way off, three worried punchers found small satisfaction in that. They would sooner face an angry silver-tip, or a cougar with young, than to intrude upon the vision of that insignificant but odorous " 'phoby cat." Each of them knew of instances, related by others, where men bitten by a skunk had gone raving mad; but none of them, personally, ever had seen any such case; and none of them had any intention of letting the other two see any such a shocking spectacle in the immediate future.

The little animal emerged from the tent and appeared to be undecided as to which way to go; and no roulette ball ever possessed the fascination nor furnished the thrills that took hold of the three staring watchers. It took a few steps one way and a few steps the other, and then started straight for the thicket where Art Fleming shuddered and swore under his breath. Two sighs arose on the air concurrent with the cursing.

"Just my cussed luck!" gritted Fleming. "Get out of here, cuss you!" he whispered fiercely, and raised his Colt. No sane man, with his firm beliefs regarding skunks, would hesitate when forced to choose between probable death from a bullet or certain and horrible death from hydrophobia. The skunk reached the edge of the thicket, five feet from the perspiring puncher, and was blown into a mass of reeking flesh.

Fleming groaned miserably. "They shore dies game!" he swore, half-nauseated. "They're cussed strong finishers! Why couldn't he 'a' headed for one of th' others? I got to move, right now."

He did so, slowly, cautiously, painfully; but the scent moved with him. He stopped, mopped his face, and then held his hand away from him. His sleeve, vest, and sombrero proclaimed their presence with an enthusiastic strength and persistence.

"Cussed if he didn't *hit* me! An' I might just as well go back to th' ranch, so far's huntin' Nelson is concerned. He could smell a day before he caught sight of me!" A sickly grin slipped over his face, for he was blessed with a keen sense of humor. "Won't Gates an' Quigley be indignant when I odors in upon 'em!"

Purdy rolled his head in silent mirth, one hand over his nose; and Holbrook alternately chuckled and swore, wishing that the soft wind would shift and spare him.

"Laugh!" blazed Fleming, angry, ashamed, and disgusted, removing his vest and throwing it into the clearing. His sombrero followed it and then there was a ripping sound and a red flannel shirt sleeve joined the other cast-offs. The little, persistent flame on the stick blazed higher and revealed the collection of personal effects.

"If he peels off th' rest of his shirt an' shucks his pants, he'll smell near as bad," chuckled Purdy gleefully.

"Dan'l Boone Number Two!" said Holbrook, tears in his eyes. "But I shore wish he had enticed it off aways before he shot it!"

Dawn stole from the east and the magnificent sunrise passed unnoticed. Fleming, sullen, angry, odorous, trudged doggedly to his horse, which regarded him with evil eyes, mounted and rode away at a gallop in his desire to create a breeze; and in this the horse needed no urging. Back in the canyon Purdy and Holbrook scouted diligently, but with caution, covering ground slowly and thoroughly as they advanced.

Under a tangled thicket near the camp there was a sudden movement, and Johnny, hands and face covered with blood from the scratches of thorns, slowly emerged and followed the scouting rustlers at a distance. Satisfied that they would not return he circled swiftly to the south of the camp and caught a glimpse of Fleming as that unfortunate plodded dejectedly over a distant ridge on his way to his horse.

Johnny watched for a moment, and then, turning hastily, slipped back to the camp, where he collected what he could carry, packed it into blankets, put on the well-worn, heavy boots, fastened the pack on his back and dashed into the cover again, desperately anxious to gain his objective.

He knew what would happen. As soon as Fleming reached the ranch-houses he would reclothe himself and return with those of his friends who were able to accompany him; and it would not be long before the Twin Buttes section would be thoroughly combed. He could not hide his trail, so it was wise to lead them to a place they could not search.

Slipping on the treacherous malpais and loose stones, fighting through the torturing locust and cactus hidden in the grass, he pushed through matted thickets of oak brush and manzanito by main strength, savagely determined to gain his goal well in advance of the creeping, cautious cattle-thieves who crept, foot by foot, down the canyon on the other side of the butte.

A black bear lumbered out of his way and sat down to watch him pass, the little eyes curious and unblinking. Several white-tailed deer shot up a slope ahead of him in unbelievable leaps and at a remarkable speed. He leaped over a fallen pine trunk and his heavy bootheel crushed a snake which rattled and struck at the same instant; but the heavy boots and the trousers tucked within them made the vicious fangs harmless. Flies swarmed about him and yellow-jackets stung him as he squashed over a muddy patch of clay. A grinning coyote slunk aside to give him undisputed right-of-way, while high up on the slope a silver-tip grizzly stopped his foraging long enough to watch him pass.

For noise he cared nothing; the up-flung butte reared its rocky walls between him and his enemies; and he plunged on, all his energies centered on speed, regardless of the stings and the sweat which streamed down him, tinged with blood from the mass of smarting scratches. Malpais, cunningly hidden in the grass, pressed painfully against the worn, thin soles of his boots and hurt him cruelly as he slipped and floundered. He staggered and slipped more frequently now, and the pack on his back seemed to have trebled in weight; his breath came in great, sobbing gulps and the blood pulsed through his aching temples like hammer blows, while a hot, tight band seemed to encircle his parched throat; but he now was in sight of his goal.

Beginning at a rock slide, a mass of treacherous broken rock and shale in which he sank to his ankles at every plunging step, a faint zigzag line wandered up the southern face of the butte. He did not know that it could be mastered, but he did not have time to gain the easier trail, up which he had led his horse. Struggling up the shale slope, slipping and floundering in the treacherous footing, he flung himself on the rock ledge which slanted sharply upward.

Resting until his head cleared, he began a climb which ever after existed in his memory as a vague but horrible nightmare. Rattlesnakes basked in the sun, coiling swiftly and sounding their whirring alarm as he neared them; but blindly thrown rocks mashed them and sent them writhing over the edge to whirl to destruction in the valley below. Treacherous, rotten ledges crumbled as he put his weight on them, and he saved himself time and time again only by an intuitive leap nearly as dangerous as the peril he avoided. At many places the ledge disappeared, and it was only by desperate use of fingers and toes that he managed to pass the gaps, spread-eagled against the cliff while he moved an inch at a time, high above the yawning depths, to the beginning of a new ledge.

Scrawny, hardy shrubs, living precariously in cracks and on ledges, and twisted roots found his grip upon them. At one place a flue-like crack in the wall, a "chimney," was the only way to proceed, and he climbed it, back and head against one side, knees and hands against the other, the strain making him faint and dizzy. Below him lay the tree-tops, dwarfed, a blur to his throbbing eyes.

A ledge of rock upon which he momentarily rested his weight detached itself and plunged downward a sheer three hundred feet, crashing through the underbrush and scrub timber before it burst apart. On hands and knees he crossed a muddy spot, where a thin trickle of water, no wider than this thumb, spread out and made the ledge slippery before it was sucked in by the sunbaked rocks. A swarm of yellow-jackets, balancing daintily on the wet rocks, attacked him viciously when he disturbed them. He struck at them blindly, instinctively shielding his eyes, and arose to his feet as he groped onward.

The pack on his back, aside from its weight, was a thing of danger, for several times it thrust against the wall and lost him his balance, threatening him with instant destruction; but each time he managed to save himself by a frantic twist and plunge to his hands and knees, clawing at the precarious footing with fingers and toes.

At one place he lay prostrate for several minutes before his will, shaking off the lethargy which numbed him, sent him on again. And the spur which awakened his dulled senses proved that his frantic haste was justified; for a sharp, venomous whine overhead was followed by the flat impact of lead on rock, and a handful of shale and small bits of stone showered down upon him. The faint, whip-like report in the valley did not penetrate his roaring ears, for now all he could think of was the edge of the butte fifty feet above him.

Never had such a distance seemed so great, so impossible to master. It seemed as though ages passed before he clawed at the rim and flung himself over it in one great, despairing effort and +grass and flowers. Down in the valley the persistent reports ceased, but he did not know it; and an hour passed before he sat up and looked around, dazed and faint. Arising, he staggered to the pool where Pepper waited for him at the end of her taut picket rope.

The water was bitter from concentration, but it tasted sweeter to him than anything he ever had drunk. He dashed it over his face, unmindful of the increased smarting of the stings and scratches. Resting a few minutes, he went to the top of the easier trail, up which he had led the horse, and saw a man creeping along it near the bottom; but the rustler fled for shelter when Johnny's Sharp's suggested that the trail led to sudden death.

Having served the notice he lay quietly resting and watching. The heat of the canyon was gone and he reveled in the crisp coolness of the breeze which fanned him. As he rested he considered the situation, and found it good. He was certain that no man would be fool enough to attempt the way he had come while an enemy occupied the top of the butte; the trail up the north side could easily be defended; the other Twin, easy rifle range away, was lower than the one he occupied and would not be much of a menace if he were careful; he had water in plenty, food and ammunition for two weeks, and there was plenty of water and grass for the horse.

Safe as the butte was, he cheerfully damned the necessity which had driven him out of the canyon: the question of sleep. Dodging and out-witting four men during his waking hours would not have been an impossible task; but it only would have been a matter of time before they would have caught him asleep and helpless.

Returning to the pool, he saw how closely Pepper had cropped the grass within the radius of the picket rope, changed the stake and then built a fire, worrying about scarcity of fuel. Since he could not afford to waste the wood he cooked a three-days supply of food.

Eating a hearty meal, he made mud-plasters and applied them to the swollen stings, binding them in place by strips torn from an undershirt, and then he sought the shade of the ledge by the pool for a short sleep, which he would have to snatch at odd times during the day so as to be awake all night, which would be the time of greatest danger.

CHAPTER XVIII
At Bay

It was late in the afternoon when he awakened from a sleep which had been sound despite the stings. Removing the plasters he made a tour of the plateau, satisfying himself that there was really only one way up and that the rustlers were not trying to get to him. Returning to the camp, he filled a hollow in the rock floor with water, bathed, put on his other change of clothes, and then made a supper of cold beans and bacon. Filling another hollow, he pushed his soiled clothes in it to soak over night.

When he passed a break in the rampart-like wall near the top of the trail, which at that point shot up several feet above the top of the butte, a bullet screamed past his head, so close that he felt the wind of it. Peering cautiously across the canyon he saw a thin cloud of smoke lazily rising over the top of a huge, black lava bowlder on the crest of the other butte. A head was just disappearing and he jerked his rifle to his shoulder and fired.

"Five hundred an' little more," he muttered. "I got it now, you wall-eyed thief!"

Another puff of smoke burst out from the lower edge of the lava bowlder, the bullet striking the rampart below him. His reply was instantaneous; and was directed at a light spot which ducked instantly out of sight, just a little too quickly to be hit by the bullet, which tossed a fine spray of dust into the air and put a leaden streak where the face had been. He fired again, this time at the other side of the bowlder, where he thought he saw another moving white spot, and he thought right.

After a quick glance down the trail, Johnny took a position a hundred yards to the left, trying to find a place where he could catch a glimpse of the hostile marksman. But Fleming had a torn and bloody ear and a great respect for the man on the southern Twin, and henceforth became wedded to caution. Curiosity was all very well, but his was thoroughly satisfied, and discretion meant a longer life of sinful activities.

"I had my look, three of 'em," growled Fleming. "An' three looks are enough for any man," he added quizzically, binding up his bloody ear with a soiled and faded neckerchief, which should have given him blood-poisoning, but did not.

"Now that we got him treed, there ain't no use goin' on th' rampage an' gettin' all shot up tryin' to get him. All we got to do is wait, an' get him when he has to come down. It'll be plumb easy when he makes his break. A man like him is too cussed handy with his gun for anybody to go an' get reckless with. If we keep one man near th' bottom of that trail, he's our meat. I don't know how he ever got up that scratch on th' wall; but I'll bet there ain't a man livin' that can go *down* it."

Johnny grew tired of watching for Fleming, and wriggling back to where he could safely get on his feet he arose and made the rounds again. When he reached the place where he had floundered over the edge to safety he critically examined the faint trail from cover, and the more he saw of it the more he regarded his ascent as a miracle.

"Only a fool would 'a' tried it," he grinned. "It's somethin' a man can do once in a hundred times; only he's got to make it th' very first time, or th' other ninety-nine will shore be lost. I'll never forget it, not never."

Watching a while, he wondered if it were guarded, and grinned at the foolishness of the idea; but he slowly pushed his sombrero out around a rock to find out. An angry *spang!* and a wailing in the sky told him the answer. The flat report in the valley became a mutter along the distant hills.

"Good shootin'," he grunted. "Glad you was out of breath, or excited, or somethin' this mornin'."

Back at the top of the other trail he found two large rocks lying close together near the edge, and he crawled behind them and peered out through the narrow opening for a closer look at the canyon.

It was a chaos, dotted with bowlders of granite, sandstone, and lava, some of them as large as small houses, their tops on a level with the tops of the nearest trees. It was cut by rock ridges, great backbones of stone that defied Time; and dotted with heavily wooded draws which extended up to the foot of the great pile of detritus embracing the foot of the buttes. Down its lowest levels ran a zigzag streak of bright, clean rock, the water-swept path of the torrents sent roaring down by melting snows and an occasional cloudburst. Several pools, fed by a dark trickle of water from the springs back in the upper reaches, could be seen. Of timber there was plenty, heavy growths of pine extending from the edge of the creek bed to the edge of the detritus, with here and there an opening made by the avalanches which had cut into the greenery for short distances. At other places even the stubborn pines could not find a grip, and a thinning out of the growth let him see the rocky skeleton below; but these were so few that he easily memorized their positions. Trouble would come a-winging to any careless rustler who blundered out onto any of them.

The opposite butte took his attention and he marveled at it. Under its lava cap and the great layer of the limestones was a greater layer of clay and shale and other softer sandstones. These had been harassed and battered by the winds and rains and frosts of ages and the resulting erosion had chiseled out wonderful bits of natural sculpturing. At one place he could see, and with no very great strain upon his imagination, part of a massive building with its great buttresses, where a harder, more enduring streak of rock had offered greater resistance to the everlasting assaults.

Farther to the right was a wonderful collection of columns and pinnacles, and some of the openings between them ran back until shrouded in darkness; great caverns in which houses could be built.

As the sun sank lower the shadow effect was beautiful, and even Johnny's practical mind was impressed by it. The color effect he had seen before—the streaks of black, gray, red, green, maroon, and white. Bits of crystal and quartz were set afire by the sun's slanting rays and some of them almost dazzled him.

To the west the sky was a blaze of color and the lengthening shadows made an ever-changing picture. Below him the dusk was beginning to shroud the bottom of the canyon, creeping higher and higher as the minutes passed. To see better, he wriggled closer to the edge, and a venomous whine passed over his head to die out swiftly in the air.

"Huh!" he grunted. "Fine target I must 'a' been for that thief down there, with such a sky behind me. I've got to remember things up here, or I'll lose my rememberer. I'm on a skyline that *is* a skyline. An' I ain't goin' to answer every fool that cuts loose at me, neither. I got plenty of cartridges, but I won't have if I start gettin' foolish with 'em. An' before dark I'm goin' to rustle me a blanket; it's gettin' cooler by jumps."

He made another visit to the south side of the butte for a glance down the trail of misery, and then dismissed it from his mind. In view of his experiences with it in daylight, he knew that no human being could climb it in the dark.

"It's as safe, day *an'* night, as if Red or Hoppy was layin' right here—an' that's plenty good enough for me," he smiled. "William, Junior's, bobcat kitten won't never grow big enough to climb that place—an' it's th' only thing on earth that he can't climb, blast him!"

Returning to his camp he had a drink and a smoke, and then, taking up a blanket and a pan of cold beans, he went to the head of the trail, there to keep a long and wearisome vigil.

Darkness had descended when he reached his chosen spot, and wrapping the blanket around him he sat down cross-legged, laid his rifle near him, and leaned back against a rock to watch the trail and wait for daylight. Faint, long-drawn, quavering, came the howl of a wolf, and from a point below him in the blackness of the canyon a cougar screamed defiance. He was surprised by the clearness with which occasional sounds

231

came up to him, for he distinctly heard the crack of dead wood where some careless foot trod, and he heard a voice ask who had the second shift on the south side of the butte.

"Turn in," came the answer. "We ain't watchin' that side no more. You relieve me at midnight, an' don't forget it!"

For some time he had been hearing strange, dragging sounds which seemed to come from the foot of the trail; and had been fooled into believing that an attack was under way. Then several low crashes gave him the distance, and he again leaned back against the rock, slipping the Colt into its holster.

A tiny point of light sprang up in the darkness, whisked behind a bowlder as he reached for his rifle, and grew rapidly brighter. Then it soared into the air and curved toward the foot of the trail, and almost instantly became a great, leaping flame which soon lit up the trail, the towering walls of the buttes, and the glistening bowlders in the canyon.

He stared at it and then laughed. "They ain't satisfied with watchin' th' trail an' listenin' with both ears, but they has to light it up! There ain't no danger whatever of me tryin' to get down now; an' I'd like to see anybody try to get up it while that fire's burnin'! They're shore kind to me."

"You be careful an' keep it out of th' brush,"

warned a faint voice. "If she catches, this canyon will be a little piece of hell. Everythin's so dry it rustles."

"Ain't you turned in yet?" demanded the guard. "You never mind about th' fire. You get to sleep; an' you get awake again a twelve."

"Huh!" came the laughing retort. "We can *all* go to sleep while *that's* blazin'. Go gnaw yore bone an' quit growlin'."

Johnny laughed loudly, derisively. "I may set it on fire myself!" he jeered. "An' if I don't, th' rainy season is purty near due—an' when it comes you'll need a boat. Fine lot of man-hunters you are. All you can shoot is boots an' skunks!"

A flash split the darkness, and the canyon tossed the report from side to side as though loath to let it die. When the reverberations softened to a rolling mutter he jeered the marksman and called him impolite names. The angry retort was quite as discourteous and pleased him greatly.

An hour passed, and then Johnny arose and crept softly down the trail, hugging the rock wall closely. When he reached a small pile of broken branches, caught in a fissure, he gathered an armful and carried them up on the butte. Firewood was too scarce for him to neglect any opportunities. A second trip enabled him to find a few scattered pieces and they were added to his store. Then he went to his horse, removed the picket rope, and going to the edge of the cliff at a spot over the trail he tied one end of the rope around a rock and lowered the rest of it over the rim. Another trip down the trail was necessary to make the free end fast to a dead fir that lay along the wall, and having tied it securely he slipped back to the plateau, hurried to the rope and pulled on it in vain. Try as he might he could raise only one end of the log.

"Cuss it!" he grunted; then he grinned and whistled a clear note. A few minutes passed and soft hoofbeats came slowly nearer. Then a black bulk loomed up beside him and nuzzled his neck. "I forgot th' saddle," he said. "You wait here, Dearly Beloved," and he slipped away, the horse following him.

They returned together and Johnny made the line fast to the pommel of the saddle, took hold of it himself to show his good will, and spoke to the horse.

"Oh, you don't know nothin' about haulin', huh?" he grunted, dropping the rope and taking the reins. "Come on, now easy does it. Easy! Easy! Keep it there—th' cussed thing's got stuck on th' edge." In a moment he returned. "All right! *Over* she comes."

The man at the foot of the trail hurled more wood on the fire and then tried a few shots when the noise above caught his ear. Then as the flames shot up he grunted a profane question and stared at the animated tree trunk which climbed sheer cliffs in the dark.

"Well, I'm cussed!" he grumbled. "Firewood! An' me lettin' him get down there to tie that rope!"

Johnny peered over the rim and noticed that the flashes came from one place, and getting his rifle he kicked a few rocks over and fired instantly at the answering flash. Two guns in the canyon awakened the echoes and he stepped back to let the whining lead pass over his head.

"There I go!" he snorted. "Wastin' cartridges already! But I wish—gosh! *I* got it!"

Grinning with elation he felt his way along the butte until he was directly over the fire, where he stopped and began to search for rocks and stones, and he did not cease until he had quite a pile of them. Approaching the rim he peered over cautiously and searched the canyon within the radius of the firelight, but without avail. He noticed, however, that there seemed to be a nest of rocks and bowlders on the outer edge of the circle of illumination and he surmised that it was there the guards were lying. He heaved a big stone and watched it whiz through the lighted arc. It fell short and he tried again. The second rock struck solidly and made quite a noise, and choice bits of profane inquiry floated up to him. Several more rocks evoked a sudden scrambling and more profanity, and a lurid bayonet of fire flashed from a dark spot.

"Now he's took to heavin' rocks!" growled a peeved, angry voice. "Damned if he ain't th' meanest cuss I ever saw!"

Johnny threw a few more missiles and a deep curse replied from the pit. Close to the edge of the wall was a large rock, nicely balanced. It was the size of a small trunk, and a grin crept across his face as he walked over to it. Putting his shoulder, all his wiry strength, and plenty of grunts into the task, he started it rocking more and more, and, catching it at the right instant, he pushed it over and rolled it to the edge, where it threatened to settle back and remain; but another great effort rolled it slowly over the edge and it disappeared as if by magic. Striking a sharp bulge in the great wall when about half way down, it bounced out in an arc; and when it struck the bowlder pile it was a real success, judging from the noise it made. The canyon roared and seemed to shudder as the crash boomed out; and the huge missile, shattering into hundreds of fragments, lavishly distributed itself through the brush and among the bowlders like a volley of grape.

Deep curses roared from the canyon and several flashes of flame darted out.

"Lay on yore stummicks, fightin' mosquitoes, an' heavin' wood on that fire at long range, huh?" jeered Johnny, throwing another rock. "These are better at night than cartridges, an' they won't run out. I'll give you some real troubles. I only wish I had a bag of yellow-jackets to drop!"

Another jet of flame stabbed upward, but from a new place, farther back; and a voice full of wrath and pain described the man on the butte, and with a fertile imagination.

"What's th' matter with *you?* An' what's all th' hellaballoo?" indignantly demanded another and more distant voice. "How can a man sleep in such a blasted uproar?"

"Shut up!" roared Purdy with heat. "Who cares whether you sleep or not? He cut my head an' near busted my arm with his damned rocks! Mebby you think they ain't makin' good time when they get down here! Only hope he stumbles an' follers 'em!"

"He's a lucky fool," commented Fleming, serene in the security of his new position. "Luckiest dog I ever saw."

"Lucky!" snorted Purdy. "*Lucky!* Anybody else would 'a' been picked clean by th' ki-yotes before now. For a cussed fool playin' a lone hand he's doin' real well. But we got th' buzzard where we want him!"

"Lone hand nothin'," grunted Fleming. "Didn't he have that drunken Long Pete helpin' him?"

Purdy growled in his throat and gently rubbed his numbed arm. "There's another. It just missed th' fire. Say! *That's* what he's aimin' at!"

"Mebby he is," snorted Fleming; "but if he is he's got a cussed bad aim. Judgin' from where they landed, I bets he was aimin' em all at me. I got four bits that says he wasn't aimin' at no fire when he thrun them little ones. One of 'em come so close to my head that I could hear th' white-winged angels a-singin'."

"White-winged angels a-singin'!" snorted Purdy. "Hell of a chance you'll ever have of hearin' white angels sing. Yore spiritual ears'll hear steam a-sizzlin', an' th' moans of th' damned; an' yore spiritual red nose will smell sulphur till th' stars drop out."

"I'm backin' Purdy," said the distant voice. "They don't let no skunk perfume get past th' Pearly Gates."

"They won't let any of you in hell," jeered a clear voice from above. "You'll swing between th' two worlds like pendulums in eternity. Cow-thieves are barred."

A profane duet was his answer, and he listened closely as Holbrook's voice was heard. "Say!" he growled, killing mosquitoes with both hands and sitting up behind his bowlder. "Can't you hold your powwow somewhere else? Want him to heave rocks all night? How can I sleep with all that racket goin' on? Yo're near as bad as these singin' blood-suckers; an' who was it that kicked me in th' ribs just now?"

"If you wouldn't sprawl out in a natural path an'

take up th' earth you wouldn't get kicked in th' ribs!" snapped Fleming.

"Yo're a fine pair of doodle-bugs," sneered Holbrook, sighing wearily as he arose. He lowered his voice. "Here he is over this end of th' trail an' givin' you a fine chance to sneak up an' bushwhack him; an' all you do is dodge rocks, cuss yore fool luck, an' kick folks in th' ribs. Don't you know an opportunity when you see one?"

"Is *this* an opportunity?" mumbled Purdy sarcastically, rubbing his arm and fighting mosquitoes.

"With that fire showing up everything for rods?" softly asked Fleming with heavy irony. "Who's been puttin' loco weed in *yore* grub?"

"'Tain't loco weed," growled Purdy. "It's red-eye. He drinks it like it was water."

"No such luck," retorted Holbrook; "not while yo're around. It ain't no opportunity if yo're aimin' to have a pe-rade past th' fire," he continued in a harsh whisper; "but it shore was a good one if you had cut down through th' canyon a couple of rods below th' end of th' trail, an' then climbed up to it an' stuck close to th' wall. You could 'a' been up there now, a-layin' for him when he went back on guard. It's cussed near as simple as you are."

"You must 'a' read that in that joke book what come with th' last bottle of liniment," derided

Purdy. "Fine, healthy target a man would make if he didn't get over th' top in time! Lovely job! You must think he's a fool."

"Don't be too sarcastic with him, Purdy," chuckled Fleming. "He does real well for a man that thinks with his feet."

"You fellers make me tired!" muttered Holbrook in sudden decision as another rock flew into pieces on a bowlder and rattled through the brush. "I'd just as soon get shot on a good gamble as die from these whinin' leeches. I'm all bumps, an' every bump itches like blazes. I never thought there was so many of 'em on earth. You watch me go up there—an' cover me if you can. Jeer at him an' keep him up there heavin' rocks as long as you can."

"Watch you?" grunted Purdy. "That's just what I'm aimin' to do. I'm aimin' to watch *you* do it. We don't have to take chances like that. His grub will run out an' make him come down. Time is no object to us. We can afford to wait."

"You can't do it, Frank," said Fleming, dogmatically, ducking low as another rock smashed itself to pieces against a bowlder.

"Huh!" snorted Holbrook, picking up his rifle and departing.

His friends chose their positions judiciously and shouted insults at the man on the butte; and after a few minutes they saw Holbrook, bent double, dart swiftly across a little open space, disappear into the brush and emerge into sight again, vague and shadowy, near the base of the wall a dozen yards below the end of the trail. He crept slowly over a patch of detritus which sloped up to the wall, and began his climb, which was not as easy a task as he had believed.

The wall, eroded where rotting stone had crumbled away in layers, was a series of curving bulges, each capped by and ending in an out-thrust ledge. He forsook his rifle on the second ledge and went slowly, doggedly upward, but despite all his care to make no noise, he dislodged pebbles and chunks of rotten stone and shale which lay thick upon the rocky shelves. When half way up he paused to search out hand and foot holds and became suddenly enraged at the amount of time he was consuming; and he realized, uneasily, that he had heard no more crashing rocks. The knowledge sent caution to the winds and drove him at top speed, and it also robbed him of some of the jaunty assurance which had urged him to his task. Fear of the ridicule and the jeers of his sarcastic friends now became a more compelling motive than the hope of success; and he writhed and stretched, twisted, clawed, and scrambled upward with an angry, savage determination which he would have characterized as "bull-headed" in anyone else. Then another smashing rock revived his hopes and made him strain with renewed strength.

At last his fingers gripped the crumbling sandstone of the trail's edge and by a fine display of strength and agility he swung himself over it and rolled swiftly across the slanting ledge to the base of the wall, where he arose to his feet and leaped up the precarious path. The ascent was twelve hundred feet long and it swept upward at a grade which defied anyone to dash along it for any distance. Walking rapidly would have taxed to the utmost a man in the pink of condition; and his pedal exercise for years had been mostly confined to walking to his horse.

The footing was far from satisfactory and demanded close scrutiny in daylight, while in the dark it was a desperate gamble except when attempted at a snail's pace. Ridges, crevices, stones, pebbles, drifts of shale and rotten stone, treacherous in their obedience to the law of gravity when the pressure of a foot started them sliding toward the edge of the abyss; places where the soft sandstone had split in great masses and dropped into the canyon, taking parts of the trail with them and leaving only broken, narrow ledges of the same rotten stone, all these conspired to make him use up precious minutes.

Below him to his right lay a sheer drop of two hundred feet; above him towered the massive wall; behind him and unable to help him, were his friends, and the fire, which was not bright enough to let him see the footing, but too bright for his safety in another way; before him stretched the heart-breaking trail, steep, seemingly interminable, leading to the top of the butte, where the silence was ominous, for somewhere up there was an expert shot defending his life. He had heard no more crashing rocks, and the insults of his friends had not been answered; and to hear such an answer or the crash of a rock he would have given his season's profits.

He paused for breath more frequently with each passing minute and his feet were like weights of lead, the muscles in his legs aching and nearly unresponsive. He was paying for the speed he had made in the beginning.

The great wall curved slightly outward now and he hugged it closely as he groped onward, and soon emerged from its shadow to become silhouetted against the fire below. And then a spurt of flame split the darkness above him and a shriek passed over his head and died out below as the roar of the heavy rifle awoke crashing echoes in the canyon.

Below him lurid jets of fire split the darkness and singing lead winged through the air with venomous whines, which arose to a high pitch as they passed him and died out in the sky. He knew that his friends were firing well away from the wall, but he cursed them for the mistakes they might make. Another flash blazed above him, and the sound of the lead and the roar of the gun told him that his enemy was now using a Colt. Ordinarily this would have given him a certain amount of satisfaction, for everyone knows that while a rifle is effective at such range, a hit with a revolver is largely a matter of luck; but as he leaped back into a handy recess a second bullet from the Colt struck the generous slack of his trousers and burned a welt on that portion of his anatomy where sitting in a saddle would irritate the most. It was a lucky shot, but Holbrook was too much of a pessimist at the moment to derive any satisfaction from the knowledge.

"I'm in a hell of a pickle!" he growled as the shadows of the recess folded about him. "I can't go up, an' I can't go down—I can't even *sit* down. I got to wait till that fire dies out—an' suppose they don't let it die? Five minutes more an' I would have won out."

"Hey, Frank! Are you all right?" asked a voice.

"That's Fleming, th' fool," growled Holbrook. "I suppose he wants me to step out on th' edge of th' platform an' speak a piece for him."

A laugh rang out at the head of the trail. "Answer th' gentleman," said Johnny in a low voice, fully appreciating Holbrook's feelings. "Don't it beat all how some folks allus pick th' wrong time in their yearnin' for conversation? I've been there; more'n once. You promise to go down an' give him a lickin' an' I won't pull a trigger on you while yo're on th' trail!"

"Hey, Frank! *Oh,* Frank!" persisted Fleming.

"Tell him to shut up," chuckled Johnny. "Here, I'll do it for you: Hello!" he shouted. "Hello, you loquacious fool! Frank says for you to shut up!"

Fleming's retort was unkind.

"Frank says he ain't smelled no skunk since he left th' canyon!" jeered Johnny. "Don't you get upwind of me!"

Fleming's retort was even more unkind.

"Hey!" yelled Purdy, cheerfully. "You ought to 'a' heard what Quigley said when Art odored into th' house! Dan'l Boone was scared it would get in his wounds an' poison him to death."

"Yo're a sociable ki-yote!" jeered Fleming.

Johnny laughed. "I'm that sociable I carries callin' cards, like you read about in th' mail-order catalogues. They're snub-nosed an' covered with grease, which I mostly rubs off because of th' sand stickin' to it. I'm 'most as sociable as th' dogs that drove me out of my valley, burned my cabin, stole my cows, an' put me out of th' game. I'm 'most as sociable as th' three skunks that laid for me that night. I told Quigley in Pop Hayes' saloon what I'd do if I was pestered; an' I've been doin' it. An' I ain't through yet, neither. Here's one of my cards now," he jeered, sending a .45 down the trail to let Holbrook know that he was not forgotten.

"You stopped my play, an' stole my cows," he

said. "So I'm goin' take all them that you got in yore sink. When I gets through *I'll* be th' owner of th' QE ranch, all by myself; an' there won't be none of you left to bother me. Noggin' a free country is a game two can play at, an' you shore got a good pupil when you taught me th' game. I'm aimin' to set up a record for th' cow-country. I never heard tell of a man shootin' off a whole outfit an' takin' their ranch; but that's just what *I'm* goin' to do unless you fellers get out of th' country while you can."

Jeering laughter and ridicule answered him; and then Purdy had an inspiration and voiced it with unnecessary vigor and quite a little pride.

"Hey, Frank!" he yelled. "If yo're all right, heave a rock over th' edge!"

There was a moment's silence and then a faint crash sounded in the canyon.

"There," called Johnny pleasantly. "Does that satisfy you, or shall I heave another?"

Fluent swearing came from below, in which Holbrook fervently joined, *sotto voce,* and he heaved another rock.

Johnny laughed loudly. "There's another in case you didn't hear th' first. I'm tellin' you about it because I don't want to deceive you. Mebby one of you fellers would like to sneak up here an' drag yore friend down?"

Holbrook reviewed the situation and could not see that he gained anything by keeping silent.

"*I* heaved them rocks!" he shouted savagely. "I'm all right. Now you put out that fire an' gimme a chance. I don't want to stay up here forever!"

"All right, Frank," called a new voice, which Johnny recognized as belonging to Quigley.

"Shore," jeered Johnny. "Run out an' kick it apart an' smother it with sand," he invited, reaching for his rifle. "But you want to do a good job. An' if he's still there at daylight you won't have to bother about him no more. I mean business now. I gave three of you thieves yore lives th' night you burned my cabin; but I'm shootin' on sight now."

"You got too cussed much to say!" snapped Holbrook angrily.

"An' I'll have more to say if yo're there at sunup," retorted Johnny. "An' lemme tell you, fire or no fire, you ain't down in th' canyon yet!"

Holbrook laughed. "You'll be as savin' of yore cartridges as you are of yore grub. How long do you reckon you can hold out?" he sneered.

"It only takes four bullets to clear a way for me," retorted Johnny.

New sounds came from the canyon. Rock after rock curved into the arc of illumination and landed in the fire, knocking it apart and sending blazing sticks flying toward the wall of the butte. Quigley warned his men to be careful and not set the brush on fire. There was a sudden puff of steam and the light dimmed quickly. Several other hatfuls of water turned the blazing embers into a black, smoking mass, where only an occasional red speck showed in the darkness.

The trail was blotted out and Johnny sent a .45 whining along it. A flash from below replied to him and he listened for a sound which would tell him that Holbrook had started on the return trip. But that individual, boots in hand, made no noise as he slipped along the wall. Coming to another recess, he sought its shelter, tied the boots together with his neckerchief, slung them over his shoulder and started down again.

Quigley ordered his companions not to shoot. "You might get Frank; an' he's in danger enough as it is. Yore flash will give that coyote a fair idea of where th' trail is."

"Did you hear what that ki-yote said about takin' our ranch?" asked Purdy.

Quigley laughed. "Yes; an' I admire his gall. He's got three of us, if he got Ackerman; but we wasn't awake to his game then." Another flash came from the top of the butte, and he growled when he heard the spat of the bullet. "He ain't lost th' trail yet, but he's puttin' 'em high."

"He'd be a handy man to have around," said Fleming. "I wonder if he'd 'a' throwed in with us, 'stead of rustlin' by hisself?"

"I'd 'a' found that out if Ackerman hadn't 'a'

been so dead set ag'in him," grunted Quigley, not refusing to take credit for an idea that was not his own. "I wonder," he mused.

"Offer him a share," suggested Purdy. "If we change our minds later, that's our business. We're losin' a lot of time with him; too much."

There was a sudden rattle of shale and pebbles, low-voiced profanity and a crash of breaking branches. "Cuss them rotten ledges!" said a voice not far distant. "An' damn these cactus an' locusts! I owe him more than he can ever square up, blast his hide!"

"Thank th' Lord," muttered Quigley in sudden relief.

"But mebby he *is* workin' for Logan," objected Fleming. "Hey, Frank! Over here."

"If he is it's about time for th' CL to hunt him up," Purdy growled anxiously. "We'd shore be in a fix if they caught us down here!"

"CL or no CL, we stays!" snapped Holbrook, rounding a bowlder and swearing at every step. "We got him now; an' we ain't goin' to let him go!"

"Shore!" endorsed Quigley. "They drove me off th' range; but I'll stay in these hills if I dies for it. Once we get this feller out of th' way an' get back to th' ranch we can put up an awful fight from th' houses, if we're forced to. They're stocked good enough to last us six fellers over four months. It's a show-down for me, come what might; but any man can take his share of th' money an' get away, if he wants."

Growls answered him, and he laughed. "That's th' way! Well, Frank; now what do you think of th' grand opportunity?"

"It was there; I started too late!" snapped Holbrook angrily. "If Art an' Purdy had any sense, one of 'em would 'a' jumped for that trail when th' first rock came down, instead of duckin' around these bowlders like a pair of sage hens. I didn't wake up till th' show was 'most over; an' I got within a hundred yards at that. Five minutes more an' I'd 'a' been layin' behind a rock waitin' for him to come back. It would 'a' been all over by now."

"Well, don't try it again," said Quigley. "He's got all th' best of it up there. We'll give him a week for his grub to peter out before we force things. An' there ain't no use of all of us stayin' out here. This is th' only way he can come down. Two of us out here is plenty, takin' turns watchin' th' trail. An' if you keep a fire burnin' you both could almost sleep nights. He'd never tackle it. Purdy, you an' Art clear out for th' ranch at day-light. Me an' Holbrook will stay here tomorrow an' tomorrow night, when you fellers can relieve us. I'd feel better, anyhow, if there was somebody besides Ben an' th' cook in them houses. You can't tell what might happen. It'll be light in an hour, so I'll go over an' start some breakfast."

"Say, Tom," said Fleming. "Make yore camp up on th' other Twin, an' get out of this cussed hole with its heat an' its pests. Th' man off guard could get a real sleep up there. But, of course, you'll have to do th' cookin' down here, where there's water handy."

"See about that later," answered Quigley. "Anyhow, we can sleep up there without shiftin' th' camp," and he disappeared in the darkness.

Fleming rolled a cigarette by sense of touch and thoughtlessly struck a match. *Spang!* said a bowlder at his side. *Ping-ing-ing-gg!* sang the ricochet down the canyon.

"Put it out!" yelled Holbrook, diving for cover.

"You damned fool!" sputtered Purdy from behind a pile of rocks.

"Beats all how careless a feller will get," laughed Fleming as he slid behind a rock. "I plumb forgot!"

CHAPTER XIX
An Unwelcome Visitor

Dawn broke, and as the light increased Holbrook saw a column of smoke arising from the southern Twin like a faint streamer of gauze. A slender pole raised and stood erect, and his suspicious mind sought a reason for it.

"Wonder if he's tryin' to signal somebody? Long Pete! I reckon he don't know Pete's dead. He'll not see *him* this side of hell," he muttered, settling in a more comfortable position to go to sleep.

The pole swayed as a rope shot over it and grew taut, and then a faded shirt, heavy with water, came into view and sagged the rope.

Holbrook grinned and picked up his rifle. "Gettin' th' wash out early. An' he must have plenty of water, to waste it like that."

He raised the sight a little and tried again. "Can't tell where they're goin'," he grumbled, and tried the third time. The edge of the shirt flopped inward as the garment momentarily assumed the general shape of a funnel.

"He ain't th' only ki-yote that can shoot,"

chuckled the marksman. "Fleming couldn't 'a' done any better'n that. Bet he's mad. Serves him right for havin' two. He ain't no better than me, an' I only got one, since Ackerman took my other one. Cuss it!" he swore, blinking rapidly and spitting as a sharp *spat!* sent sand into his face.

He shifted, wiped his lips, and peered out at a spot on the other butte where a cloud of smoke spread out along the ground. Then he poked his sombrero over the breastwork and wriggled it on a stick, but waited in vain for the expected shot.

"He ain't bitin' today; an' he's savin' his cartridges. Well, I got plenty; so here goes for that shirt again."

Again the inoffensive garment flopped; and then a singing bullet passed squarely through Holbrook's expensive sombrero.

"You stay down from up there!" grunted Holbrook at the hat. "Plumb center! I got a lot of respect for that hombre. He got th' best of th' swap, too. I spoiled a worn-out shirt, an' he ventilated a twenty dollar Stetson. He owes me a couple more shots!"

The next shot missed, but the second turned the shirt into another funnel.

"Hey!" shouted an angry voice. "What you think yo're doin'?"

Holbrook's grin turned into a burst of laughter as the pole swiftly descended, and he again poked up his hat, hoping for a miss and another wasted cartridge; but, failing to draw a shot, he gave it up and crawled back to a safer and more comfortable place where he lay down to get some sleep.

Johnny, full of wrath, worked along the edge of the butte in a vain endeavor to catch sight of his enemy, and he took plenty of time in his efforts to be cautious. Any man who could hit a shirt plumb center and nearly every time, at that distance, shooting across a deceptive canyon and against the sky, was no one to get careless with. After waiting a while without hearing any more from his humorous enemy, he looked down each trail and then went to the other end of the butte.

Not far from him a slender column of smoke arose from a box-like depression which lay beyond a high ridge and was well protected from his rifle. Peering cautiously over the rim of the butte, his head hidden in a tuft of grass, he critically examined the canyon, bowlder by bowlder, ridge by ridge. A puff of smoke spurted from a pile of rocks and a malignant whine passed over his head. Wriggling back, he hurried to another point fifty yards to his right, where he again crept to the edge and looked down. Another puff of smoke and a bloody furrow across his cheek told him that the marksman had good eyes and knew how to shoot. Johnny drove a Sharp's Special into the middle of the smoke and heard an angry curse follow it.

"Hey, Nelson!" called a peeved voice from the rocks. "Nelson!"

"What you belly-achin' about?" demanded Johnny insolently.

"How'd you like to join us instead of fightin' us?"

"Yo're loco!" retorted Johnny. "Can't you think of anything better'n that? I cut my eye-teeth long ago."

"I mean it," said Quigley, earnestly. "Mean it all th' way through. We talked it over last night. It's poor business fightin' each other when we might be workin' together. Laugh if you want to; but lemme tell you it ain't as foolish as you think. It's a lazy, independent life; an' there's good money in it. You'd do better with us than you'd 'a' done alone."

"I've shore fooled 'em!" chuckled Johnny softly. Aloud he said: "I can't trust you, not after what's happened."

"I reckon you *are* suspicious; an' nobody can blame you," replied Quigley. "But I mean it."

"Why didn't you make this play when I was in my valley, pannin' gold an' gettin' a little herd together?" demanded Johnny. "*You* knowed I wasn't after no gold; an' you knowed what I *was* after. But no; you was hoggin' th' earth an' too cussed mean to give a man a chance, an' make another split in yore profits. You burned—oh, what's th' use? If you want my answer, stick yore head out an' I'll give it to you quick!"

"I know we acted hasty," persisted Quigley;

255

"but some of us was ag'in it. Three of 'em are dead now; Ackerman's missin'. We'll give you th' share of one of 'em in th' herd that we got now; an' an equal share of what we get from now on. That's fair; an' it more than makes up for yore cabin an' them six cows. As far as *they* are concerned, we'll give you all of what they bring. How about it?"

"Reckon it's too late," replied Johnny. "I ain't takin' nobody's share. I'm aimin' to take th' whole layout, lock, stock, an' barrel. Why should I give you fellers any share in it? What'll you give me if I let you all clear out now?"

"What you mean?" demanded Quigley.

"Just what I said," retorted Johnny. "There's six of you now. It ought to be worth something to you fellers to be allowed to stay alive. I'll throw off half for th' wounded men—let 'em off at half price. What are you fellers willin' to pay me if I let you leave th' country with a cayuse apiece an' all yore personal belongin's?"

"This ain't no time for jokin'!" snapped Quigley angrily.

"I ain't jokin' a bit! I'll have yore skins pegged out to dry before I get through with you. Yo're a bunch of sap-headed jackasses, with no more sense than a sheep-herder. I'm 'most ashamed to get you; but I'm stranglin' my shame. You pore muttonheads!"

Quigley's language almost seared the vegetation and he was threatened with spontaneous combustion. When he paused for breath he swung his rifle up and pulled the trigger, almost blind with rage. Johnny's answering shot ripped through his forearm and he felt the awful sickness which comes when a bone is scraped. Half fainting, Quigley dropped his rifle and leaned back against a rock, regarding the numbed and bleeding arm with eyes which saw the landscape turning over and over. Gathering his senses by a great effort of will, he steadied himself and managed to make and apply a rough bandage with the clumsy aid of one hand and his teeth.

"I'll give you till tomorrow mornin' to make me an offer," shouted Johnny; "but don't get reckless before then, because th' temptation shore will be more than I can stand. Think it over."

"Damn his measly hide!" moaned Quigley, his anger welling up anew. "Give him our ranch, an' cows, an' *pay* him to *let* us leave th' country! Six of us! Six gun-fightin', law-breakin', cattle-liftin' cow-punchers; sane, healthy, an' as tough as rawhide rope, payin' *him,* a lone man up a tree, to let us leave th' country! All right, you conceited pup; you'll pay, an' pay well, for that insult!"

He still was indulging in the luxury of an occasional burst of profanity when Holbrook approached the bowlders on his hands and knees.

"I'm still hungry; an' I can't sleep unless I'm full of grub," apologized the rustler. "An' I heard shootin'. What's th' matter, Tom? Yore language ain't fit for innercent ears!"

"Matter?" roared Quigley, going off in another flight of oratory. "Matter?" he shouted. "Look at this arm! An' listen to what that——carrion-eatin' squaw's dog of a——had th'——gall to say!"

As the recital unfolded Holbrook leaned back against a rock and laughed until the tears washed clean furrows through the dust and dirt on his face; and the more he laughed the more his companion's anger arose. Finally Quigley could stand it no longer, and he loosed a sudden torrent of verbal fire upon his howling friend.

Holbrook feebly wiped his eyes with the backs of his dusty hands, which smeared the dirt over the wet places and gave him a grotesque appearance.

"Why shouldn't I laugh?" he choked, and then became indignant. "Why shouldn't I?" he demanded. "I've laughed at yore jokes, Fleming's stories, Cookie's cookin', an' Dan'l Boone's windy lies; an' now when something funny comes along you want me to be like th' chief mourner at a funeral! I'm forty years old an' I've met some stuck-up people in my life; but that fool up there has got more gall an' conceit than anybody I ever even heard tell of! I'm glad *I* didn't hear him say it, or I shore would 'a' laughed myself plumb to death. Did you ever hear anything like it; drunk or sober, *did* you?"

"No, I didn't!" snapped Quigley. "An' if you've got all over yore nonsense, suppose you take a look at my arm, an' fix this bandage right!"

"Sorry, Tom," answered Holbrook quickly; "but I was near keeled over. Here, gimme that arm; an' when I get it fixed right, you make a bee-line for th' ranch. There ain't no use of you stayin' out here with an arm like that. Good Lord! He shore made a mess of it! Them slugs of his are awful; an' that gun is th' worst *I* ever went up ag'in. *I* want that rifle; an' I speaks for it here an' now. When we get him, I get th' gun."

"It's yourn," groaned Quigley. "Gimme a drink of whiskey before I start out. But I don't like to leave you to handle this alone. I can stick it out."

"It's a one-man job until somebody comes out," responded Holbrook. "All I got to do is lay low an' not let him come down that trail. A ten-year-old kid can do that durin' daylight. But you ain't goin' to go till you feel a little better," he ordered, producing a flask. "You wait a while— th' sun won't be hot for a couple of hours yet. An' would you look at th' mosquitoes! They must 'a' smelled th' blood. Here, wrap yore coat around it or they'll pump it full of pizen."

Two hours later, Quigley having departed for the ranch, Holbrook lay on the top of the northern Twin, glad to have escaped from the attacks of the winged pests which had driven him out of the canyon; and hoping that his enemy would try to take advantage of the situation, if he knew of it, and try to escape. He had decided that he could guard the trail as well from the top of the butte as he could from the canyon, for the whole length of the steeply sloping path lay before him. Cool breezes played about him, there were neither flies, mosquitoes, nor yellow-jackets to plague him, and the opposite butte and the whole canyon lay under his eyes. And he also had better protection than the canyon afforded, for there was always present a vague uneasiness, no matter how well hidden he might be, while his good-shooting enemy was five hundred feet about him. Food and water were close to his hand and he enjoyed a smoke as he lazily sprawled behind his protecting breastwork of rocks and set himself the task of keeping awake and alert.

He had seen no sign of his enemy, although he had closely scrutinized every foot of the opposite butte. Quigley, he thought, must have reached the ranch by that time and no doubt Fleming or Purdy was on the way to relieve him. As he glanced along the canyon in the direction that his friend would appear he saw a movement of the brush near the bottom of the much watched trail and he slid his rifle through an opening between the rocks covering the center of the disturbance.

It was too early for Fleming or Purdy, he reflected; and his eyes narrowed as he wondered if it could be some friend of the man he was watching.

The bushes moved again and a grizzled head thrust out into view, slowly followed by a pair of massive shoulders as a great silver-tip grizzly pushed out into the little clearing where the guarding fire had been, and slowly turned its head from side to side, sniffing suspiciously. Satisfied that there was nothing to fear, it crossed the clearing and ripped the bark off of a dead and fallen tree trunk, licking up the grubs and the scurrying insects. Shredding the bark and thoroughly cleaning up the last of the grubs, it sat down and lazily regarded the towering butte.

Holbrook watched it with interest, for there was something almost human in the great bear's actions, a comical gravity and a deftness of paws which brought a grin to his face.

The bear arose clumsily, scratched itself, and proceeded toward the trail in that awkward, lumbering way which conveys such a vivid impression of tremendous strength and power. Holbrook knew that the lazy, clumsy shuffling, the indolent thrust of the rounded shoulders and the slow, deliberate reaching of the great legs, the forefeet flipping quickly forward, hid an amazing, deceptive quickness and agility, and a devastating strength. Sleepy, peaceful, and good natured as the beast appeared, its temper was always on edge and its heart knew nothing of fear when that temper was aroused; and he also knew that the vitality in that grub, insect, and berry-fed

261

body was almost beyond belief, that a clean, heart shot would not stop it instantly.

The animal waddled onto the trail and paused to turn over a rock, licked up a few scurrying bugs and waddled on again, the great shoulders rising and falling with each deliberate step. A pause, and the red tongue wiped out a procession of hard-working ants, and again it lumbered upward.

"Nelson is due to have company; an' plenty of it!" chuckled Holbrook; "an' if he slides any lead into th' wrong place under that flea-bitten hide he'll find that butte is a cussed lot smaller than he ever thought it was. Ah-ha! Cussed if th' yellow-jackets ain't declarin' war on him! Just wait till his snout gets well stung, an' he'll be ready an' eager to fight anything that lives!"

The bear was moving swiftly now, but pausing frequently to scrape his smarting snout with one paw or the other, and it was beginning to show signs of irritation as the swarming yellow-jackets warmed to the attack.

"Gettin' riled more every minute!" grinned Holbrook. "I'd hate to run foul of him now! Mr. Nelson shore is goin' to have a grand an' busy little seance up there, unless that Sharp's of his gets home plumb center th' first crack. He'll mebby wish it was a repeater. That old varmint must be nine feet long, an' just plumb full of rage. I can imagine them wicked little eyes of hisn gettin' redder an' redder every minute. An' one swipe of them paws would cave in th' side of th' biggest steer on th' range. It's a cussed good thing grizzlies ain't got th' speed an' habits of mountain lions—they'd be th' most dangerous things on earth if they had."

The bear sat down suddenly and dragged himelf a few feet, and then ran on at top speed.

Holbrook roared with laughter. "Ho! Ho! Ho! This is goin' to be as much fun as a circus! Damned if I'd miss it for a week's pay! Go on, Old Timer; steam up!"

Free at last from the stinging attacks of the yellow-jackets, the great bear suddenly stopped, squatted back on his haunches and rubbed his head and snout with both paws; and then, looking across the canyon at the place the laughter was coming from, slouched back on four legs and waddled rapidly upward, his huge body twisting ponderously at each step. Reaching the top he paused while he surveyed his immediate vicinity, looked back down the trail, glanced across the canyon again, and then slowly disappeared among the rocks and bowlders.

Holbrook shifted his rifle to a more comfortable position across his knees and leaned forward expectantly, grinning in keen anticipation, his cigarette cold and forgotten between his lips. It was just possible that there might be more in the coming show for him than amusement, for Mr.

Nelson, intent, very, very intent, upon his part of a game of tag among the bowlders, might forget for a moment and carelessly show himself long enough to become a promising target.

"Wonder how much he'll take, purty soon, to *let* Ol' Silver-tip leave th' country along with us?" he chuckled. "I wish Tom was here!"

Johnny opened his eyes at Pepper's snort and glanced at the horse, which trembled in every limb and whose big eyes were ablaze with terror. She had jerked the picket rope loose from under the rock which had held it, but was rigid with fear. Sitting bolt upright as he jerked out a Colt, Johnny glanced in the direction of Pepper's stare and then left the blanket to take care of itself. Twenty paces distant was the Sharp's, loaded and lying on a rock, and he hotly cursed the stupidity and carelessness which had caused him to go to sleep so far away from the weapon. It was the first time such a thing had happened in weeks, and he instantly resolved that it never would happen again. Between him and the rifle was the biggest, meanest looking grizzly it ever had been his misfortune to face.

The unwelcome visitor had finished a pan of beans and a pan of rice and had its nose jammed in the last can of sugar that Johnny owned. Observing his unwilling host's acrobatic leap and the flying blanket, the huge animal pushed the sugar can from its swollen nose with a cunningly curved paw, and heaved itself onto its four legs, regarding the puncher with a frankly curious and belligerent stare. The little eyes were wicked and bloodshot and one of them was nearly closed from the stings of the yellow-jackets. Altogether it was as unpleasant a sight as anyone would care to look upon at such close range.

Behind Johnny was the rock wall, rising fifteen feet above the bottom of the little rock basin, and it curved slightly outward at the top. On one side were scattered several great bowlders, and he kept these in mind as he glanced quickly behind him at the wall, which was smooth and devoid of handholds.

He had killed a grizzly with a six-shooter, but no such animal as the one facing him; and a Colt was not a weapon to be eagerly used, especially at such close quarters, where a sudden rush might be fatal to the user. He knew the thickness of the bone over the little brain, and keenly realized the smallness of the eyes as a target in the slowly moving head; if he could maneuver the animal to give him a heart shot he would have a fair chance.

"G'wan away from here!" he ordered peremptorily, with an assurance in his voice which he did not feel. "Pull your stakes, you big tramp, or I'll bust yore neck!"

Bruin refused to heed him; instead, the animal shuffled forward, its head wagging, and Johnny also stepped forward, on his toes, yelled loudly and waved his arms. Bruin paused and looked him over. Johnny side-stepped toward the rifle, but the bear pivoted quickly, swung around and declared its intentions with a low but entirely sufficient growl.

Johnny figure quickly. He might beat his visitor to the gun, but he strongly doubted if he would lead by a margin large enough to have time to swing the weapon to his shoulder and obtain the nicety of aim necessary to stop his pursuer as suddenly as the occasion demanded. The bowlders remained as his other alternative, and as the bear took its second step, which was the beginning of the rush, Johnny made a very creditable leap in the direction of the bowlders, gained the first by ten feet to spare, vaulted the second, dashed around the third and streaked up the slope leading to the top of the rocky wall behind the pool.

As he gained the top a bullet hummed past his head, but it received no recognition from him, for the bear also was hustling up the slope, thoroughly aroused and abrim with energy and ambition. Jerking out his Colts, he emptied one of them into the rushing animal as he leaped aside to get behind another bowlder. The bear slowed for an instant as the six heavy slugs ripped into it, and then, loosing a roar that awoke the echoes, it gathered speed and slid around the rock, clawing desperately to make a short turn. Johnny emptied his second gun into the enraged animal as he dodged around another rock, and then, dropping both Colts into their holsters, he sprinted for the top of the wall as Holbrook's second bullet loosened a heel and almost threw him.

Reaching the edge he launched himself from it, recovered his balance like an acrobat and dashed for his rifle as the grizzly, reaching the edge, checked himself barely in time and hunted hurriedly for a way to get down the wall. Giving it up in an instant, the animal drew up its forelegs with a pivoting swing, and started at full speed along the edge, to go down the way it had come up. This exposed its left side, and the Sharp's, already at Johnny's shoulder, steadied upon the vital spot as he timed the swing of the great foreleg. There was a sharp roar, and an ounce and a quarter of lead smashed through skin and flesh, squarely into the animal's heart. The great beast collapsed, slid around and raised its head; but again the heavy rifle spoke and the massive head dropped limply, for the stopping power of a Sharp's Special is tremendous.

Johnny jerked out the smoking shell, slid another great cartridge into place, and then sat down on the rock, wiping his face with his sleeve.

"Hey!" called a distant voice. "Want any help with th' varmints?"

Johnny grabbed his rifle and slipped to the edge of the butte. Holbrook called again, carelessly exposing his shoulder; and then cursed the bullet which grooved it.

"Can I do anything more for *you?*" jeered Johnny.

CHAPTER XX
A Past Master Draws Cards

Back on the CL the foreman was worried about his new, two-gun man, and had almost made up his mind to order the outfit into the saddle and to lead it up into the Twin Buttes country to aid Johnny. While he was turning the matter over in his mind he entered the bunk-house and saw Luke Tedrue, the oldest man on the ranch, dressed in a clean shirt, new trousers, and a pair of new boots. Luke looked surprisingly clean and he was busily engaged in cleaning and oiling the parts of an old .44 caliber Remington six-shooter, one of those early models which had been transformed from its original cap-and-ball class into a weapon shooting center-fire cartridges. It had been the butt of many joking remarks and the old man cherished it, and had defended it in many a hot, verbal skirmish. Considering its age and use it was in a remarkably fine state of preservation.

Luke had played many parts in his day, for he had been a hunter, frontiersman, scout, pony-express rider, miner, and cavalryman, and as an Indian fighter he had admitted but few masters.

Tough, wiry, shrewd, enduring, of flawless courage and bulldog tenacity of purpose, he had behind him long years of experience; and his appearance of age was as deceptive as the pose of a basking rattler.

The lessons of such a long, precarious, and daring life as he had led were not easily ignored, and now as a cow-puncher, riding out his declining days on the range, there were certain habits which clung to him with the strength of instinct. One of these was his faith in a weapon almost universally condemned on the range. It mattered nothing to him that times and conditions had changed; he had proved its worth in years of fighting, and now he refused to lay it aside. There had been a day when Bowie's terrible weapon had entered largely into the life of the long frontier.

Logan, worried and preoccupied as he was, could not keep from smiling at the old man's patient labor.

"Luke, you waste more time an' elbow grease on that worn-out old relic than most people do with *real* guns. Th' whole outfit, put together, don't pamper their six-guns th' way you do that contraption. Why don't you throw it away an' get a *good* gun?"

Luke snorted, and screwed the walnut butt-plates into place. Then he slipped the cylinder into position, slid the pin through it, swung up the old ramrod lever and snapped it into its catch under the barrel. Spinning the cylinder, he weighed the heavy weapon affectionately, and looked up.

Luke grunted. "Huh! Mebby that's why old Betsy is a better gun today than any in this outfit. Why should I get a new one? This old Rem. has been a cussed good friend of mine. She's never balked nor laid down, an' she puts 'em where she's pointed. An old friend like her ain't goin' to rust if I can help it."

"Rust?" inquired Logan, chuckling. "Why, there ain't been enough moisture in th' air lately to rust anything, let alone any gun that's as full of grease an' oil as that contraption. Wait till th' rainy season hits us before you worry about rust. An' what are you all dressed up for? When I saw you this mornin' you was th' dirtiest man on th' ranch; an' now you fair shines! Ain't aimin' to go an' hitch up with no female, are you?"

Luke shoved home the last greasy cartridge, snapped shut the hinged flange, laid the gun aside, and pointed to a pile of wet clothing on the floor near his bunk.

"There ain't no female livin' can put a rope on me no more," he grinned. "See them clothes? I done fell in th' crick. Some slab-sided nuisance shifted th' planks an' was too lazy to put 'em back right. They tip sideways. I got half way acrost an' up she turns. Lost my balance an' lit belly-whopper. But I put 'em back just like I found 'em."

"An' you'll get an innercent man."

"There ain't none in this outfit," grunted Luke. He searched the foreman's face with shrewd eyes. "John, worryin' never did help a man. Get shet of it, or it'll get shet of you."

"Easy said, Ol' Timer; but it ain't so easy done," replied Logan.

Luke kicked his wet holster toward the clothes and took down one belonging to someone else, and calmly appropriated it, belt and all.

"Two most generally splits a load about in half," he observed, shoving the gun into the sheath. "An' it allus helps a lot to talk things over with somebody."

"Well, I ain't heard a word from Nelson since he left that note tellin' me where he was goin' an' for me not to bother about our five-day arrangement; an' he shore started off to wrastle with trouble."

"Huh!" snorted Luke grimly. "Dunno as I'd do much worryin' about him. Real active, capable hombre, he is. Chain lightnin', an' an eye like a hawk. A few years more an' he'll steady down an' get sensible. Lord, what a fool *I* was at his age! Beats all how young men ever live long enough to become old ones."

"But he's been gone a month," replied Logan. "It's been two weeks since I heard from him, an' longer. He's playin' a lone hand ag'in them fellers, an' it ain't no one-man job, not by a damned sight! He was to find out certain things an' then come back here an' report. Why ain't he got back?"

"Busy, mebby," grunted Luke. "I have an idea th' job would keep one man purty tolerable busy, with one thing an' another turning up. He don't want to get seen an' tip off his hand; an' keepin' under cover takes time."

"I should 'a' taken th' outfit up there an' combed th' hills, regardless what anybody said about squarin' up old scores."

"What you should 'a' done, an' what you *did* do don't track," replied Luke. "An' I ain't shore that you oughta 'a' busted loose like that a-tall. It's a good thing most generally to know where yo're goin' to light before you jump. What you should 'a' done was to 'a' sent me up there, either alone or with him. 'Tain't too late to deal me a hand. Where'd he say he was goin'?"

"West of Twin Buttes. But if you go it'll be a one-man job again, an' I don't like it."

"Uh-huh!" chuckled Luke. "That's just what it is; an' I *do* like it. I drove stage, carried dispatches through Injun country, an' was th' boss scout for th' two best army officers that ever fit Injuns. Reckon mebby if th' Injuns couldn't lift my scalp, no gang of thievin' cow-punchers can skin it off. An' I'm cussed tired of punchin' cows. I ain't no puncher by nature, hopes, or inclinations. I'm a scout, *I* am; an' I'm goin' up there somewhere west of th' Twins an' find Nelson, if he's still alive, get them facts an' bring 'em back."

"I don't like th' idea," muttered Logan.

"Huh! I ain't got them fool notions that Nelson has. I ain't no Christian when I'm on a war trail. He worries about givin' th' other feller an even break; but I worries if I lets him have it. Mexicans, thieves, an' Injuns—they're all alike; an' they don't get no even break from me if I can help it. I puts th' worryin' right up to them. I'll bet he's alive, an' workin' all th' time; but he ain't got no chance to get quick results; an' it's his own handicappin', too. When a man's scoutin' around a whole passel of rustlers, a gun has got its limits. Gimme a pair of moccasins an' ol' Colonel Bowie."

"I likes you purty much; but damned if I thinks much of any man that uses a knife!"

Luke laughed grimly and got the knife from his bunk. "There he is. He don't make a man no deader than a bullet; an' he don't make no noise. There ain't nothin' handier in a mix-up—an' a good man can drive it straight as any bullet, too. I'm gettin' het up considerable about all this palaver about this knife an' me; an' I'm goin' to lick th' next man that rides me about it. It's a' honest weapon. It was ground out of a two-inch hoof file, an' when it cuts through th' air it takes considerable to stop it. When I was younger I could send it so far into a two-inch plank that you could feel th' pint of it on th' other side. Just feel th' heft an' balance of that blade!"

"Feel it yoreself!" snapped Logan. "That ain't fair fightin'; an' if you don't like that, you can start in here an' now an' lick me."

"I never said I was a fair fighter," grinned Luke, slipping the weapon into a scabbard sewed to the inside of his boot; "but old as I am, I can put yore shoulders in th' dust. We'll argue instead. Them fellers ain't fair fighters; they dassn't be even if they wanted to be; an' when I'm tanglin' up with 'em I ain't polite a-tall. I just fights, knife, gun, teeth, hands, feet, an' head, any way as comes handy. That's why I'm still alive, too. Now I'm goin' up somewhere west of th' Buttes an' look around from there; an' Colonel Bowie goes with me, right where he is. Tell th' cook to give me what grub I wants. An' I reckon I better take Nelson some ca'tridges an' tobacco."

"Tell him yoreself; an' if he won't do it, I'll tell you who moved th' planks," grinned Logan. "But I hate to see you go alone."

"An' I'd hate to have anybody along," grunted Luke. "I'll be busy enough takin' care of myself without botherin' with a fool puncher."

The old scout sauntered into the kitchen. "Mat, you sage hen; th' next time you shifts them planks, put a stone under th' edges that don't touch th' ground. You near drownded me in three inches of water an' a foot of mud. Now you

275

gimme a chunk of bacon, couple pounds of flour, three pounds of beans, couple of pounds of that rice, 'though I ain't real fascinated by it, couple handfuls of coffee, handful of salt, an' a pound of tobacco. I may be gone a couple of months an' get real hungry. Nope; no canned grub. I want this fryin' pan, that tin cup, an' a fork."

He sniffed eagerly and strode to a covered pan. "Beans, ready cooked! Mat, you was hidin' them! Dump some of 'em into a cloth—now I won't have to cook my first couple of meals. Stick all th' stuff in a sack, them on top," and he hurried out.

Fifteen minutes later Logan entered Mat's domain. "Where's Luke? What, already? Must 'a' been scared I'd change my mind. Why, he left his pipe an' smokin' behind," pointing at the table.

Mat grinned. "He says a smoker can't smell, an' gets smelled. An' he says for somebody to go up to Little Canyon for his bronc. He's leavin' it there tonight, hobbled. An' take that pipe out of here; I don't want them beans ruined."

Luke was crossing the CL range at a gallop, anxious to cross the river and get past the Hope-Hastings trail before dark. Reaching the Deep-water he forced his indignant horse into it and emerged, chilled, on the farther bank. Hobbling the animal, he put his boots on the saddle, slipped on a pair of moccasins, fastened the pack on his back and swung into the canyon, his mind busily forming a mental map of the country.

Placing Hope at one end and Hastings at the other, he connected them by the trail, putting in the Deepwater, the Barrier, and Twin Buttes.

"They comes to Hastings 'stead of Hope, which says Hastings is nearest. He said west of Twin Buttes. Then I'll start at th' Buttes an' go west till I find his trail; an' if I don't find it, I'll circle 'round till I finds *something!* I'd know that black cayuse's tracks in a hundred.

"Logan sent Nelson up here because nobody knowed him an' that he was workin' for us. Huh! What good will it do 'em to know a man if they never see him? An' they won't see me, 'less I wants 'em to. That water feels colder than it ought to—reckon I'm gettin' old. I shore ain't as young as I uster be. Got to move lively to get thawed out an' dry these clothes."

Crossing the main trail after due observation, he saw an old and well-worn trail leading westward into a deep valley.

"Huh! Hit it first shot. You just can't beat luck!"

Choosing the cover along one side of the smaller trail, he melted into it and plunged westward, swinging along with easy, lazy strides that covered ground amazingly and with a minimum of effort. His long legs swung free from his hips, the hips rolling into the movement; his knees were rather stiff and as his feet neared the ground at the end of each stride he pushed them ahead a little more before they touched. This was where the swaying hips gave him an added thrust of inches. And like all natural, sensible walkers, his toes turned in.

Night was coming on when he neared Twin Buttes and a rifle shot in their direction drew a chuckle from him. Throwing off the pack he ate his fill of Mat's cooked beans, shoved the wrapped-up remainder into his shirt, hid the pack and slipped into the deeper shadows, his rifle on his back, the old Remington in one hand and Colonel Bowie lying along the other, its handle up his sleeve and the keen point extending beyond his fingers.

A coyote might have heard him moving, but the task was beyond human ears; and after a few minutes he stopped suddenly and sniffed. The faint odor of a fire told him that he was getting close to a camp, and a moment later a distant flare lit up the treetops in the canyon proper. Looking down he noticed the buckle of his belt, thought that it was too bright, and wrapped a bandanna handkerchief around it. Slipping the six-shooter into its holster he moved forward again, bent over, going swiftly and silently, his feet avoiding twigs, branches, and pebbles as though he had eyes in his toes. Rounding the southern Twin he melted into the darkness at the side of a bowlder and peered cautiously over the rock.

A great, crackling fire sent its flames towering high in the air from a little clearing at the lower end of a path which went up the side of the butte and became lost in the darkness. Examining the scene with shrewd, keen, and appraising eyes, he waited patiently. A burst of fire darted from the top of the northern Twin and a strange voice jeered softly in the distance. From the top of the southern butte came an answering jeer in a voice which he instantly recognized.

"Treed, by God!" he chuckled gleefully. "Reckon he'll be tickled to see me. Wonder how long he's been up there?"

A piece of wood curved into the circle of illumination and landed on the blazing fire, sending a stream of sparks soaring up the mesa wall.

"There's Number Two," soliloquized Luke cheerfully, "feedin' th' fire an' watchin' th' trail. Cuss him for a fool! Some of them sparks will get loose, an' hell will be a nice, quiet place compared to this canyon. Well, now I got to rustle around an' locate 'em all; an' this ain't no place or time for no shootin', neither."

Half an hour later Fleming tossed more wood on the fire and settled back to fight mosquitoes. A glittering streak shot through the air and he crumpled without a sound. A shadow moved and a silent form wriggled through the brush and among the bowlders and retrieved the knife, took the dead man's weapons and wriggled back again. It slipped noiselessly across the canyon, searched along the base of the northern Twin, found the wide, up-slanting trail and flitted along it, pausing frequently to look, sniff, and listen. Reaching the top of the butte, it wriggled from bowlder to bowlder, ridge to ridge, systematically covering every foot of the plateau, and steadily working nearer the southern rim.

Holbrook yawned, stretched, and yawned again. He picked up his rifle and scowled into the canyon, where the fire engaged his critical attention.

"That lazy cuss is lettin' it burn too low," he growled. "Wonder if he's asleep!" He laughed and shook his head. "Nope; don't believe even Art could sleep down there, with them mosquitoes pesterin' him. *This* suits me, right here!"

He looked around uneasily. "I do so much layin' around out here in daytime that I can't sleep nights," he grumbled, not willing to admit that he felt uneasy. "Funny how a man's nerves will get hummin' when he's on a job like this. It shore is monotonous." Looking around again, he shifted so that he could see part of the mesa top behind him, and tried to shake off the premonition of evil which persisted in haunting him.

"How many cows you thieves sold so far?" called a voice from the other butte.

"Nowhere near as many as we're goin' to get," retorted Holbrook, laughing. "Changin' yore mind?" he jeered.

"Not me; I wouldn't work with no teethin'

infants. I'd rather work alone. I associates with *men, I* do."

"You'll 'sociate with dead men purty soon," sneered Holbrook. "We got you just where we—" the words choked into a gurgle and a lean, vague figure moved slowly forward from behind a ridge.

"What's th' matter?" ironically demanded the man on the southern Twin. "Swaller yore cigarette? That's a good thing. You want to practice swallerin' hot things because tomorrow yo're goin' to swaller a snub-nosed Special." Pausing, Johnny waited expectantly for an answer, but receiving none, he grunted cheerfully. "All right; go to blazes!"

The fire burned lower and lower and Johnny became suspicious. If the rustler on the other butte hoped to keep him engaged in snappy conversation when the fire grew low, there was no telling what the man in the canyon might do; so he crept to the top of the trail and peered down it, scanning the wall intently, half expecting to glimpse some swift, shadowy movement; but his alertness was not rewarded.

"Wonder how long Hoppy or Red would loaf on a game like this," he grinned, "if they was down there! But there ain't many of their breed runnin' around."

An hour passed and the fire was a mass of glowing embers, now and then relieved by a spasmodic burst of flame, which flickered up and died. Across the little clearing a shadowy form moved slowly backward, chuckling softly. If there were any more rustlers around, one of them certainly would have investigated why the fire was allowed to die; and Luke felt quite confident that he had accounted for all of them who were in the vicinity. Still, he argued, nothing was a certainty which depended upon circumstantial evidence, and he did not relax his caution as he moved away.

Johnny, straining his eyes in trying to discover signs of enemies on the trail, suddenly stiffened, listening eagerly with every nerve taut. Again came the voice, barely audible. Moving to the other edge of the butte he peered over cautiously, well knowing that he could see nothing.

" 'Tell Red his pants wear well,' " floated up to him out of the canyon.

Johnny moved a little and leaned farther over after a glance at the black sky assured him that he would not be silhouetted for a marksman below.

" 'Does William, Junior, chew tobacco?' " persisted the whisper.

Johnny wriggled back and sat bolt upright, incredulous, doubting his senses. "What th' devil!" he muttered. "Am I loco?"

" 'We was scared he'd die,' " continued the canyon.

Taking another good look down the threatening trail, Johnny wriggled to the edge and again looked down.

"'Pete paid Red th' eight dollars,'" said the chasm, a little louder and with a note of irritation.

"Who th' devil are you?" demanded Johnny loudly.

"Not so loud. Luke Tedrue," whispered the darkness. "How many of them skunks are around here?"

"Yo're a liar!" retorted Johnny angrily. "An' a fool!"

"Go to th' devil!" snapped the canyon.

"Come around in daylight an' I'll send you to him!" growled Johnny. "Think I'm a fool?"

There was no answer, and, fearful of a trick, Johnny wriggled back to his snug cover at the head of the trail, finding that the fire had become only a dull, red mass of embers which gave out almost no light.

"You shore got me guessin'," he grumbled; "but I reckon mebby I'm guessin' purty good, at that. You just try it, cuss you!"

Luke explored the canyon again to make assurance doubly sure, and again approached the great wall.

"'Does William, Junior, chew tobacco?'" he demanded.

Johnny squirmed, but remained where he was. "You can't fool me!" he shouted peevishly.

"Reckon not; yo're as wise as a jackass, a dead one," said Luke. "You stubborn fool, listen to this: 'Don't look for no word from me. I'm goin' west, to try it from back of Twin Buttes. They've drove me out.'" The voice was plainer now. "How many of 'em are out here?"

Johnny grinned suddenly, for in the increase in the power of the voice he recognized a friend.

"Hello, Luke, you old skunk!" he called, laughing. "Glad to see you. There's four been hangin' around but there's only two now, or three at th' most. Look out for 'em. Goin' to try to come up?"

"No, not a-tall," replied Luke. "There's enough of our outfit up there now. I only found two of th' thieves, but th' third may be hid som'ers well back, 'though I've shore hunted a-plenty."

"Found two?"

"Yep; one down here, an' t'other up there. Colonel Bowie pushed 'em over th' Divide. Comin' down?"

"When that fire's out."

"How'd they come to drive you up there?"

"I come up myself. Couldn't watch while I slept; an' I had to sleep. Now that there's two of us it's all right."

"You called th' turn. Get yore traps together an' I'll fix th' fire. Where's yore cayuse?"

"Up here. Don't bother with th' fire. Be right down."

Half an hour later Johnny reached the bottom of the trail and paused.

"'Red's pants,'" said a humorous voice.

"Come on, Luke. We'll hold up somewhere an' get th' relief shift when it comes out from th' ranch."

"Shore. Where's th' ranch?"

"'Bout three miles west; an' it's a cussed fine one, too."

"All right; get movin'. I want to dry out these pants. They must be all cotton from th' way they feel. We'll go back a ways an' start a fire."

"No, we won't; too dangerous," growled Johnny decidedly. "We got this game won right now if we don't let 'em know there's two of us."

Luke grinned in the dark. "Suits me. You wait here a minute," he said, disappearing. When he returned he grunted with keen satisfaction, for Fleming's trousers felt snug and warm. "How many are left?" he asked, leading the way toward his hidden pack.

"Quigley, Purdy, Gates, an' th' cook."

"Them names don't surprise me," grunted Luke.

"How'd you get so wet?"

"Swimmin'," growled Luke.

"Yore shirt feels dry."

"It is, around th' shoulders; but th' tail feels like th' devil. But it's wool, all through."

"Was you trailin' Ackerman an' Long Pete?"

"Nope; didn't trail nobody a-tall. How many cows they got?"

"Plenty, damn 'em!" growled Johnny.

"What you been doin' up here all this time; an' how many have you got?"

"Three; I've been busy."

"Why, you had time to get 'em all."

"Didn't dare do any shootin' till I had to," replied Johnny. "Didn't want 'em to know I was up here. A gun makes a lot of noise."

Luke chuckled grimly. "Shore! That's what I *allus* said; an' that's why I use Colonel Bowie. He don't even whisper."

Johnny snorted with disgust. "Huh! I ain't knifin' or shootin' from ambush. There's *some* things I won't do!"

"Uppish, huh?" chuckled Luke. "Well, young man; mebby ambushin' ain't yore style, but I feels free to remark that it's mine in any game like this. Them pants feel good. That river's gettin' colder every year."

"River!" said Johnny, pausing in his surprise. "What river?"

"Deepwater, of course. How many rivers do you reckon we got out here?"

"Th' devil!" muttered Johnny. "Say! When did you leave th' ranch?"

" 'Bout three o'clock. I'd 'a' been here sooner, only I hoofed it from th' river. Cayuses can't go where a man can; they make a lot of noise, an' a man sticks up too cussed prominent in a saddle. They ain't worth a cuss in this kind of country when trouble's afoot."

"Well, I'll be hanged!" grunted Johnny.

"Pull up; here we are," said Luke, stopping and bending over some rocks, which he rolled aside. "Rocks are reg'lar telltales. They has a dark side an' a light side; an' th' deeper they're set in th' ground, th' bigger th' dark side is. When you want to cache with 'em, you picks them that sets on th' ground; an' you don't turn 'em wrong side up, neither. Then a little sand used right will fix things so that only me or an Injun can tell that anything's been moved. Here's yore ca'tridges an' tobacco. Tote 'em yoreself."

"Much obliged. But how did you find me so cussed quick?" demanded Johnny, breaking open the boxes and distributing their contents about his person.

"Smelled you," chuckled Luke, fixing the pack on his back.

"Yo're an old liar!" retorted Johnny. "Tell me about it."

"Can't; there ain't nothin' to tell," replied Luke, winking at the sky "It's just experience, instinct, brains, knowin' how, an' a couple more things. Us old-timers done better'n that, forty years ago. I'm glad to get my hand in ag'in; punchin' cows shore does spoil a man. Now, you know this layout; where we goin' now? An' what you goin' to do with that four-laigged nuisance?"

"Put her in a draw east of here. She'll stay where I leave her."

"Then she ain't no fe-male. It just can't be did. I know 'em!"

"You an' our Pete oughts get acquainted with each other," chuckled Johnny. "You fellers has th' same ideas 'bout some things."

"Foreman, or owner?"

"Just a plain puncher."

"He oughta be th' foreman; he's got sense. I buried one, an' left two more. You can't fool me about th' sex."

"Yo're a reprobate. Come on, Pepper," said Johnny, whistling to the horse, who heeled like a dog. "It'll be light purty soon, an' we want to hide this cayuse."

"It's yore say-so; I'll string along, ready to chip."

CHAPTER XXI

Scouting as a Fine Art

Quigley, favoring his injured arm, led the way toward Twin Buttes to relieve the men on guard, Purdy close behind him; and he did not stick to the trail, but cut straight for his objective along a way well known to both. He was not in good shape for hard work or hard fighting, but he felt that his place was on the scene of action, as befitted a chief; and he had stubbornly battered down all the reasons advanced by his companions at the ranch by which they sought to dissuade him. It had to be either him or the cook, for he was not as seriously wounded as Gates.

The chief was the best man for leader that the outfit contained, and if he had erred in being slack and over-confident it was only because they never had been molested seriously since they had taken to the Twin Buttes country, and, with the exception of Ackerman, he secretly felt less security than any of the others. Thanks to his earlier activities and clever distortion of facts as to why he had crossed the Deepwater to live in the Buttes, the outfit had not been bothered; and the

Twin Buttes section had become taboo, in recent years, to everyone, no man caring to risk his life in penetrating that locality until Johnny Nelson appeared. And although Ackerman had preached disaster, he had preached it so long and so much that he was regarded as a calamity howler.

There were two comparatively safe ways to reach the Buttes, when once the last high, intervening ridge was attained. One led to the far side of the northern Twin and was hidden by it from the sight of anyone on the other butte; the second course swept to the south, running through arroyos and draws, and sheltered by the dense growths of pine; and it not only was a shorter and easier course, but allowed an occasional glimpse of the way Johnny had scaled the great southern wall.

Reaching the ridge, Quigley paused to rest, and weighed the merits of the two approaches. He could be as clever and cautious as the next man when he felt that the occasion demanded it; and the events of the last few days told him that such an occasion had arrived. Easing the bandages, he chose the southern course and led the way again.

"There's his smoke," grunted Purdy, trudging along in the rear. "Wonder how much grub that ki-yote's got?"

"Don't know; an' don't care much," replied Quigley. "It don't make no difference. Th' time will come when he's *got* to come down, an' bein' there when he does is our job. If I was plumb shore he was workin' on his own hook my worries would simmer down a whole lot; an' until I *am* shore, I ain't overlookin' nothin'."

"You ain't got no business comin' out here with an arm like that," growled Purdy. "Three of us are enough."

"I ain't got no business bein' nowhere else," retorted Quigley. "An' as long as yo're ridin' that subject again, lemme tell you that from now on till we get him, I'm goin' to stay right there. My eyes are all right, an' my Colt arm is th' same as ever. Bend low here an' foller my steps close—on th' jump, *now!*"

Reaching the end of the wide valley they came to a great widening of the lower levels, where the canyon emerged from between the Buttes and became lost in the great sink which surrounded the Twins. Quigley knew the sink from former explorations, and he chose ridges and draws without hesitation and kept well hidden at all times from anyone up on the butte. In order to continue in this security it was necessary to go almost to the eastern wall of the sink in a wide detour, and the chief unhesitatingly chose that route.

Because of an instinct born from years of woodcraft, Quigley's eyes missed nothing. Had he been riding down Hastings' single street he unconsciously would have observed every tin can, every old boot, and his memory, automatically photographing them with remarkable fidelity, would have filed the pictures away for future reference. Crossing a sage hen's track he unconsciously observed it minutely, and he could have told quite an interesting and intimate tale of what the bird had been doing.

Plunging into a deep gully, he swung up the opposite slope on a diagonal, and stopped suddenly, his busy mind instantly sidetracking its cogitations to take care of a matter immediately under his eyes. Three small stones lay, dark and damp, against the sun-dried, whitish rock stratum which formed the surface of the ridge. Above the level of his shoulders several green twigs were well chewed, two of them bitten clean off, and a dried lather still clung to them. Shoving his elbows out from his sides to check his companion, he looked closely at both signs, and then, bending over, hurried along the slope searching the ground and swiftly disappeared around a bowlder. Purdy followed and bent over beside him. In a small patch of sand and clay which filled a hollow in the rock floor was the print of a hoof, and extending in front of it lay the imprint of the forward half of a moccasin.

Quigley glanced up quickly at his companion. "Fresh made!" he grunted. "Leads away from th' butte. Might be two men, one of 'em ridin'. Wait here, an' lay low!"

Going on a few steps he shook his head slowly and disappeared around a thicket. Ahead of him was a wide streak of sand and gravel and he hurried to it.

"*Two* men on foot, leadin' a hoss!" he growled. "Wish I had time to foller these tracks; but there's no tellin' how far they go." He paused a moment in indecision, tempted to go on, but shaking his head he wheeled and ran back to Purdy, cursing the increased throbbing of his arm.

"Purdy!" he whispered incisively; "somethin's rotten! One cayuse; two men. Wait a minute!" and he sent his thoughts racing over every possibility. "They can be strangers that blundered through here; or friends of Nelson's. If they was strangers, an' passed th' Buttes, as that back trail indicates, they wouldn't try to keep hidden, an' either Art or Frank would 'a' seen them, an' follered them. If they was friends of his—damn it! Wish I had taken th' trouble to hunt up th' tracks of that black cayuse some place where they showed up plain an' deep!"

Purdy thoughtfully rubbed his head. "Mebby that cayuse wandered down, an' th' boys led it off to hide it."

"*Both* of 'em?" snapped Quigley. "One had to stay on guard. An' they can't turn boots into moccasins. Cuss it! Why would innercent strangers wear moccasins in this kind of country? They wouldn't, unless they was up to some deviltry. Purdy, we got a job on our hands. First, we'll see Art an' Frank—no *we* won't: *I* will. You foller these tracks an' find out what you can. Don't foller 'em longer than an hour. We'll meet right here. If you hear three shots so close together that they sound like a ripple, you cut hell-bent for th' ranch, by a roundabout way," and he was gone before Purdy could answer him.

Purdy ran forward, his gaze on the ground, and every time the trail became lost on clean, hard rock, he swore impatiently and ran in ever-widening circles until he found it again. Suddenly he crouched low and froze in his tracks. In an opening at the bottom of a deep, heavily wooded draw lying just ahead of him he caught sight of a black horse, saddled, cropping grass. The animal threw up its head, looked at him, flattened its ears and backed away, ready to bolt. And under his eyes lay four pairs of moccasin prints, two of them pointing back toward the Buttes.

"It's *his* bronc!" growled Purdy under his breath. "How th' devil—!" Wild conjectures filed into his mind in swift confusion, and, wrestling with them, he wheeled sharply and dashed back the way he had come, his Colt ready for action.

Quigley, calling into play every trick of wood-craft that he knew, kept on toward the Twin Buttes canyon, silent, alert, never once leaving cover. The smoke of the fire up on the butte was barely discernible now and the smoke from the rustlers' fire at the foot of the trail could not be seen at all. Eagerly he scrutinized the tops of the two buttes, but in vain.

Working steadily forward with the caution of an Indian, he followed and kept close to the eastern wall of the sink until directly back of the place where the trail guard should be, and in line with that and the lower end of the trail. His progress now became slow, and he exercised an infinite caution and patience. Cover followed cover, and every few yards he stopped and waited, his senses at the top pitch of their efficiency. Drawing near the position used by him and his men in guarding the mesa trail he passed within fifty feet of Luke Tedrue, and neither knew of it. Had he gone ten feet farther forward he would have died in his tracks.

He stopped. It was now Art's or Frank's turn to show some sign of life. Neither of them had any need to remain quiet, and he knew that under such circumstances a man is almost certain to make some kind of a noise within a reasonable length of time.

The minutes passed in absolute silence, and finally he could wait no longer, for each passing minute was precious to him, and he silently backed away, to approach from another direction. As he crept past a bowlder, avoiding every growing thing and every twig or loose pebble, he glanced along a narrow opening between some rocks and a thinning of the brush, and saw two sock-covered feet, toes up. It took him a long time to maneuver so that he could see enough of the body to be sure of its identity, and when he was sure he choked back a curse.

"Fleming!" he breathed. "Knifed through th' throat! An' they took his pants an' left a pair of blue ones. Nelson wore black! An' Frank, up there on th' other butte—I can't get up *there* without bein' seen. Frank, my boy; if yo're alive, you'll have to look out for yoreself!"

As he crawled and wriggled and dashed back over his trail his racing thoughts threw picture after picture on his mental screen, until every possible solution was eliminated and only the probable ones remained; and from these two there loomed up one which almost bore the stamp of certainty. The CL outfit, either wholly or in part, had arrived on the scene, and even now might be attacking the ranch-houses. Dashing around a pinnacle of granite, he sped down the slope of the draw where Purdy, behind a thicket, awaited him.

"Here, Tom!" softly called the waiting man, arising.

"Quick!" panted Quigley. "Hell's broke loose with all th' gates open! What you find?"

"Nelson's bronc. Th' two men that led it cached it in a draw an' went back again towards th' Buttes. What's up?"

"Everything, I reckon. Fleming's dead—knifed," panted Quigley, leading the way westward. "Frank—I don't know—about him. Never—had a chance—Art didn't. Good thing—I reckon we come—th' way we did. There—ain't no tellin'—what we might a' run—up ag'in. Damn 'em! I'll never leave—th' hills! Dead or—alive, I stays!"

"I've located here—permanent myself," growled Purdy. "Fleming knifed, huh? Mebby—mebby they're Injuns! Knife-play an' moccasins! I—betcha!"

"Damn fool!" gritted Quigley savagely; and then, remembering his companion's declaration of permanent location, he relented. "He wasn't—scalped!"

"Apaches—don't scalp!" grunted Purdy doggedly.

"But they make—tracks, don't they?" blazed Quigley. "I tell you—I know Injun tracks—like I know my name. They're—white men!"

CHAPTER XXII

"Two Ijuts"

Luke Tedrue brushed flies. Since a little after dawn he had brushed them continually, insistently, doggedly, with an enforced calmness and apathy which only an iron, stubborn will made possible; and had they suddenly desisted in their eager explorations he would have kept on brushing from sheer force of habit. But while his hands and arms were moving mechanically, his mind was having an argument with itself concerning his ears, and a vague uneasiness made him restless.

He suspected that he had heard a sound, one which only a moving body would have made; but it had been so slight that he had not recognized it at the time, and it was only through the persistent, indefatigable urging of some subconscious sense that he was now trying to force his memory to repeat it for him, to give him a hold upon it that he might describe and classify it. Exasperated, fretful, uneasy, he called himself a fool with too zealous an imagination; but he kept straining at his reluctant memory, trying to force it to leap back and grasp the elusive impression. Vexed and anxious, he at last wriggled back among the bowlders which sheltered him, determined to prove or disprove the haunting subconscious sense. It had become maddening, a ghost he simply had to lay.

Realizing that the moving object is the more readily seen, Luke moved slowly and with no regard for dignity; and he proceeded, an inch at a time, upon his lean, old stomach. Nothing was too small or insignificant to escape his notice, for his eyes, close to the ground, first took in the entire field of vision with one quick, sweeping glance, and then, beginning with the more distant objects, examined everything in sight as though he had lost something of great value and of size infinitesimal. Another few inches of slow, laborious progress, and another searching scrutiny, his ears as busy as his eyes. In half an hour he had covered ten feet, and at the end of an hour he had made it to twenty. And then, as he glanced around to obtain a general and preliminary view of a new vista, his eyes passed over a little patch of sand, and instantly flashed back to it, regarding it with an unwinking intentness.

He hitched forward again, more rapidly, and gained three feet before he stopped to peer about him. At last he came to the sand patch, which lay between a bowlder and a clump of dry, dead, and rustly brush, which accounted for its having a story to tell. It was the only way a cautious man could have proceeded, and the print of the heel of a hand and the five little dots where the tips of thumb and fingers had rested was well to one side of it. Furthermore, there was a smooth streak across it which contained two other streaks along the outer edges of the first one. The story was plain: a stomach, followed by two legs, had been dragged across the little patch of sand.

Luke raised his educated eyes and looked around him, but now his field of vision was considerably constricted, for he paid attention only to those few spaces in the brush and among the rocks which a clever man would be likely to use; and being a clever man himself, he unerringly picked certain openings and almost instantly riveted his gaze on a sign: a toe print at his left. Close to it was another, and the way in which the sand had been pushed up told him that the first had been made by a man crawling west; and the other announced to him that it had been made by a man moving east. Luke deduced that the same man, returning over his own trail, had made the second as well as the first.

Luke was relieved, and, having a safe trail to follow, he pushed on rapidly but silently, soon reaching the place where it ended; and in plain sight of him, through the thin growth of brush, was Fleming's body. One glance at it and Luke turned, following the trail back as he had come;

and an hour later, having learned a great deal, he ran and crept, leaped and wriggled up to the place where his friend lay and petulantly cursed the flies.

"Ijut Number Two," said Luke pleasantly, "where are you?"

"Talkin' to hisself again," grumbled a low voice from the mysterious passages under a great, tumbled mass of bowlders. "If a body meet a body, reachin' for th' rye," continued the vexed voice, "whose treat is it?"

"Depends on who can't keep still," answered Luke brightly. "We are two ijuts," he said positively and flatly.

"Well, I allus like a man that speaks his mind, even if he *is* a liar," commented the mysterious voice. "Damn these flies! I crawled in here to get rid of 'em; but they come right along. An' a little while back I smelled a striped kitty-cat. I knowed what it was because th' wind wasn't blowin' from yore direction."

"Cuss his impudence!" said Luke. "He takes me for a wild flower! A rose, mebby. An' me comin' out here to save his worthless life!"

"You didn't do nothin' of th' kind," contradicted the sepulchral voice. "You come out here to practice with Colonel Bowie! I can prove it before any fool jury. Damn th' flies!"

"What flies?" innocently demanded Luke, his voice suggesting a hot curiosity and a thirsty yearning for knowledge.

"Time," said the other. "Time flies; an' I've had these flies all th' time. It's time they flies away, to fly back another day. You leave yours behind you, Cow Face, if you visit me."

"Ain't got none; an' ain't seen none," replied Luke cheerfully.

"Twice a liar," observed Johnny pleasantly. "Why don't you learn to speak th' truth sometimes? I'm worried about yore soul."

"I'm worried about my belly an' my knees. They're scraped clean, wrigglin' over rock."

"'Tain't possible; not at yore age," commented Johnny. "Th' accumulations of years can't be got rid of so easy, Old Timer."

"No wonder they chased him off th' Tin Cup," grinned Luke. "We are two ijuts."

"Listen to th' jackass," said Johnny. "Th' flies that flew an' flied; th' flies that crawled an' died; th' flies that buzzed an'—an'—holy hell! Did you *ever* see so many of 'em?"

"I done listened to th' jackass," grunted Luke. "An' now I observes, gentle but firm: We are two ijuts."

"We are *one* ijut," corrected Johnny. "You are th' one. A soft answer turneth away wrath."

"I am an ijut; an' you are an ijut," replied Luke with exaggerated patience. "That makes two; an' so we are *two* ijuts."

"Can't you say nothin' else, One Ijut?" demanded Johnny peevishly. "Yo're tiresome;

yo're a repeater, rim fire, Chestnut, model of 1873. I'm lazy by nature; but doin' nothin' *all* th' time is hard work. It don't set right. They have taken her to Georgia, there to wear her life away. An' my neck aches from lookin' up, an' holdin' my head out on th' end of it. My stummick an' my elbows, my knees an' my toes all, all ache. They are rock-galled. As she toils 'mid th' cotton an' th' corn.'"

"Cane," corrected Luke. "Yore appalin' ignerence is discouragin'. We are two ijuts."

"All right; I quit," said Johnny wearily. "Have it yore own way; mebby we are. But it could 'a' been corn just as well as cane, anyhow. Why are we two ijuts?"

"Because we are holdin' th' bag," said Luke sadly.

Johnny turned around and stuck his head out. "Yes?" he inquired, with a rising inflection. "I'm plumb insulted. I ain't never held no bag; not never!"

"'Tain't never too late to learn," said Luke sorrowfully. "Th' snipe has come, an' went; an' we're *still* holdin' th' bag."

"Let's fill it full of flies," suggested Johnny. "Say! If you ain't seen no flies, how did all of them get squashed on yore face?"

"Come flyin' out of yore cave just now an' bumped into me full speed," replied Luke, grinning. "We have been out-guessed, we have.

They smelled us out. We're two tenderfeet in a wild, bad camp. Somebody's likely to hurt us, first thing you know. What did you see when you wasn't killin' flies?"

"Th' sky, th' canyon, an' th' butte."

"Uh-huh; so did I. I saw th' butte, th' canyon, an' th' sky. Then I moved an' saw hand prints, belly prints, toe prints, knee prints, an' other kinds of prints. Yore friends stacked th' deck on us an' dealt 'em from th' middle. Now what?"

"First, we eat," said Johnny, arising with alacrity. "Then, mebby, we eat again. We drink an' we wash. I'm near half as dirty as you. What have you found out?"

"Did you ever see two calves, wobble-kneed, friskin' around lookin' saucy an' full of hell an' wisdom; but actin' plumb foolish?"

"I shore did. I never saw no other kind, unless it was sick. Stiff back, humped in defiance; tail tryin' to stand up; stiff-laigged, when they didn't buckle unexpected; jumpin' sideways, tryin' to butt, an' allus hungry. I did, Old Timer; lots an' lots of times."

"Well, them's us," sighed Luke. "You hold yore trap an' listen while I speaks my piece. I saw them signs, like I said. Th' cuss that made 'em sneaked right up to my back door, went around th' side of my house, stopped just in time for his health, backed off, saw his friend's body, an' my pants, an' backed off some more. Then he climbed up

304

on two good feet an' made toe prints plumb deep. He didn't run; no, ma'am; he just telegraphed hisself; never stopped for nothin'. He sped, he shot, he *moved!*"

"An' us two ijuts layin' out here in th' sun till we was cussed near jerked meat!" growled Johnny. "I call that blamed unpolite."

"Didn't I tell you we was two ijuts? When an older man speaks you want to keep yore mouth shut an' yore ear tabs open. Th' young bucks go out an' steal th' horses an' lift th' scalps; but th' old fellers make good talk around th' council fires. Stick *that* in yore peace pipe an' smoke it. Might be good for your health sometime."

"Yo're a purty spry scalper yoreself," admitted Johnny. "Regular old he-whizzer; but you got no morals, an' a very bad, disgustin' habit. I'm surprised you didn't take scalps, too!"

"You let the Colonel alone," warned Luke. "Now, that rustler is some he-whizzer hisself, an' he won't need nobody to tell him what he saw. He's done told his tribe about that; an' bein' a stranger here I'm only guessin'. Say what's on yore mind."

"Th' young buck will now talk at th' council fire," grinned Johnny. "Yo're right, for once. It wasn't th' cook. I never saw a cook yet that could move around so nobody could hear him. It wasn't Gates, because he's wounded several; an' I don't think it was that other feller, because somehow I

305

ain't feverishly admirin' his brains. That leaves Quigley; an' he ain't no fool *all* th' time. I can see him beatin' hell an' high-water to his three stone shacks, where his friends are, an' where his guns, grub, clothes, an' other things are. I can see four men lookin' out of four loopholes. They are if they ain't jumped th' country; an' if they has, we'll let 'em go.

"Takin' a new, fresh holt, I'd say that they don't know that we'd let 'em go; an' they don't know how many we are, or where all of us are located. They don't aim to lead us a chase; that is, mebby they don't. Them shacks are shore strong; an' they don't know how far they might get if they run for it. 'Tain't like open country—they got just four places to ride out of that sink an' they all can be easy guarded."

"They won't come out th' way they went in," said Luke. "That would be risky an' foolish; so they's only three places left."

"A wise man never does what he ought to do," said Johnny. "Now, I'll bet they are either in them stone houses, or some place else," he grinned. "Th' only way, after all, to see a good man's hand, is to call it. Me an' you, bein' amazin' curious, will do just that. If they're in them houses they'll be expectin' us; they'll turn th' 'Welcome' sign to th' wall an' smoke up them loopholes. Don't interrupt me yet! I'm long-winded an' hard to stop. Th' question is: Are you primed to wrastle this thing out, just me an' you, or shall I watch 'em while you go back to th' CL for help? That—"

"I *will* interrupt!" snorted Luke heatedly. "If it wasn't that yo're only a fool infant, damned if I wouldn't fan yore saddle end! I ain't never yelled for help when it wasn't needed; an' lots of times when it was needed I forgot to yell. Too busy, mebby. You've been running things with a high hand out here, an' yore head reminds me of th' head of a cow bit by a snake. It's swelled scandalous. I'm goin' to show you how to get four men out of them loopholes. Bein' young an' green, you'd likely want to crawl in an' pull 'em out. But me, bein' wise, will use brains, an' more brains. I can make a cat skin itself."

"You want to be plumb shore that it ain't one of them striped kitties—they look a lot alike in a poor light; an' that entrance canyon is shore poor light. I reckon we won't eat, yet. We better rustle for their ranch."

"But Logan wants to know them facts that he sent us after," growled Luke regretfully.

"We ain't got 'em; an' we can't get 'em. Them fellers won't do no rustlin' now, so how can we trail 'em? They're too cussed busy lookin' out for their skins about now. An' only two of 'em ain't wounded; Purdy an' th' cook."

"How many cows they got?"

"Near two hundred."

"Holy Jumpin' Jerusalem!" snorted Luke.

"We're lucky that we still got th' ranch-house an' th' river!"

"We're wastin' time," growled Johnny, impatiently. "There's no telling what they're doin'. Come on. Bein' desperate, mebby they're roundin' up to make a drive. Come on!"

It was past mid-afternoon when the two punchers looked down into the QE valley and found relief at the sight of the cows lazily feeding. They were scattered all over the range and both men knew that no attempt had been made to round them up.

Going down the blind-canyon trail, they crossed the range, climbed the opposite cliff and finally stopped in front of the stone houses. A gun barrel projected from a loophole in the south wall of the house nearest the canyon, and four saddled horses were in the smaller corral.

"There they are," said Johnny. A bullet stirred his hair and he drew back from the rim. "We got to get 'em. Start skinnin' that cat, Old Timer."

"It'll shore take a lot of skinnin'," growled Luke.

"Not if we uses 'brains an' more brains,'" jeered Johnny. "Th' young buck will now be heard shootin' off his mouth at th' council fire; an' you listen close, One Ijut!"

"Have yore say," said Luke, covering a loophole which showed signs of activity.

"We've got to move fast, before they learn that there's only two of us," said Johnny. "When them houses was built they was laid out with th' idea of men bein' in *all* of 'em; an' they'd be cussed hard to lick, then. But I reckon they're all in that one house. There ain't men enough to hold 'em all; an' so they favored th' one near th' canyon. We got to keep that door shut so they can't get out an' away. I'll do that after dark; an' I'll stampede them cayuses. That leaves 'em no chance to make a dash an' ride for it. Now you see that little trickle of water flowin' under th' houses? That's their water supply; I know something about that crick; but that's another job for th' dark. Take a look over there, where it turns. See that dirt bank, on th' bend? That's where they turned it out of its course an' sent it flowin' in th' ditch leadin' to th' houses. Do you reckon you could cut that bank with Colonel Bowie an' throw a little dam across th' ditch? 'Tain't wide; only a couple of feet. I—"

Luke fired, and grunted regretfully. "Missed him, damn it!" he swore, reloading. "Gettin' so you can find work for my knife, huh?" he chuckled. "Not bein' blind, I see th' bank an' th' bend. An' if I can't turn that water back th' way it used to go, I'll fold up an' die. This is like old times. You must 'a' had a real elegant, bang-up time out here, crawlin' around an' raisin' hell with 'em. What a grand place for th' Colonel! I shore missed a lot; but I'm here now, an' with both feet! Sing yore song; I'm listenin'."

"It's sung," grinned Johnny; "an' now we got to dance."

"I ain't as spry as I used to be," grunted Luke; "so I'll have to make them fellers do th' dancin'."

CHAPTER XXIII
"All but th' Cows"

Gates, the wounded, tossed restlessly in his bunk, and finally rolled over and faced the dark room.

"Never was so wide awake in my life," he grumbled. "Been settin' around too much lately. If I wanted to stay awake I'd be as sleepy as th' devil."

"Better try it again," counseled Quigley, shifting from his loophole. "You don't want to be sleepy tomorrow when yo're on guard."

"Tom," said Gates, ignoring the advice. "I've been doin' some thinkin'. A feller does a lot of thinkin' when he can't sleep. We made a couple of mistakes, holin' up like this. In th' first place, if we had to hole up, we should 'a' occupied *both* end houses, 'stead of only one. This way, they can walk right up to within twenty feet of us, use th' cook shack, th' grub in th' store-house, an' them store-house loopholes, which is worse. If we had both end houses, two men in each, they couldn't get anywhere close to us except along th' crick an' up on th' cliff."

"Yes; I reckon so," said Quigley. " 'Tain't too

311

late yet, mebby. I didn't like th' idea of splittin' up our forces. As far as grub is concerned, we're near as well off that way as we are in our water supply. We got grub in here for two months, an' plenty of cartridges if we don't get reckless with 'em. Of course, I wish that other case was in here, too; it'd give us another thousand rounds for th' rifles; but I ain't worryin' none about that. An' I'm purty near shore, now, that there's only two of 'em fightin' us: Nelson an' that Tedrue, judgin' from th' knife-work."

"That's th' way I figger it," agreed Gates. "An' that's why we shouldn't 'a' holed up like this. Me an' th' cook could 'a' held this house, while you an' Purdy was on th' outside stalkin' 'em. Any man that can stalk like you can is plumb wastin' his time cooped up in here; an' you could 'a' made things sizzlin' hot for them two fellers, good as they are. This way, they've got us located, an' they only have to look for trouble in front of 'em. They know where to expect it all th' time. It was a big mistake."

"Mebby," grunted Quigley. "We'll try it in here tonight an' tomorrow, an' then if we don't have no luck, I'll fade away tomorrow night an' give 'em a taste of Injun fightin'. There ain't no moon this week, so we can pick our time to suit ourselves."

Purdy leaned his rifle against the wall and groped for the water bucket. "I'll make a try for that extra case of cartridges right now, if you say th' word," he offered. "Huh! We shore drink a lot of water," he grunted. "I filled this pail before sundown, an' it's near empty now. Too much bacon, I reckon."

Quigley laughed softly. "Water is one thing we don't have to worry about at all. That ditch was a great idea."

Could he have followed the ditch in the dark he would have been surprised to have seen the dam across it, and the cut through the artificial bank, where Luke Tedrue and a commandeered shovel had released the little stream and let it flow to Rustler Creek along its old, original bed down a shallow gully. That was Johnny's idea; but after the old scout had carried it out, he had an idea of his own which pleased him greatly, and he acted upon it without loss of time.

The cook stirred and sat up, feeling for his pipe, which was always his first act upon awakening. He grunted sleepily and sat on the edge of his bunk. "This is a whole lot like bein' in jail," he yawned. "An' what do you think? I dreamed that somebody had just tapped a keg of beer, an' when I sidled over to see that none of it was wasted, why I woke up! That's allus my luck. How soon'll it be daylight? That dream made me thirsty. Where's that cussed water bucket?"

"Right where it was th' last time you found it," grinned Purdy. "It ain't moved none at all."

"Yo're right, it ain't," grumbled the cook,

scraping a tin cup across the bottom of the pail. "It never does unless *I* do it. I'll bet four bits that I've filled it every time it got empty; an' I'll bet four bits more that I ain't goin' to fill it *this* time," he chuckled. "There's just enough here for me. Th' next gent that wants a drink will be observed bendin' over th' trapdoor an' fillin' it for hisself. Here's how! An' damn th' beer what only comes in dreams."

Gates crawled out of his bunk and limped to the bucket. "Get out of my way," he growled. "Speakin' of beer started my throat to raspin'. No you don't; not a-tall," he grumbled, pushing the cook aside. "I'll wait on myself, slugs or *no* slugs. I ain't no teethin' infant, even if I *am* full of holes." He crossed to the trapdoor and fumbled around in the dark. "Huh! I knowed it couldn't get far away. I've been kneelin' on it all th' time!"

"Better lemme do that," offered the cook, advancing.

"Better yore grandmother," said Gates. "No, ma'am; you put on too many airs, you do." He raised the door. "You might strain yore delicate back, Cookie, old hoss. An' anyhow, I'm aimin' to spite you for that unnecessary remark about openin' a keg of beer. This ain't no time to talk about things like that." He leaned down and swung the bucket, but there was no splash, only a rattling, tinny thump. "Why," said his muffled voice, "there ain't no water here! Mebby I missed it. Why, damn it, there ain't no water here a-tall! What th'—" His voice ceased abruptly and a solid, muffled thump came up through the opening.

The cook, leaning forward in the position he had frozen in when he had grasped the significance of the sound of the striking bucket, moved toward the trap, feeling before him. He touched the edge of the opening and swiftly felt around it. Gates was not there.

"Damn it, he's fell in!" he muttered. "It wasn't no job for a wounded man like him, bendin' over that way. Here, Purdy!" he called. "Gimme a hand with Ben. He plumb keeled over an' fell in." He reached down impatiently and felt around. "Hell!" he yelled as an up-thrust hand gripped him, jerked him off his balance and pulled him down through the opening. "Look out, fellers!" he shouted.

A second thump, softer than the first, ended the cry and Purdy, leaping forward, slammed shut the trap and bolted it. "More knife-work!" he gritted, pale with rage. Arising, he leaped toward the cabin door, yanked it open and dashed along the house, staggering as a finger of flame spurted from a loophole in the wall of the store-house, but recovered his balance and turned the corner. As he did so he caught sight of a thickening in the darkness, which moved swiftly and silently along the ditch, and he fired at it. Something whizzed past his neck and rang out, sharp and clear as a bell, on the end wall of the house. He answered it with another shot and saw the blot stagger and fall.

From the ditch came a spurt of fire and Purdy plunged forward, firing as he fell. Another shot answered him and again he fired, but with a weak and shaking hand. Then from a loophole behind him Quigley's rifle poked out and sent shot after shot along the ditch, firing on a gamble.

As the rifle spoke, a shadow flitted past the corner of the store-house, passed swiftly and silently across the space between the two houses and plunged through the open door of the rustlers' stronghold. It tripped over a box and sprawled headlong just as Quigley wheeled and sent a bullet through the space Johnny had occupied an instant before.

Leaping to his feet, Johnny hurled himself upon the rustler, wrenched the rifle loose and gripped the owner's throat. Plunging, heaving, straining, they thrashed around the room, smashing into bunks, breaking dishes; hammering, gouging, biting, choking, they bumped into the door, plunged through the opening and carried the struggle out under the sky.

Quigley, his face purple and his eyes popping out, almost senseless on his feet, and fighting from instinct, managed to break the grip on his throat and showered blows on his enemy's face. Sinking his teeth in Johnny's upper arm, he got both of his hands around Johnny's throat and closed his grip with all his weakened strength.

Across the yard they reeled, bumped into the corral and along it, following the slope of the ground without thought. Johnny, suffocating, thrust the heel of his right hand against his enemy's nose and pushed upward and back, while his left hand, leaving the gripping fingers around his throat, smashed heavily into Quigley's stomach. The hands relaxed, loosened their grip and fell away, and before they could regain their hold, Johnny's chin settled firmly against his chest and protected his windpipe. Just in time he caught Quigley's gun hand and tore the Colt out of it, whereupon Quigley hammered his face with both hands. Shoving, wrestling, reeling, they came to the edge of the ravine through which flowed Rustler Creek, and, plunging over the steep bank, rolled to the bottom and stopped in the mud and water of the creek itself, where they fought lying down, each trying desperately to remain on top.

Quigley's hand brushed one of Johnny's guns, gripped it, drew it out and shoved the muzzle against his enemy's side. As he pulled the trigger Johnny writhed swiftly and turned the muzzle away. Squirming on top, he again turned the muzzle away as Quigley fired the second time. At the roar of the shot the rustler grunted and grew suddenly limp.

• • •

Logan pushed back from the dinner table and glanced out of the window. Shouting an exclamation he leaped for the door, the rest of the outfit piling pell-mell at his heels.

A black horse, carrying double, stopped near the door and eager hands caught Luke Tedrue as he fell from Pepper's back. Johnny, covered with mud, dust, blood, and powder grime, his clothes torn into shreds and his face a battered mass of red and black and blue flesh, swayed slightly, grasped the saddle horn with both hands and sat stiffly erect again.

"Good Lord!" shouted Logan, jumping to him. "What th' hell's up?"

"Rustlin'," muttered Johnny. "Luke's brains got foundered in th' head an' he pulled three of 'em out of a hole; but I made Quigley skin th' cat."

"Are they *all* gone under?" yelled Logan incredulously.

"All but th' cows," sighed Johnny, and strong arms caught him as he fell.

Center Point Large Print
600 Brooks Road / PO Box 1
Thorndike ME 04986-0001 USA

(207) 568-3717

US & Canada:
1 800 929-9108
www.centerpointlargeprint.com